once written twice shy

book one

carey decevito

This book is an original publication of Emberlust Press.

Decevito, Carey
Once Written, Twice Shy / Carey Decevito—Paperback edition
ISBN: 1481268589
ISBN-13: 978-1-4812685-8-5

Cover photography by Eric David Battershell
Cover Model Burton Hughes
Cover design by Clarise Tan, CT Cover Creations
Edited by Karen Hrdlicka

DEDICATION

For Nick and Isabella.

PROLOGUE

I stared at the overly large bags that lay by the front entrance, with what must have been the world's largest *what the fuck* look on my face.

"I can't do this anymore," she said.

Her words tore me to shreds.

"What do you mean you 'can't do this anymore'? Julie, you haven't been doing anything to fix *this*."

"I'm done, Paxton."

I ran my hands through my hair, pulling at the handful of blonde tresses gripped between my rigid fingers. The prickle in my scalp did enough to keep my temper in check and diffuse some of my anger. "You've got to be kidding me."

I couldn't believe it, but then again, part of me could.

She was giving up on everything.

My love, our life, our family; it had all disappeared in the blink of an eye.

I still loved her, but in all honesty, I can also state I haven't been in love with her for quite some time.

We've been together for nearly five years. In that time, we had built a home, one that was graced with our beautiful three-year-old son, Jasper.

My hand ran down my face.

Christ, how am I going to explain this to Jasper?

I was willing to try and work things out. Hell, I'd even mentioned marriage counseling on multiple occasions, but like everything else, work came first and the sessions she'd promised had never materialized.

I looked up at the woman, who stood in the entrance to what I had considered our home; frustration, anger, bitterness, and that subtle feeling of failure were all too overwhelming. "Fine," I said. "But what about Jasper?"

"Can you keep him for this week? It's just until I get situated. We can discuss custody later."

"Where are you going?"

"Todd asked me to move in with him," she said, as if I'd known about her relationship with the man the entire time. I'd suspected she'd maintained her infidelity but I didn't know for sure until now.

I huffed, "So he's still in the picture." I hadn't asked, so much as accused her. She nodded. "How long have you two been—" I couldn't finish the sentence.

Bile rose from my stomach.

"Does it matter?"

"You can go," I said in a defeated tone. I looked down at my feet, when all I wanted to do is ask her what happened to *can we try and work things out?* I groaned at the memory and shook it out of my head in dismay. "Get out."

"Pax—" She made to step toward me with an outstretched hand.

I shook my head to stop her, my blood pressure rising with her lack of departure. "I said *get out!*" I pointed toward the door, my stomach contents churning further.

The woman took off like a bat out of hell.

And that was it.

I was tired of having a one-sided relationship and was thus relieved at the woman's departure.

The news of her continued adultery had shocked me, especially when she had sworn to make an effort to sort things out between us. It explained why we had remained in our separate rooms all of this time, living our lives apart as though we were roommates. It more than proved we were better off without each other. This was really the end of my marriage.

When I married, I had intended it to be for life.

Well, I guess life had a plan of its own, huh?

With each passing day, I picked up the broken pieces of me. I hadn't realized that I had stifled so much of myself over the years to try and please a woman who seemed to never be sated with anything I said or did.

Fueled by my feelings of loss and neglect, I made a decision, which led me to rediscover an old love.

The proverbial flame was rekindled and I began to write again.

For what felt like an eternity, I wrote. When I was done, I read my piece over so many times that my words no longer made sense, forcing me to put it down and go back to it later.

I stared at my finished manuscript displayed on my screen.

What am I going to do with this?

I had discovered a site, a few months before. It had been recommended by a colleague. The venue allowed people from around the world to peruse and read various works written by amateurs. Some of the work on there I found horrid, while others, despite their various grammatical and punctual flaws, you wished you could set your hands on an edited and printed copy, they were so great.

What the hell?

I decided to chance it.

With a bit of copy and paste, and a little restructuring, I hit the *publish* button and there it was. My first written piece was out for the world to see.

It wasn't until a few months after I had posted my work

that I stumbled upon a comment I couldn't dismiss. I ached for constructive feedback, but the lack of it was getting to me due to the site being overrun by teenagers. I debated getting rid of my profile altogether up until that fateful day.

That short message was where things began to change for me. With simple words of appreciation, intellectual and heartfelt thoughts, followed by a click of her mouse, Alissa had made me smile.

I sought her profile out and found that she was a fellow amateur writer just like me.

She's gorgeous, had been my first impression. Despite her evident beauty, something else could be seen in her profile photo; something that beckoned me further, begged my curiosity to look beyond the surface. It was in her eyes.

Loneliness.

Or was I reading into things too much, since I was such a novice at these social media-like sites?

For a few weeks, I sat on Alissa's words alone as I read through some of her work.

She was good.

Better than good even.

I thought I'd end up with one of those written numbers that didn't make much sense or that glittered in the night, featuring vampires and werewolves. Boy was I wrong!

The woman sure knew how to paint a vivid picture. She pulled off the hot and sexy but kept it real all at once by adding emotion, drama, even a bit of action and suspense to her mix. Her work was altogether something reminiscent of everyday life: the good, the bad, the ugly, the... Well, you get the picture.

A few days after reading her last novel, a dream influenced by her work prompted me to finally write out an acknowledgment to her comment.

From there, we began to chat through private messages on a near daily basis.

We never stopped…

CHAPTER 1

Just short of a year later...

Waiting in the airport terminal, I couldn't remember the last time I had felt like this. The anxiety that consumed me was reminiscent of my first date with my first girlfriend as a teenager.

I looked up at the screen and saw that US Airways Flight 2583 to Jacksonville, North Carolina had landed. In a matter of minutes, Alissa would be standing before me in the flesh. My thoughts flittered to that first day, nearly a year ago, when we first made contact.

The conveyer belt that carried the luggage snapped me out of my reverie when it ceased moving and the area around me had become deserted.

Had something gone wrong, had she stood me up?

I lowered myself to the bench behind me and let my head drop into my hands. I sighed. "Serves you right for thinking she'd show," I mumbled.

I was trying to convince myself I should leave when I felt a soft hand on my shoulder. "Paxton?" a soft-spoken woman said at my side, her voice familiar from our numerous phone calls and Skype conversations.

She's here.

My heart thumped out of my chest. I felt foolish for thinking the worst and excited I was proven wrong. I got up to face Alissa, who had a beaming smile splayed on her face. Boy was that smile contagious! My lips tugged upward instantly.

She let out a giggle and after dropping her bag, she jumped me with a hug. Without hesitation, my arms found their way around her waist to return her enthusiastic greeting.

"You looked like a man deep in thought."

I set her back but held on to the sides of her arms. "Can I be honest?"

I breathed easier when she nodded, "I wouldn't expect anything less from you."

I shrugged my shoulders sheepishly and averted my gaze from her momentarily before eying her. "I thought you weren't coming."

She looked as if I'd slapped her.

"Paxton, I would have called or emailed. Hell, I would have messaged you if anything had come up. We've talked about meeting for months. I wouldn't—"

Call it insanity or whatever you will, I did the only thing my brain could process at the time and took the one step toward her. Standing toe to toe, I let go of her arms, grabbed her face, and crashed my lips to hers in an effort to shut her up. What was most surprising was how natural the act felt.

Her hand flew to her mouth as soon as I pulled back, eyes wide. No big surprise that I hadn't been the only one shocked at my actions.

Where had this sudden forwardness come from? Maybe it

had been the relief she was finally standing before me in person. Maybe it was that she'd proved, with her flustered rambling, I hadn't been the only one looking forward to our meeting.

Yes, things had gotten personal with our countless chats. But despite the numerous times we had flirted, exchanged photos, talked dirty, and even discussed how she had come up with some of the steamy scenes from her stories, I worried I had crossed a line.

Even when this feels completely natural.

"Alissa, I'm—"

She shook her head and lifted her hand. "I knew that was coming at one point or another. I just didn't expect…" With a small upward quirk of her lips, she waved her hand in a dismissive gesture. "Never mind. That was nice."

I instantly breathed easier and grabbed her carry-on luggage. "Let's get out of here." I offered her my hand to hold. "Assuming you're still up for it, after my mauling you and all."

She giggled nervously but grasped my proffered grip in hers. I walked us out of luggage claim, toward the parking structure, with a certainty I hadn't screwed things up so quick out of the gate, but maintained a level of wariness nonetheless.

With her luggage stowed in the back of my SUV, I headed to open the passenger side door for her.

If I'm going to be honest, my mind was presently stuck on our brief kiss.

Apparently I wasn't the only one.

Before I knew what hit me, Alissa had me pinned against the side of my vehicle, her body and lips smashed against mine.

My hands reached for her hips, pulling her into me as I licked her bottom lip, begging for entrance. The small taste of her in luggage claim had proven one thing: I wanted more and as long as she was handing out samples, I wasn't going to decline her offer.

With a light moan, she granted me access while her hands found their way around my neck and into my hair. We breathed each other in.

Alissa pulled away first, her chest heaving for air. I was none the better. The woman knew how to kiss. So much so that a certain part of my anatomy had begun to stir with that more thorough taste of her.

Don't judge, it's been a while.

She hid her face in my chest.

I pecked the top of her head. "I guess we're even, huh?" She groaned, making me chuckle. I grabbed her chin, tilting it to reveal a beautiful crimson. A chaste press of my lips to hers seemed to alleviate her sudden embarrassment. "Let's get going." But that flush of color in her cheeks was so becoming I simply had to tease her. "I can't have you all over me for everyone to see." I winked. Her blush had barely begun to fade as my words caused it to flare up once more, gaining me the reaction I was looking for. "I love that look on you, by the way."

She waited for me to get behind the wheel before asking, "What look?"

"Your blush," I said and buckled myself in. "I know you told me about it but it's nothing like I had pictured. You're gorgeous."

She clasped her cheeks with her hands in an effort to conceal another wave of red and failing miserably. "You need to stop that."

In a mocked tone of innocence I said, "What?" I leaned over the middle console to flick her nose with an index finger. "It's true."

A soft laugh escaped her and she nodded toward the steering wheel. "Get to driving, will you?"

I dropped her luggage as soon as we crossed the threshold. Kicking the door shut, I pulled Alissa so her back was against my chest and hugged her from behind, setting my chin on her shoulder and savored the feel of her against me.

A perfect fit.

"I can't believe you're actually here. You hungry?" It was nearly dinnertime and although I'd had a late lunch, my stomach grumbled.

She giggled at the noise. "A little." She wrapped her arms over mine. "What do you have in mind?"

I'm no culinary savant or anything, but I'm not the type of person to cook until I set fire to my kitchen either.

Until tonight apparently.

Part of it was Alissa's fault, despite the fact that she would beg to differ.

With a faltering grip, white powder filled the room after she recommended I use either cornstarch or flour to thicken the gravy. Flour, as it turns out, was all I had.

A fit of laughter consumed us as we attempted to clean up, making more of a mess out of ourselves than anything else.

She proceeded to wipe at me with a damp tea towel. When she got a little too close to a certain area, I grabbed her wrist to stop her. I pulled the cloth from her grip and wiped at her face, while I felt her cool fingers wiping at mine.

Our eyes connected and locked.

Our laughter subsided.

The braised pork chops and boiling potatoes forgotten, we found ourselves wrapped in each other like a pair of randy teenagers. There was no telling who had started it. The chemistry was instantaneous.

When we came up for air, Alissa said, "Is it me or is it getting hot in here?"

As soon as she'd said it, something captured my attention from the corner of my eye, making me turn to look.

Our indulgence had resulted in the potatoes becoming an overboiled pile of mush. The braised chops were charred, as the pan had caught fire. And the gravy did thicken—to the consistency of a dried up hockey puck stuck to the bottom of its pot.

Suffice it to say; dinner was effectively ruined.

Alissa was giggling into my back as I managed to put a stop to the tiny blaze with the help of a box of baking soda and an expired kitchen fire extinguisher.

Taking a deep breath, and looking over my shoulder at the woman still trying to gain her composure I asked her, "How do you feel about takeout?"

"I think it's a safer bet."

CHAPTER 2

When the kitchen was tidied up, the pots having been left to soak in the sink, and our food ordered, I offered Alissa a shower.

"You go ahead," she said. "I'll take mine after."

"I've got two bathrooms. You can use the one in my room since this is where you'll be staying. I'll take—"

"I can't kick you out," she said. "I could—"

"I didn't want to assume anything and I wanted you to be comfortable. The spare room doesn't have a bed yet, so I'll take the pullout couch. It's fine." I nodded toward the ensuite bathroom. "Go ahead, it's through there. I'll take the main bath down the hall."

In a rush to get cleaned up and return to Alissa, I was fresh out of the shower when I realized I hadn't grabbed any clean clothes to change into.

I wrapped the towel around my waist and headed out to gather something to put on.

Just as I slipped into my room, hoping to make a quick exit without being caught, I was graced with a sight that made my heart stop and start up again at a staccato pace.

Bent over, rummaging through her bag for what I presumed was a shirt, Alissa's heart-shaped ass, covered in a tight pair of blue jeans, was facing me along with her blonde locks dripping down her back.

I took a step forward and hadn't expected the floorboards to creak, giving my presence away.

She stood up ramrod straight and whirled around to face me, grabbing the first thing out of her bag to cover herself with.

I looked at it and burst out laughing. "You might need something more than that, sweetheart."

Her eyes looked down in horror when she found herself clutching a black lace bra. Blushing, her mouth opened as if to say something but nothing came out. Instead, I saw her gaze moving up my towel-clad torso, to my chest, her head tilting to the side, eyes widening, and her breathing picked up.

Grabbing her discarded towel, she quickly covered up and said, "I think I'm just going to—" She started to make a quick dash for the hallway with a mortified look on her face.

My hand clasped her arm to stop her. "Let me just grab the few things I didn't earlier and get out of here."

Turning away from her, I searched through my closet and pulled the few items I needed and headed for the exit. "I'll see you when you're done." I paused at the bedroom door before leaving her. "Has anyone ever told you you're hot when you're flustered?"

I didn't wait for a response. A few steps down the hall, I could hear the woman grumbling to herself and smiled. Things were definitely far from boring with Alissa around.

The pizza arrived while Alissa was still getting herself straightened out. I figured that she was done by now, but she was dealing with some residual embarrassment before coming downstairs to join me. In the short amount of time since her arrival, I had come to think of her meek demeanor as a rather endearing quality of hers.

I poured some wine for us after getting the plates ready, knowing she wouldn't be that much longer.

I smiled as I replayed the earlier series of events in my head.

Like any normal hot-blooded male out there, I'd be crazy if I said I didn't want to get laid by the woman currently holed up in my bedroom. We had chemistry, there was no denying that, but the gentleman in me urged me to slow things down a bit. There was something greater to lose here; a friendship that I wasn't willing to part with.

And maybe something greater?

The couch dipped beside me and the wine in my goblet sloshed about, bringing me back to the present.

"So, I guess you didn't lie when you said you knew how to make a towel look good, huh?" She smirked.

I eyed her amused face, surprised at her overtness and humored all the same. "I deserve that. I'm sorry for barging in. I—"

She placed a hand on my arm and squeezed lightly. "It's okay. You just took me by surprise."

"Here." I handed over her glass of wine, watching as she took a large gulp of the cabernet sauvignon. Trying to get my head back in the game had proved useless with my next statement. "For what it's worth, those jeans look fantastic but I have to confess, my imagination is running wild with pictures of you wearing that black lace bra you were holding on to."

She laughed. "Boy, you're a cheeky one, aren't you?"

I smiled, happy that our familiar playful banter from our online conversations had begun to creep into our face-to-face setting as time went on. I was starting to see more of the Alissa I had grown to know over the last ten months. Witnessing a genuine physical reaction instead of those stupid emoticon faces or some video rendition of her was a refreshing change. I was able to read her like one of her books, and what I took in only made me want to be around her more. There was a level of comfort between us that I hadn't seen coming, despite our few moments of awkwardness.

After dinner, I noticed Alissa fighting off the urge to fall asleep as our movie went on, so I pulled her legs on top of my lap in order to let her stretch out and be more comfortable.

When the credits began to roll, I turned the TV off and lifted the sleeping woman into my arms. By instinct, her arms wrapped themselves around my neck. Nuzzling against my jaw, Alissa mumbled something indiscernible while I carried her to my bedroom.

I set her down on my bed and tried to pull back but she woke and latched onto my shirt, capturing me with those cerulean eyes of hers.

I froze.

"Please don't go," she whispered and pulled me down. I had to brace myself to prevent from toppling over and crushing her.

Butterflies fluttered about in my stomach. "Are you sure?"

She bit down on her lower lip, making me wish I could nibble it myself. That simple innocent action of hers had been driving me crazy every time she'd done it.

I felt her fingers around the belt loops to my jeans, forcing me lower.

Her lips brushed against mine. "This is your house, it's a big bed, and you're not sleeping on the couch."

I played with her hair and studied her. "It's not so bad."

"Pax?" Her gaze flittered between my mouth and eyes.

"Hmm?" I leaned toward her.

"Kiss—"

I never let her finish, knowing that we both wanted the same thing.

She ran her hands from my belt loops to around my hips and under my shirt. The feather-like contact as her fingers traced about my lower back heated my flesh. She nibbled on my lip. Her soft tongue met mine as we sought closeness. She tasted sweet and I wondered what the rest of her would taste like, or if I'd be lucky enough to find out. Something told me I was well on my way with the way things were heating up.

I let my hand wander from her side down to her hip. Her leg folded up at the knee, allowing me better access to squeeze her jean-clad cheek, causing her to moan into my mouth. I kissed the length of her jaw, down to the side of her neck, up to her ear.

"You have no idea how much I want you right now," I said.

Her body trembled.

I nipped her lobe, eliciting a whimper from her as her hands came free of my shirt and made their way to my hair. I felt the prickling of my scalp, followed by a rush of arousal as she pulled.

My pants tightened further. If she had any question as to how much she turned me on, the vixen that lay beneath me had a feasible answer as I pressed my lower half into hers.

Alissa rolled us over and straddled my waist with a wry grin. "If you want something, Paxton, you've got to take it." She grabbed on to the hem of my shirt and I arched my back to help her remove it.

A look of hunger twinkled in her eyes as she studied my upper body. A finger ran up the middle of my stomach, starting at the waist of my jeans, circling my navel. The tickling digit changed to an open palm, which rubbed my chest as she leaned forward to bring her lips inches from mine.

I reveled in all things Alissa.

The woman was a temptress, a mistress at seduction, and she behaved as if she had no clue to her prowess. That hot and moist tongue of hers, mixed with her nips and the series of open-mouthed kisses heading down my torso, was wreaking havoc on my senses. An internal fight broke out between my urge to flip her over and exact my sensual revenge, and staying put to see where she was going to end up next.

Reduced to breathlessness, I managed, "Allie?"

Her fingers toyed with the button at the top of my jeans. Her mouth latched onto one of my nipples, flicking that wicked tongue of hers over the hardened disk. "Hmm?" The vibrations sent electrical currents throughout my body.

She leaned up to kiss my mouth. I felt her smile against my lips and saw the crinkling at her eyes when the button snapped out of its eyelet.

In that moment, something snapped in me also.

I flipped us over, grabbed her hands, and pinned them above her head with one of mine. My other hand roamed free to find the exposed flesh around her stomach from her shirt riding up.

"Too many layers," I grunted my disapproval.

She helped me with stripping her shirt and discarded it to the floor, much like mine had been. I looked upon her as her blonde hair draped over my pillow, garnishing her head as if it were a halo. She looked delicious, and I was desperate to taste more than just her mouth.

"So soft," I said against the middle of her stomach, while depositing soft kisses on my way up to those lace-covered mounds of hers.

I slid my hand underneath the band and took a breast in my hand, pinching its nipple and rolling it. She gasped and arched toward me.

Junior swelled to desperation in my jeans. I knew I'd have to at least unzip myself to allow for a bit of breathing room, and soon.

I pulled myself off of her and kneeled between her legs. Her face was flushed, her breathing was labored and her eyes... *Wow!* They were the brightest deep blue I had ever seen.

My hands reached for her fly and button. She tilted her hips up in permission and I pulled her denim off.

Damn! The woman sure knew her lingerie.

I grunted my approval at the sight of the matching black

lace accentuating her slender, toned legs, and looking forward to the time they would be wrapped around me.

Amusement could be seen all over her face as she observed me taking her in.

"You look like a kid who's visiting an amusement park for the first time." Her voice had turned husky. "Your turn. Take off those pants, stud."

I mock saluted, gaining me a giggle while I proceeded to stand beside the bed and dropped *trou*.

Feeling her urge to stay close, she knelt on the edge of the mattress. Her palms met my chest; leaving a burning trail from the moment they made contact. Our eyes met and all playfulness, all mischievousness, was absent. In its stead, vulnerability dominated.

In that moment, I was reminded of Alissa's past relationship troubles. She knew of my hang-ups as much as I knew about hers. Honestly, she'd been the one to make me see there was more to life than just existing. That there was someone out there who was better suited for me than my ex-wife ever had been.

Julie.

Talk about a proverbial bucket of iced water to cool things down a notch.

I need to tell her.

Here she was, single, hot and ready and even though she knew of my separation, I felt like a cheat.

A moron.

A liar.

Yeah, definitely a lying cheat of a moron.

CHAPTER 3

Taking a step back, I averted my gaze from hers and shook my head. "I can't do this."

Alissa's hands froze and she slumped back to sit on her knees. "Why?" The look of complete confusion mixed with rejection and disappointment on her face just about did me in.

What had I done?

I dropped to my knees in front of her and grabbed her hands before she could withdraw from me completely.

I sighed. "Let me explain." She stayed silent and unmoving. "Promise me you won't leave until you've heard me out." She gave me a hesitant nod. "Allie, there's something I need to talk to you about before anything can happen here."

She pulled her hands away and swallowed hard. "You still love her, don't you?"

"What? Allie, no!"

"Oh." She looked down at her clasped hands. "Then what is it?"

"No matter how I try to word it in my head, it won't come out right." I rubbed my face with both hands.

"Pax, you're making me nervous here."

And I'm a world class jackass. "I'm still married," I blurted, and I took her silence as a vantage point to expand on that line. "I mean, we're not together in any sense of the word—"

She snickered dryly and crossed her arms over her chest. "Except for the legal sense." Okay, so sarcasm was warranted, and so was her defensive posture. "Pax, why would you let me think that you were divorced? You said—"

"I didn't. Well, I guess I did but not deliberately. I never thought that this," I pointed between her and me, "would ever happen. Truth is, I should be divorced by now."

"But it is happening, Paxton." She sighed. "Were you ever going to tell me if we hadn't gone this far? What else is there, why would you think you'd be divorced? *Why* aren't you?"

"I planned on telling you when everything was finalized," I said. "A few months after our separation, I filed the papers. That was the day you learned about the divorce. I didn't think there'd be an issue. I mean, Julie had a boyfriend and it seemed pretty cut and dried. You would think—"

"That still doesn't explain why you're still married to her though, does it?" Her tone had taken an accusatory edge. She was pissed and rightly so.

"She's refusing to sign, Allie."

"What? Why?"

"Julie can be a vindictive woman. Whenever I ask her about the papers, there's always a different reason," I said. "What's worse is that she likes to use Jasper as a bargaining chip. I don't want to lose my son, Alissa. It's why I haven't pushed her into signing the papers. And since I wasn't pursuing anyone…"

I left it at that.

For Jasper's sake, we'd been trying to keep things amicable where our split was concerned. I see Jasper every other week with our shared custodial rights. He had more than enough to adjust to with his parents living in separate households; he shouldn't be aware of the animosity between us.

And then there was Todd, my ex's beau—note the sarcasm. Am I jealous? Hell no! I just don't want my son's mother to be shacking up with every Tom, Dick, and Harry out there, leaving poor Jasper wondering where he fit in with this new family dynamic.

There, the truth was out and it was up to the woman in front of me to decide how things would go from here on out.

"Sounds to me like she wants it all," she said hotly. I nodded and got up to sit on the bed beside her. "I'm sorry," she added.

I had told her everything, risking losing our friendship and there she was apologizing?

"I'm the one who's sorry," I said. "I should have said something before now. I understand if—"

"Do you think she ever will? Sign, I mean?" she asked.

"I don't know. This is the first time where I feel the need to bring lawyers and a judge into this so it ends."

She didn't say anything.

Silence, the ominous lack of sound that made me ache to know what Alissa was thinking. I knew I hadn't earned the right to ask. She should have gotten up, gotten dressed, and headed for the nearest hotel, and I wouldn't have blamed her one bit. Hell, I would have driven her there and paid for her stay myself.

Instead, a warm hand grasped mine and squeezed.

My heart sank when she did get up. She didn't go far though; only turned to stand facing me.

I looked up at her, seeing the concern in her eyes. I knew I had hurt her, yet there she remained before me.

"Is that all, there's nothing more?" I shook my head, indicating the negative. "Good." Her hands cupped my cheeks and she bent so her face was a breath away from mine. "Now kiss me."

Her kiss was hard and demanding, almost punishing in nature. She moaned into my mouth when I returned her passion.

My hand reached up and brushed a strand of hair behind her ear. "Are you okay with this?" I asked. "I'm sorry, I really fucked this up. This internet friendship thing is all new to me. I guess we got so busy talking about everything else that we missed the boat on a few things, huh?" I sighed.

"I agree, but…"

I pulled her closer so the side of my face rested against her bare stomach, just below those luscious mounds of hers.

"But?"

Her hands braced themselves on my shoulders. In a few seconds, she was straddling my lap. "There's one thing that can't get miscommunicated, though."

I smirked. "And what's that?"

Her mouth collided with mine and my hands fell to release the catch on her bra. The feel of her bare ample chest against mine made my shaft pulse with more need than earlier.

I stood, making Alissa wrap her legs around my waist as I turned us toward the bed. I tried to be gentle as I laid her down beneath me, but having a woman hang on to you like a spider monkey can cause a shift in a guy's balance.

To continue in the day's awkward fashion, we tumbled and I landed over her with a grunt as our sexes crushed together over our underwear, while Alissa giggled at the turn of events.

I snapped the elastic to her underwear and her laughter ceased. "These have got to come off." My fingers slid to the sides of her hips and began tugging at the undergarment.

I kissed downward, vowing I'd return to her breasts after paying my respects to the rest of that beautiful body of hers. The closer I got to her core, the more I smelled her arousal. It made me want to hurry things along.

When my boxer briefs were off, I towered over her on my knees, taking in the sights. Her hips were wide, waist narrow. Built like the finest sports car, those curves of hers could make any grown man obsessive about running their hands all over them. Her womanhood, well, let's just say I could see myself spending all night in that haven. Shaved, smooth as a baby's bottom, and its juices were begging me to take her in my mouth and ravage her until she screamed out my name.

Repeatedly.

Our eyes met when I brought my face to hers. "You're beautiful."

I smiled at her blush, kissed her nose and went to work.

From her lips, I trailed kisses, licks, and bites, along with letting my hands and fingers do some of the talking down her torso.

Her breathing picked up, her body wriggled as she attempted to bury her butt into the mattress.

She was at my mercy.

I latched on to one of her pert nipples and sucked it in, nipping it before washing the sting away with my tongue. She gasped and her hands found their way into my hair, keeping me where I was for a while, before guiding me to the other to repeat my erotic punishment.

"Pax…"

I continued.

Her hands left me to grasp the linens.

The moment I reached her navel, circling my tongue around it, my finger entered her and she exploded in her first orgasm. I smiled against her heated skin.

When she began to descend, I thrust a second finger into her, feeling her muscles clamp down on me in tiny little tremors. She was tight, hot, and smelled divine.

"I need to taste you." I slipped my tongue between her folds and swiped it up to her nub. Her thighs twitched and she let out a deep guttural moan.

Her hips began to lift off the mattress, urging me deeper. I used my free hand to push them back down before pressing my lips to her clit and sucking. I savoured her essence.

"Oh! Oh, God! Pax!" Tremors climbed in intensity inside her depths and I pulled my fingers out, letting my tongue give her one last pleasurable lick which made her body shiver from head to toe. "What are you doing?"

"I can't wait," I said. I climbed up to kneel right at the junction between her thighs. She looked at me with urgency and grabbed on to my dick, pumping it.

My head fell onto my shoulders and my eyes began rolling into the back of my head. I was at her mercy and so aroused for her that it hurt.

"Allie, you need to stop." I stilled her hand. "You'll put an end to this before it really begins." I reached over to the drawer in the bedside table and pulled out a condom.

She grabbed it from me. "Let me."

Sweet mercy!

With my hand over hers, we both guided me to her entrance. I pushed into her and watched as her eyes began to roll back and close.

I stopped midway inside her and kissed her long and hard. "Look at me," I said and nuzzled her nose. She obliged, releasing my cock and running her hands up my chest as I filled her. "Fuck." I felt myself bottom out as she took me to the hilt. I groaned, "Baby, you're so tight." I remained stationery and washed tender kisses all over her face, while her fingers caressed my scalp and my urgency to spill myself ebbed.

She moaned into the side of my neck when I shifted and she wiggled around slightly. "Pax, I can't wait." She arched her hips into me and our pelvises pressed closer. "Please."

I began to thrust, pulling myself out and then pushing back into her heat until I bottomed out again. Her hips ground against mine in a circular motion, our gazes fused to one another as the tension built.

Alissa met with every one of my thrusts, our rhythm increasing with our need. I was dying to feel her clamp down on me, my urge to spill growing dangerously close.

She brought a hand down between us and began to massage her clit. "Damn, Allie." My eyes went wide at the show and the feeling I was about to blow was unavoidable. "Baby, I need you to come." I picked up the pace. Her body writhed in ecstasy and I shifted to hit her G-spot on the next few thrusts.

"Oh, yes! Oh, God, yes, Pax!"

Her climax caused her insides to grip me like a vise, squeezing me until all it took was a few more thrusts before I cried out my release, extending hers.

Spent, I collapsed, letting my face fall into the crook of Alissa's neck. My entire body quivered every time I felt an aftershock-type tremor from her core.

I pulled back to kiss her lips and she graced me with a smile. "That was amazing."

I nuzzled her nose before rolling us over to tuck her into my side. "Oh yeah."

She released a contented sigh as she settled into me.

I hadn't realized, until then, I'd missed the postcoital closeness one could share with another person.

Looking down, Alissa had fallen asleep. I kissed the top of her head and revelled in the contentment I felt.

Soon enough, the darkness of slumber fell upon me and whisked me away.

CHAPTER 4

I woke up, my arm numb with the annoying sensation of pins and needles. I was about to roll over when I realized I had something—or rather someone—weighing me down.

Last night's events came flooding back like a freight train. The scent of her shampoo fluttered through the air, courtesy of my open window, and my heart began to flutter. I turned to look at Alissa, who was curled up in a ball on her side, and smiled.

It wasn't a dream.

I pulled her back into my chest and she uncurled her body, allowing it to lean into me. Kissing her shoulder, I settled my head down with my cheek pressed against the back of her head. Forgetting all about my dead arm, I closed my eyes.

Just a bit longer.

Alissa stirred.

I groaned when she performed a small cat stretch that propelled her butt into my crotch. The sensation made me dizzy with lust and I felt my cock harden. I was thankful she had rolled over onto her back so I didn't have to embarrass myself.

I smiled down at her. "Good morning."

"Hi." She returned my smile and rolled onto her side to hug me. Her head pulled away as she looked up at me, her brow arched and she giggled. "Well, someone's happy this morning."

"Ignore *him*." I laughed and kissed her forehead. Pulling her closer, she groaned. "You okay?"

"Yeah, I just need the bathroom."

Jumping out of bed, she grabbed the bedsheet and wrapped it around herself before disappearing into the bathroom.

I rolled onto my back and laced my fingers behind my head, thinking of what to do for the day. Rummaging through memories of various online conversations between us, I remembered Alissa loved the outdoors, so I figured I'd conjure something up to do with one of our common interests. It looked like it was going to be a nice day, according to the sunshine beaming through the edges of my curtains.

My mind was so busy finalizing the details to my plans that I hadn't noticed her presence in the room until I felt the mattress dip beside me.

"What are you thinking so hard about?" she asked.

I grabbed her hand and pulled her closer. "If I told you, I'd have to kill you, and I can't have that. I like you too much." My free hand pulled on the sheet so it fell away from her.

Quick as a cat, she bunched the material in a fist and clutched it to her chest but never made a move to tuck it back in.

The glimmer of mischief filled her eyes.

"I bet I could make you spill," she said and let go of the sheet. It pooled around her butt and thighs. She sat there, hovering above me with dishevelled hair, her skin bared from the waist up.

I swallowed hard. "And how would you do that?"

You've got to love that feminine wile, and Alissa had it in spades right then.

She laughed and traced her fingertips over my chest, down my stomach. "Oh, I have my ways." She bit down on her lower lip. She kissed me nice and slow. "Mmm," she mumbled against my lips before pulling away, robbing me of the chance to coax more out of her. "I should get ready for whatever you have planned for us though."

She dismissed the sheet altogether, got up, and I watched those naked hips of hers sway from side to side, heading toward the bathroom once more.

I groaned and sat up. "Tease!"

Turning to look at me over her shoulder, she said, "You can join me, but only if you tell me what your plan is." With that, she shut the door.

Moments later, I heard the water turn on and debated if I should give in.

Fuck it!

I walked into the bathroom, pulled the shower's sliding glass door to the side, and attempted to get in with her.

The vixen stood in front of me, blocking the entrance with an expectant look. "You better be ready to talk, stud."

I eyed her tanned legs and smirked. "You better be ready to spread 'em, sweetheart." She gasped at my retort. "I'm not ruining my surprise, and all you need to know is we'll be going for a ride and spending lots of time outside. Happy now?"

She grabbed my hand and pulled me into the shower with her. "No, not yet."

Her lips crushed mine.

I bit on that bottom lip she so loved to nibble on and she opened for me. I revelled in the feel of her velvet tongue against mine, the feel of her soapy wet skin, like silk against my roughened own as my arms surrounded her.

"How 'bout now?" I asked, trying to catch my breath, my

hands loosening their hold to travel downward and clutch her butt.

She giggled. "Just a bit," she said, her thumb and forefinger held a few centimeters apart.

I arched my brow.

Her arms pulled me back in and I denied her, presenting my cheek just before her lips met mine. She rebelled by getting up on the tips of her toes and nipping my earlobe.

I shuddered, my knees feeling weak. "You have no idea what you do to me."

"I think I have a slight idea."

Her hand lowered itself and left a wet, steaming trail down my front. She snaked it lower, grabbed my cock and began to pump. My jaw went slack and the hot water felt cold against my skin as the raging inferno within was fed. My eyes closed and my head tilted back. She had cocooned us into our very own bubble of bliss, where I was only aware of the contact she had on my throbbing dick.

My eyes snapped open. "Oh, God!" I said when I felt her lips wrap around the flesh that had made her scream out my name last night.

I looked down and our eyes locked.

She hummed around me and I felt my balls tighten. I strung my fingers through her wet hair.

I was close.

So close.

She took me in as far as she could stand, and I felt her throat muscles working as she swallowed me down further. The look of pure enjoyment and her fierce determination had me on the cusp.

"Holy! Mmm…Allie," I rasped.

Her teeth lightly grazing my length threw me over the edge.

I exploded with a guttural moan that shook me to my core, my hands reaching out to either side of me to make sure I maintained my stance as she sucked, licked and swallowed me clean.

When the urge to collapse receded, my hands released the walls and framed her face. Pure satisfaction graced her expression and those swollen lips, those molten eyes, made me pull her up to her feet for a searing kiss.

"Now I'm happy," she said before pecking me on the mouth and turning around. "Mind washing my back?"

I stood there, dumbstruck.

What the fuck was that? "You're a devil woman, you know that?" I shook the carnal haze out of my brain and reached around her for the soap. "But it's my turn now," I whispered into her ear and watched the goosebumps spread on her skin.

I was itching to see Alissa's reaction with what I had in store for us, so when she said she was finished eating, I left money on the table that would cover both the bill and leave our waitress a hefty tip.

I grabbed Alissa's hand, rushed us out to my SUV, and drove us to a ranch on the outskirts of town, thankful no one was home when we arrived.

She looked around after I'd helped her out of my car. "Where are we?"

Her eyes were fixed on the fields of wildflowers. "You like?" She nodded. "It's my parents' place. I brought you here because we needed to pick up a more suitable ride for what I've got planned." I grabbed her hand and led her to the rear of the barn. "Come on."

"What are you up to, Paxton Lowell?"

I pushed the two heavy sliding doors sideways to reveal a four-wheeler.

"Your chariot awaits, madam." I laughed at her wide-eyed look and the grin that followed it.

"It explains why you told me not to wear anything nice.

Let's go!" She jumped up and hugged me with a light giggle. "I haven't been on one of these in ages."

The notion of two thirtysomethings behaving like kids for a day was ridiculous, but it was well worth it to see the bright smile on Alissa's face. A smile, I might add, that had yet to disappear as we sped through the fields.

I drove on until we reached the edge of the forest and stopped where the bush trail started. "I hope you're okay with getting messy." I grinned over my shoulder. "It's been raining a lot up until this week, so I can promise that things are far from dry in there."

Her laugh was filled with mischief as she rubbed her hands together. "Do I look like I'm afraid of a little bit of dirt?"

"I was hoping you'd say that."

A while later, we hit a slight snag.

Having reached the bottom of the gully that was evidently a little deeper than I remembered, my old Honda got stuck in the mud.

I cursed.

"Don't laugh or you're walking back," I said to a giggling Alissa, despite not feeling any ire at all.

The harder I tried to get us out by rocking the wheeler back and forth for traction, the more Alissa's giggles grew.

Nothing helped.

If anything, I made more of a mess, which seemed to add to the hilarity of our situation. Despite my annoyance at our conundrum, I couldn't hide the smile on my face. It was hard to stay frustrated with Alissa looking like she was having a ball.

"You take the wheel while I push," I said, and moved to step into the massive mud hole. "When I tell you, ease onto the gas. Don't hit it too hard or else you'll make things worse." She nodded and I braced myself onto the rear rack. "Now!"

Underestimating the touchiness of the throttle, the tires spun and the machine's ass end sunk from my grip. There was no way we were getting that thing out of there until things dried up.

We were as good as pedestrians.

She turned and broke out into a full-blown belly laugh. "Oh, crap, Pax!" She clutched at her stomach. I was covered from head to toe in mud, thanks to her. "I'm sorry."

"No you're not," I said, but couldn't contain my smirk before I allowed a small chuckle to escape. "Laugh now. Just you wait, you'll get yours too." I snickered as I tried to wipe the mud off my face. "Damn stuff is as thick as tar."

I helped her off the bike so we could head back.

As luck would have it, the moment she let go of my hand, she slipped. She squealed as she tried to right herself, only to land on her ass and the mud sucked her in deeper.

It was my turn to bust a gut.

"Karma's a bitch," I said in a singsong fashion.

"Yeah, yeah." She laughed as she took my outstretched hand again.

I gave her my best angelic face and then grinned like the devil. "You know you're enjoying this."

She was wiping the mud off her hands and onto her shirt. "Can't say I wasn't." She looked up at me and grinned. "Next time, if you want to mud wrestle, just ask."

Damn this girl is fun.

After a half hour trek, I suggested we take a small break when we'd reached the fields. I collapsed onto my back and pulled on her hand so she followed me down. She had laid her head on my stomach, both of us staring up at the sky.

I don't know how long we were there for, but I was aware of the fact the mud on my skin was pretty well caked on dry.

"This shit is going to be hell to get off."

She peeled a dried chip of mud off my cheek, flicked it and said, "I think you might be right, but you'll look pretty with a more even complexion in the end."

"*Pretty?*" I lifted my head and gave her a perplexed look. She tried to hide her laugh, but it was next to impossible with her head bouncing up and down off my stomach. "I'll show you pretty. I think it's time you earned yourself a few extra laugh lines, sweetheart! Then you can talk to me about mud baths." I rolled her under me and set to tickling.

We made it back to the house, still laughing about our earlier mishap. I started the hose and sprayed her down. She squealed as soon as the water made contact.

"Damn that's cold," she said, shivering with her lips gaining a blue tint.

"A white T-shirt would have made this whole experience that much better," I said, wiggling my eyebrows.

She harrumphed and snagged the hose from me. On a smirk, she added, "Oh, it's about to get better all right."

Taking aim at me, she fired.

She soaked me good and proper as I used my T-shirt to scrub as much of the mud off as I could.

I grabbed a few towels from the house's mudroom-slash-laundry room, left a note letting my parents know what had happened to the ATV and we headed home.

I'd have to go back with the old man some other time and get it out when things got drier.

In an attempt to avoid the debacle of what was last night's dinner, I made Alissa sit at the kitchen island while I cooked.

We settled in the living room after our meal.

Alissa walked up to the built-in library and grabbed the frame that held a photo of Jasper and me.

"He looks so much like you." She graced me with a sweet smile and I could have sworn I had seen a look of longing cross her face, but as quick as it appeared, it vanished.

She put the frame back where it had been and I found myself envisioning a day where she and Jasper would meet and wondered if he would like her. Almost immediately, I was convinced that he would. However, my son getting used to her would take time, as it had with Julie's man.

"Uh oh, you've got that pensive look again. What's on your mind?" she asked, as she sat down beside me.

Before I had the chance to answer, there was a knock at the door.

"Hold that thought," I said, and got up to see who could be calling on me. I hadn't the faintest idea, nor did I expect to find the person that stood there.

CHAPTER 5

I drew my front door inward and cursed internally as soon as I saw her.

Julie.

She pushed past me. "Can I come in?"

Do I really have a choice?

Panic set in. I didn't know what to expect when Julie noticed Alissa's presence. I turned to do some damage control and took note that Alissa was nowhere to be seen. A slight shuffling noise from the kitchen told me that was where she went.

I huffed and ran my hands through my hair. Her visit was the last thing I needed. "What are you doing here, Julie?"

Within seconds, tiny arms tangled themselves around my legs. "Daddy!" Jasper cheered.

I bent down and picked him up for a big hug. "Hey, sport." I turned to Julie. "What's going on?"

She never showed up unannounced.

Since she'd left me, the extent of our interactions had been while exchanging our son or over the phone. It sounds bad, I know—*exchange*. In essence, that's what it was.

Somewhere between trades, we'd manage to discuss everything pertaining to our son. The times when I'd bring up the topic of our divorce had always led to countless excuses, from losing the papers, to forgetting them, which meant no resolution. Needless to say, I was slowly losing my battle at remaining sane.

"Can you give Mommy and me a minute, champ?" I asked and set him down.

"Okay, Daddy. I'll go get a juice," he said before running off.

"You know where they are." Then I realized I had inadvertently caused a meeting that I hoped wouldn't blow up in my face.

I waited, willing Julie for a response to my earlier question but all I got was a sniffle and then I noticed her eyes. They were bloodshot.

"We need to talk," she said.

My mind gravitated toward the worst. "Julie, what's going on?" She couldn't answer me fast enough and after several seconds, I pushed with impatience. "Julie!"

"I'm pregnant."

The crash of broken glass caused my head to snap in the sound's direction.

Shit!

Alissa stood in the kitchen's entrance, looking pale. Jasper was there holding her hand, looking down at the mess.

My son tugged on Alissa's hand and handed her his juice box when she looked at him. "I know where the broom is, Allie. I'll go get it." Then he rushed off.

I stepped toward her when Jasper was well out of earshot. "Alissa?" The shake of her head told me she didn't want me near her and I halted. "It's not—"

"Who's this?" Julie nodded in Alissa's direction. "You freaked out about Todd but you have a slut?"

"Excuse me?" Alissa said from her crouched down position, as she had started to gather up the larger pieces of glass.

My eyes bugged out of my head when Jasper returned and was handing the tools over to Alissa. I couldn't let the kid bear witness to this fiasco of a first meeting between my visitor and my ex.

"Jasper, go to Daddy's room, please."

Jasper smiled up at his new friend, whose face had regained its coloring but showed a strained smile directed at my little guy. He grabbed his juice box from the side table and ran off.

I reared on my son's mother. "I hope that you didn't drop by just to deliver that news. We both know the kid isn't mine since I haven't touched you since before you left me."

"But—"

"You know your way out unless there's more," I said. "And Julie, I don't want to hear from you unless it concerns our son or those divorce papers. If you're looking for sympathy, you're knocking on the wrong door."

"Who is she?"

"I—" Alissa began.

I held my hand up to cut her off. "It's none of your concern, Julie. As for—"

Alissa came up beside me, grasped my hand and said, "I'm his girlfriend."

I looked over at her with a dropped jaw and she offered me a small yet strained smile, much like the one she had given Jasper, but the small gesture told me she believed what I had said.

"Right." Julie's tone was skeptical, and I caught the tail end of an eye roll when my gaze turned back to her. "The guy couldn't keep me satisfied, I doubt that you're anything more than a—"

"A slut?" Alissa's lips formed a thin line. If she were a cat, I would have been able to see those hackles of hers rise.

I knew that Julie's poor choice in words—not to mention awful manners—had rubbed her the wrong way. How couldn't they? If the woman was cruising for a bruising, Alissa struck me as more than capable of holding her own. Call me crazy, but the thought of seeing her in a catfight, defending my honor, kind of turned me on.

Not the time, Paxton, I reminded myself and tried to focus.

"That's right," Julie said and crossed her arms at her chest.

I felt the tremor of anger shake my body and knew that Alissa had felt it, judging by the squeeze of her hand on mine.

"I've heard enough." I eyed daggers at my ex. "Where the hell do you get off— Hell, you don't even know her, Julie. I shouldn't have to explain myself to you since you didn't give me the courtesy of being informed while you were out gallivanting with others."

"*Three*," Julie said. "There were three, including Todd, so don't make me out to be the town whore."

"You certainly weren't Mother Theresa. Let me make my point clear." I took a cleansing breath to make sure I didn't say anything I'd live to regret later. "Alissa is not a slut, nor do I sleep around. I suggest you get the hell out of my house and go find your man. Your pregnancy problems are yours, not mine." I geared to end my rant. "How about you tell me why you've brought our son into this? It's clear enough that it wasn't to deliver your baby news."

She took the backpack I had failed to notice and set it beside the coffee table. "I'm going away on business. It's a last minute thing and Todd's busy with work. I need you to look after him," she said. "I should be back by tomorrow night."

"Next time, you might want to call ahead. Jasper!" I heard his miniature feet stomping as he came barrelling downstairs and latched on to my free hand. "Time to say goodbye to Mommy." My icy gaze meeting Julie's, I added, "she's leaving."

With a chaste kiss to his forehead, she stood erect and eyed Alissa with utmost disgust. Snorting her disapproval, the woman spun on her heel and stomped out the door, slamming it.

I swallowed the foul taste in my mouth.

Damn her.

Walking to the door, I turned the deadbolt to lock it. I was baffled at her intrusion and insulted for her callous behavior and comments toward Alissa.

Leaning forward on the door, I shook my head in frustration. I hadn't expected this turn of events.

What's done is done.

I heard some hushed whispers before a tiny set of arms wrapped themselves around my legs. Whatever ire lingered, most of it melted away in that instant.

I turned and picked my son up, ruffling his hair with my free hand, and giving him a wide grin. I wanted to talk to Alissa about what had transpired, and I worried that her evening—our day—had been ruined, but all she gave me was a genuine warm smile. I knew right then that everything would be okay.

"I see you've met Alissa, huh?"

"Yup," he said. "Daddy, can we watch a movie before bedtime? It was Allie's idea."

"What do you think, *Daddy*, can we watch a movie?" Alissa asked with a teasing smirk.

My lips quirked up at her and when Jasper grabbed my face in his hands for my undivided attention, I nodded. "Go change into your jammies while Allie and I set everything up." I handed him his bag.

"Yay!"

I left Alissa and Jasper to watch the movie in my room, while I got the pull-out couch ready for my son.

Joining them with a small plate of cookies and three glasses of milk when I finished, Alissa looked like she was having about as much fun as Jasper was, what with the giggling that was taking place.

When the movie ended, I turned to find Jasper sound asleep with his head on Alissa's lap and her fingers playing with his hair.

"You look like you're enjoying that." She grinned and nodded. I picked Jasper up and turned to face her. "Let me get him settled then we can talk."

I brought him downstairs where his bed lay ready, set him down and pulled the blankets up to his chin, not forgetting to tuck in the stuffed puppy my mother had given him the day he was born. It was the only thing he could never part with, and my heart clenched as he clutched it to his chest.

"Night, Daddy," he said in his sleepy little voice.

I bent down, kissed his forehead. "Goodnight, sport."

I returned to my room to find Alissa still sitting in the same spot I had left her in, with the TV turned off.

"I'm sorry," I said.

"Don't." She shook her head. "Don't do that."

"*Don't do* what?" I stood at the side of the bed and watched her face.

"Don't apologize for being you. You're a dad and you have obligations, routines, all sorts of special things you do with Jasper."

"It's not that." I sat down next to her, pulling her into my side for a cuddle.

She lifted her head off my shoulder and looked at me. "I really don't mind. Jasper's a fun kid." She laughed at my are-you-for-real expression. "Why so shocked? I love kids."

"It's just the fact that this was so spur of the moment. I never planned on having you two meet this way, or for Julie to have said those things to you."

"I'm a big girl, Paxton. It's fine," she said. "So, what to do tomorrow, Daddy?" I laughed but didn't give her an answer. "I have an idea," she said before I could come up with any-thing.

"Really." I turned my body to face her, pulling her closer. "Do tell."

Her eyes shone with excitement. "I say we let Jasper de-cide what we do."

I nuzzled the side of her neck then kissed it.

She moved to straddle my lap, my hands rubbing over the bare skin of her thighs as our eyes connected.

I captured her lips in a chaste kiss. "You don't know what you're in for, Allie."

She giggled. "He's a three-year-old, Pax. And about Julie—"

"What about her?"

"Let her talk. It doesn't mean I'll listen."

I smiled and pulled her in for a kiss. "You've got it, sweetheart."

We were in the middle of a nice make out session, but as I got handsy, Alissa pulled away, her breathing heavy. She blushed. "I don't think I can do it with your son in the other room."

I grabbed her face and gave her a soft peck. "I understand. We should get ready for bed anyway."

Cuddled beneath the sheets, my lips found the skin on the back of her shoulder as we said goodnight in a spooning position. I smiled when I felt her shiver of delight against my bare chest.

I did it again.

This time, she whimpered.

I trailed my fingers down the side of her arm. "I love the feel of your skin," I whispered against the back of her neck. Retaliating by thrusting her butt into my crotch, I groaned. Her shoulders shook with silent laughs. "Let's get one thing straight here. I have no problems taking you with my son in the house."

She rolled onto her back and I kissed her before nipping at her bottom lip. She let out a soft moan. I nestled myself between her legs and kissed her harder, wrapping her legs around my waist.

"Pax," she said against my lips.

I kissed her quick and backed off. "I know, sweetie. Can't

blame me for trying though. I just needed a little more to hold me over." I winked and rolled onto my back, pulling a snickering Alissa with me to cradle her head into the crook of my neck. "Goodnight, gorgeous."

"Sweet dreams, Handsome."

Handsome… I liked that!

I woke alone, with giggling being heard from downstairs. The sweet sound put an automatic smile on my face.

I got up to search for the two of them.

Just as I thought I'd find them in the living room watching cartoons, I was proven wrong, and found them in the kitchen, cooking, no less.

Jasper was standing on a chair beside Alissa as she measured things out and let him pour the ingredients into a bowl. I leaned against the entranceway and watched the pair, who were looking like wannabe football players, sporting flour marks under their eyes.

"Ah! Ha! It's time for the blueberries!" Alissa sounded like a mad scientist on the verge of a great discovery and Jasper seemed to love it, if his giggles were anything to go by.

"Can I get them, Allie?" He bounced around on his chair. "Can I?"

Alissa freaked out with a squeal, dropping everything on to the counter, including her act, and grabbed Jasper by the arm to make sure he didn't lose his balance and fall. She picked him up and set him down on the floor.

"Go get them, handsome." Turning to stir what was in the bowl, she hummed some childhood nursery rhyme.

"I thought *I* was dubbed *handsome*," I said, which made them both jump.

"Daddy!" Jasper ran to bounce around me. "Allie and I are making pancake ex-per-mints!"

"Experiments, huh?" I asked and he nodded vehemently. I eyed Alissa and mouthed 'thank you.' She nodded in welcome, gracing me with a grin. "I can't wait to try those out."

I grabbed a cup of coffee and sat at the breakfast bar while they got back to work. It was amazing how well Jasper had meshed with Alissa. She had never said how she had gotten him to warm up to her so quickly.

When Todd had first come into the picture, it had taken a while before the little guy accepted him as an extension of his family. As much as I had hated the idea of another man in my son's life, it had taken me voicing that I was okay with him making friends with the man before he accepted him. Maybe because Allie was considered as a friend of mine, Jasper simply had accepted her by default? I shook the questions from my head.

Why mess with a good thing?

"You guys need any help? I'm feeling a little left out." I threw in a pathetic pout, gaining me an "Awe," from Jasper and a snort from Alissa.

"You can cook them, Mr. Chef." Alissa winked at me. "What do you say we set the table, buddy?" She ruffled Jasper's hair and he beamed, giving her a nod.

Half an hour later, we sat at the table, eating and discussing Jasper's choices for fun for the day. I watched Alissa's face for hints of regret to her suggestion, but she looked about as eager as Jasper did.

Huh!

"**A**re you sure you can't just drop me off at yours?" Alissa asked.

She wanted to avoid any unnecessary drama that would most definitely occur when we got to Julie's. I couldn't blame her.

"It'll be fine." I grabbed her hand and squeezed. "Besides, we're already running late. I don't know about you, but I'm not in the mood to give the woman more ammo after last night."

She snorted her dislike and then Jasper jumped into the conversation.

A few minutes of Jasper pleading and I saw her mouth a few curses, but a smile played at her lips. "Just so you know, I'm doing this for that little guy back there." She pointed toward the back seat where my son was bouncing around in his booster.

My expert three-year-old manipulator had managed to change her mind, even though I had given it my best shot. I had convinced her that she could sit in the car and wait while we went inside, but my son had managed to put a stop to that.

"Hi, Mom," Jasper said and gave her a quick hug and kiss on the cheek. "Come on, Allie."

Julie allowed Alissa entry to her house, seeing as Jasper had pretty much pulled her through the threshold before anyone could stop him.

"Come see my room," he said and kept dragging her by the hand.

"Jasp—" Julie said, but her argument fell on deaf ears.

The hostility that rolled off of Julie was palpable. I followed the two, and an irritated soon-to-be-hopefully-official-ex, to Jasper's bedroom. Unless Allie assured me that she'd be fine, there was no way I was going to leave the two women in a room alone, with or without my son.

"Okay, buddy," I said. "It's time for Allie and me to go."

"Mom, is it all right if Daddy reads me my story tonight?"

"Sure," Julie said, a little too satisfied for my liking.

"Are you going to be okay?" I whispered in Alissa's ear.

"Yeah, go ahead." She gave me a reassuring smile.

"'Night, Allie." Jasper gave her a quick hug after she'd gotten down to his height. "Can we make blueberry pancakes next time too?"

"I won't be here, but I'll make sure to teach your daddy how to make them. I'm sure he'd love your help too." I caught her amused wink. "Goodnight, handsome, and thanks for the fun today."

She kissed the top of his head and walked out of the room.

I heard Julie's feet shuffle, which told me that the vulture had turned to follow Alissa.

I came out of Jasper's bedroom to find Julie standing in Alissa's face while the woman leaned on the sofa's armrest. I stepped back and stayed unseen around the corner.

"If you think you can just swoop in and take over, you have another thing coming, lady," she said. I wanted to put a stop to all of it but something kept me rooted in my place. "I suggest you stick to wherever you came from because there's no way I'll allow you to be around Jasper. You might as well move on because I know Paxton, and he would never sacrifice his son for a little whore like you."

"I'm not going anywhere," Alissa said with determination. I was impressed with her backbone.

"You'll change your mind," she said. "No one wants a kid that isn't theirs. In time, Paxton will come to see that. When he gets bored of you, he'll dump you for the piece of ass you are. I just hope he learns a few tricks along the way, but from a woman like you, I'm sure you're doing a bang-up job at helping him out, huh?"

I turned to peek around the corner and noticed there was nothing but calmness surrounding Alissa. Hell, the woman hadn't budged.

"Are you done?" Alissa's voice was flat.

A blank expression made an appearance on my ex's face. "What—"

"It's my turn to talk," Allie cut in.

Julie's face flared crimson. "Listen here, you little—" I could have sworn I heard a growl. "There's no way in hell that I'm letting you have him. He's too good for you."

"So now he's too good? A minute ago, he wasn't good enough. Which one is it, Julie? Never mind." Alissa crossed her arms at her chest. "That's your opinion, but I can damn well tell you, based on how you've treated him, you're no better a candidate than I am." She poked the sleeping dragon in the upper arm. "What are you so afraid of, Julie?"

"*Afraid?* You think I'm *afraid?* Let me tell you what I see when I look at you," Julie said. "What I see, is a woman who thinks she can show up and take over someone's life because she doesn't know how to find one of her own. I'll tell you something, *honey*, the grass isn't always greener. Now, listen, and listen well. When you walk out of here tonight, I best not ever see or hear of you again. I don't know where you came from or what you do, but there's no way in hell I'll let some new hot number in my husband's life take over my family, do you hear me?"

"Husband?" Alissa let out a snort. "Last I checked all you had to do is sign the papers and you're both free. You do know there are other ways of getting around that, right?"

"He wouldn't dare." Julie's venom-filled voice was a few octaves lower.

Alissa got up to her full height, leaned into Julie and said, "You think? I may have only known him for a short amount of time compared to you, but I can damn well tell you what you've known for a while now. Come on, Julie, you're not stupid. The man has been lonely and deserted. He deserves better, and you know it. For once in your miserable life, let him be happy." She sighed. "I don't care if it's not with me, just let him go. He needs to move on. *You* have. For Christ's sake, you're pregnant with another man's child!" My heart skipped a beat as I heard those words from Alissa. "I don't know why you keep holding on to him, but I can tell you that there's no good payout for anyone in the end, if you don't let him go. You have Todd; what if the man wants to get married? We both know Paxton won't take you back. If anything, do it for Jasper. Don't you think your son deserves to see both his parents happy, even if it's not with each other?"

"Why you self-righteous bitch," Julie said. "You think you know it all, don't you, preaching about things you don't have a clue about."

"I know more than you—"

"Is that so?" Julie smiled, and I knew the woman was about to lay it on thicker than thick.

My feet took action and brought me into the living room. "Julie, that's enough!" My blood boiled. If it weren't about chasing off what little happiness I had and making me miserable, I'd admire my son's mother's tenacity.

Her head snapped in my direction and I came to a stop beside Alissa. I put a hand on her lower back. "Go on and wait for me in the car." I handed her my car keys. "I have a few things I would like to say to Julie," I said so my not-so-significant other could hear me loud and clear.

I waited for Alissa to disappear outside.

"She'll ruin us, Paxton," Julie said.

"You've done enough of that all on your own, Julie," I said. "Alissa's right. I'm sick of being stuck as I watch you move on with your life and I can't do the same. It's been a year since you've left, Julie. A goddamn year!"

"How long have you two known each other?"

"You sound as if I've betrayed you somehow. Last I checked, I wasn't the one who ran around or the one who gave up without a fight," I said. "We're friends. Well, we were." *Who knows now.*

"Bullshit! She said she was your girlfriend yesterday."

"You started it," I said. "You attacked her with insults. She was simply trying to get a rise out of you. I can see now that it worked, and I'm glad it did."

"What about forcing the divorce?"

"I will if I have to," I said. "You're not leaving me much of a choice here, Julie. I'm done with the games."

"Then you won't see Jasper. I won't allow him to be around that woman," she said.

"You heard Alissa, Julie. She's not going anywhere, not unless I want her gone, and that's far from the case."

"So you'd pick her over our son?" she asked.

"You know I wouldn't, but I'm not giving up on being with her either. I shouldn't have to," I said. "So you either sign those papers by Friday or I force the divorce through the courts. If you want to be a bitch and deny me my son, then I'll take that up with the courts too. Jake's always loved a good fight, or have you forgotten? I have my rights, Julie. Any judge will agree with me." I pinched the bridge of my nose and let out a cleansing breath. "You know what's right. Just do it. That's all I have to say to you."

I walked to the front door and paused when Julie asked, "What happened to you?" I turned to her, confused. "Since when have you lost your easygoing persona and traded it in for—? You've become some hard, demanding, down-to-business kind of man."

"You wanted to play dirty, Julie, so the game is on. I don't take threats of losing my son lightly. Goodbye."

CHAPTER 7

We drove back to my place in complete silence. I couldn't get Alissa's words out of my head. It felt nice to know I had someone willing to go to bat for me; someone who was loyal outside of my family. I didn't know what to think of it, but I knew when Alissa's visit was over, things between us were going to be different. They already were, if I was willing to be completely honest with myself. I only hoped my ex wouldn't ruin it all with her resistance.

"I'm sorry about Julie," I said, as I walked us up the front steps, a hand on her lower back, guiding her forward.

"It's not your fault," she said. "I just couldn't take it anymore. I know it wasn't my place, but I had to say something. You weren't there to stick up for yourself."

I nodded, unlocking the door.

She entered the house ahead of me.

I grabbed her hand and pulled her back. She turned to bury her face in my chest and my arms wrapped around her in a tight hug. "Thank you," I said in her hair.

She took a deep breath and I felt the tension leave her body. She pulled away and pecked me on the cheek before heading toward the sofa where she dropped like a rag doll.

"Enough about that infuriating woman." Reaching for the camera that we'd left on the coffee table earlier in the day, she asked, "Did you take a look at these?"

I shook my head, thankful for the change in topic.

"Come see."

Cuddled with each other, I let her control the device as we looked through each photo taken throughout the day.

"You weren't kidding when you said you were a shutter-bug."

There were photos of my son and me at the fair, the water park, the ice cream shop, and the few I had taken of her and Jasper on the park bench with their icy treats. My favorite was the one where he had nailed her on the nose with his cone and she had returned the gesture. The end result was a photo of Jasper looking up at her with a wide grin, while Allie had her head tilted back laughing, looking carefree. I had managed to get a few additional shots before I had to break them apart, sensing that a food fight was brewing.

I found myself watching her reaction while she looked through the photos I had taken. She was beautiful and the emotions that flashed through her features made her look radiant. Her expression was honest, candid even, and I was ignoring the rest of the photos because I was so taken by her.

I ended up taking the camera from her hands, turning it off, and setting it on the coffee table.

"Hey, we weren't—"

My lips were on hers, my hands framing her face, in a flash. She moaned beneath my aggressiveness.

I pulled away and smiled at the look on her face. That well-kissed expression made me want to repeat my actions again and again.

"I was expecting a 'thank you for the photos,'" she said, her voice filled with huskiness, "but I'll definitely take that."

"You're welcome." She pecked me before she leaned into my shoulder. I then laid us down. "Four more days until you leave me," I sighed, my heart feeling heavy.

She lifted her head and said, "In a rush to get me out the door already?"

"Hardly," I said and squeezed her tight. "I kind of like you here."

"Hmm." She turned so her body lie atop mine, crossed her arms over my chest and set her chin on them.

We lay there, staring at each other as I played with the loose strands of hair that ran down her back. Neither of us seemed to want to break the comfortable silence.

She began to trace the contours of my face. My eyes closed instinctively as I relaxed further into the sofa, savoring the silky feel of her fingertips.

"Keep your eyes closed," she whispered.

I smiled, obliging her.

Her lips descended onto mine with their warmth and softness. Her kiss was sweet, slow, and tender hands clasped the sides of my face. There was no doubt that she took the prize home for innocent sensuality.

I groaned my discontentment when her lips left mine. She let them skim the day-old scruff of my cheek, nuzzling as she got to my jawbone and nipped my chin. It was slow and torturous. I loved every second.

In an effort to disperse the tension that was building in my body, I slid my hands down her back and around to let them rest on her bare thighs.

Her kisses stopped, then recommenced. These were to my eyes, my nose, and my forehead. They were sweeter than the others, the kind that made you feel more than just lust. They were the kind that made you fall for a person.

Her lips brushed the edges of my mouth as she spoke. "Open your eyes."

I did.

She had pulled back a bit more so I could see her entire face smiling down at me.

"What was that for?" My voice had turned hoarse.

"For today. It was one of the best days I've ever had."

"I'm glad you had fun, despite having Jasper around to entertain," I said. "I—"

Her fingertips reached my lips. "I know it wasn't planned and it could have been under better circumstances, but I'm glad it happened, okay? I don't think I've had this much fun as a kid, to be honest. This trip was about two friends getting to know each other better. Part of knowing you includes your son, Paxton."

"*Friends*," I said and tried to hide my disappointment. "With benefits I suppose?"

She blushed. "Well…"

I laced a hand into her hair and clasped the back of her neck. Pulling her face down, I crushed her lips to mine.

I bit down on her bottom lip. She opened with a gasp and I plundered her mouth. She still tasted of the strawberry ice cream she had eaten earlier.

"Let's not kid ourselves, Alissa," I said against her skin, as I trailed hot, wet kisses down her jaw. Her head tilted back and I moved down her neck. "We're not friends with benefits, and you know it." I pulled away to gauge her reaction. Her lips were swollen and pursed, and those gorgeous breasts of hers rose and fell at a more frantic rhythm. I smirked. "I believe the word you used yesterday was *girlfriend*?"

"About that?" She bit down on her bottom lip.

"Shh." I reached up and trailed my thumb, releasing the soft flesh from her pearly whites.

Her eyes shuttered to a close, and I took advantage of the fact she was straddling me to let my fingers do the talking.

I trailed a slow path from her lips, down her jaw, and ran it out to her shoulder from her collarbone.

She shivered.

I continued down to the junction between her breasts and enjoyed the view, seeing as her shirt had inched lower.

"I don't think I can ever grow tired of how you feel against my skin," I said, but pulled my hand back. The absence of my fingers made her eyes open, and she peered down at me. "Why don't we move this to the bedroom?"

She nodded, her eyes giving off a sense of urgency.

By the time we had reached the bedroom, my shirt was off and my pants were unbuttoned. I dropped my jeans and kicked them off to the side.

Giggling, she asked, "In a rush, are we?" She attempted to make her way toward me.

"Stay," I said with my hand held up.

She froze.

A zing of arousal floated down my spine to settle in my groin. This sexual demand and control thing was heady stuff. Why I hadn't tried it before, I'll never know, but I suspected it had everything to do with the person I was with.

I walked to Alissa, grabbed her around the waist, and kissed her hard with possession. My hands found the edge of her shirt and tugged it up and over her head. Her arms wrapped around my neck, and with her lips over mine, I proceeded to undo her bottoms.

My lips left hers and moved down her body as I helped her wiggle her shorts down. I knelt in front of her and smiled at the sight of the tiny gray lacy number she was wearing. Looking up, she was grinning down at me. "I've been wondering what else you had packed like this."

I watched her face as I ran my thumb over her lace-covered lips and felt the humidity from her juices. The hand that cupped her rear felt her quiver.

Tapping each of her legs, she stepped out of her shorts. I kissed her core through the material and looked up at her again. Her head had tilted back in rapture.

"Turn around." I found myself face to her firm bottom. "Has anyone ever told you what a fine ass you have?" My hands rubbed up her legs, onto her bare cheeks before pausing on her hips. I nipped her, making her jump.

"Pax!"

I laughed at her reaction.

There was more I wanted to do to her.

So much more.

I made my ascent, letting my hands rub up her sides, to her shoulders, pushing her bra strap to the side and ran a path of kisses from her shoulder to the back of her neck. My fingers trailed down until I could wrap one arm around her waist and hold her against me.

I nipped the tender skin behind her ear and felt her body begin to shake when I rubbed my erection into her firm ass. "I want you on your back, on the bed," I said and sucked her earlobe. "Eyes closed."

Her breath caught.

I reached between us and undid the clasp to her bra with one hand before I allowed her to move away.

I lowered myself beside her, feeling her body warm mine. "This is a little something different," I explained. "I don't want you to move. I want you to listen to my voice and feel my touch." I ran a light finger over her collarbone. She hummed. "For months, you've been teasing me with your stories, your flirty comments, and toying with mention of things you would do to me if we ever met face-to-face." I nuzzled her ear. "This isn't what it's all about. Don't get me wrong, by the time the night is over, I'll have fucked you the way I know you ache to be fucked, Alissa." She whimpered.

My fingers began tweaking her pert nipples, hardening them further.

Her body's responses amazed me.

"I will ravage your body until you're begging me to stick my cock into your pussy." I shifted and nudged my knee between her legs, rubbing it against her heat. She spread her legs further for me, and dug her butt into the mattress.

"I have a plan for us, Allie." I took one nipple in my mouth and sucked hard on it before releasing it with a pop. She moaned. "You say we're friends with benefits?" She nodded with hesitance. "But you've also called yourself my girlfriend." My heart swelled when there was no hesitation with her positive response. "Sweetheart, we have a bit of a dilemma here," I said, and took her other nipple and inflicted the same treatment I had to the other. "Here's what I propose, but open your eyes first." I waited for her to do so. "By the end of this week, I swear we'll know which one of those it'll be."

I kissed her hard at first, and then softened my assault before pulling back.

"Pax."

"This is for you, baby," I said gruffly. "Tonight, I show you how hot you make me. Tomorrow, you'll know how beautiful I think you are." Our eyes connected, and those bright blue orbs of hers held a mix of softness and potent lust that entranced me. "Now, close your eyes again, but this time, tell me what you want from me."

I licked a trail back down to between her breasts. My mouth found a nipple and flicked it with my tongue, while pinching the other one and rolling it between my thumb and forefinger.

"That," she said, panting as I continued.

I nipped her and she yelped. "You're delicious." I blew hot air, making her peak stiffen up before I moved to its twin.

"Oh, God," she said, and moaned as I took the other in my mouth. "Pax! Oh! I don't think—"

I pulled away. "That's just it, baby. Don't think, just let go and feel." I bit down and laved the pert nub to soothe the sting. Her body gave way, turning boneless in my arms, the orgasm that raked through her body being one of total submission. "Good girl," I said, as I trailed down lower, her hands grasping my head as if trying to guide me to a new destination. "Tell me." I licked around her navel. "Where?" My tongue dipped into the hollow of her bellybutton.

"I-I…"

I hovered, my mouth over her covered pussy, which was pungent and drenched from her overflowing nectar, and blew.

No answer.

I knew she wanted me to eat her out, but I refused to give in to my urges if she couldn't voice hers.

"Gah!" she said when I moved down and kissed the inside of her thigh. "Pax!"

I growled out a, "Tell me," as I kept moving away from her core, but pressed my thumb to it and swiped it upward until I felt her swollen bud pulse beneath it.

"I-I…" she said again. I pinched her protruding clit and bit down on one of her thighs, making her gasp. "More. I want—"

"You want what, Allie?" I kept up with the rubbing of her throbbing clit, extending her torture, her legs twitching.

"Fu- I-" She swallowed. "I want to feel…"

"You want to feel what?" I asked. "I want to taste you, baby, but I can't do that until you—"

"Eat me! Fucking eat my pussy, Pax!"

My shaft went from concrete to steel within a fraction of a second with her vulgarity. She was normally too shy to use such language, or so she'd confessed to me before. Well, she sure as hell wasn't shy now, unleashing some of her inhibitions.

"Your wish is my command," I said, looking at her flushed face of carnal exasperation and grinned, knowing I had been the one to put that look there.

"Pax, now!" she practically growled, animalistic heat overwhelming me.

My hands grabbed the thin lace at her hips and tore her underwear down the middle, exposing the flesh I so yearned to sink into. I had a moment of guilt for destroying her lingerie.

A short-lived one.

I'll just buy her a matching set later.

I delved into her folds, lapping up her juices. "Mmm."

"Oh!"

Her hips arched up which granted me better access, and I felt the sudden urge to speed things along. My tongue plunged into her depths as I used my thumb to tweak her clit. I switched, and plunged a finger into her, massaging that sweet spot inside, while I sucked her hard and swollen bud.

When I felt her muscles tighten around my digit, I pulled it out, and with my one free hand I pushed down my boxer briefs to mid-thigh, all the while keeping my mouth on that little jewel of hers.

"I need you to come for me, baby," I said. I massaged her clit with my thumb and thrust a finger inside her. "Make yourself come with my hand."

She began to ride like a sex-crazed kitten as I tried to shimmy my underwear the remainder of the way off.

"Baby," I said and felt her buck up and boil over onto my hand.

"I need you in me right the fuck now," she demanded before I could ask her what she wanted next.

I leaned over her, grabbed the condom from the drawer, and slipped it on.

I arched her hips up by grabbing hold of her butt and slammed myself into her throbbing core in one swift motion, almost sending myself over the edge in the process.

"Oh, God!" I swear the walls shook.

Teeth grinding, I stayed buried to the hilt, unmoving. Her legs wrapped around my waist and locked into a vise-like grip, holding me to her.

"What's—"

"Fuck me, Pax," she said before I could finish.

I pulled back and gave her a hard thrust. "Like that?" She nodded. "Open your eyes, baby. I want you to watch as my cock plunges into that tight pussy of yours, see the look of pure ecstasy break out when I take us both over the edge. I want you to come with me, but only when I tell you to."

I watched as she struggled to keep her eyes open, her breath labored, and sweat glistening over her body. The sight of her tits bouncing around was disrupted as she rubbed a hand down her middle to massage her clit while she held my gaze. Her other hand moved to one of her breasts and massaged it.

"Fuck, Allie," I said through a clenched jaw as I continued to thrust.

Her passage was threatening my length and causing my balls to tighten up much quicker than I would have liked.

Still, she demanded, "Harder."

She had me entranced with her own ministrations; I couldn't do anything but control the pace, so I gave in. Her cries began to escalate and her internal muscles gave me their sign of impending eruption.

"Come," I said. "Come with me, Allie. Now!"

I cried out with her, exploding as she milked every bit of my juices. "Oh, God, baby!"

I slowed my thrusts, our erratic tremors ebbing.

When our breathing stabilized, our eyes connected again and a blush covered her entire body.

"You're so fucking sexy," I said. "That was intense," I growled into the aggressive kiss I delivered her.

I rolled onto my back and pulled her so her head lay on my shoulder, while I ran an open palm down her back and let it settle at the base of her spine.

"I think I might be addicted to you by the week's end," she said, causing both of us to laugh.

"I think I might have to tie you to my bed to make you stay," I rebutted. She shivered in my arms. "You like that idea." It hadn't been a question, more of an observation.

After a bit of playful banter, I turned off the lights and we settled under the sheets. I held on to Alissa as sleep took its claim on me.

The last thing I remember was the distinct feeling of warm lips over my heart.

CHAPTER 8

It was just before seven when I woke and the sun was peeking through the edges of my curtained window. I turned to find Alissa on her stomach, the sheets lowered to just above her bare bottom. Her eyelashes fluttered, brushing against the tops of her cheeks and a smile graced her face.

Must be a good dream.

I scooted closer to her and my fingers traced the delicate edges of her shoulder blades, making their way down her spine. She shivered when my fingers reached the edge of her breast. Her arms were tucked under her pillowed head. Even in her sleep, she responded in a way I had never seen another woman do with me before.

I thought of the previous night and the things we had done; things I had said and done to her. I couldn't explain where the urge to do so had come from. In all of my thirty-four years, I had never once been that kinky or demanding in bed. It had felt liberating to say the least, and I hoped to pull a repeat session with her sometime soon.

My focus now returned to the present, I noticed her blue orbs staring back with that amused smirk of hers splayed on her lips. "I have to say that the sight of you in thought like that first thing in the morning makes for quite a picture," she said.

"Good morning," I said and kissed her cheek.

A strand of her blonde hair fell in her face and I brushed it off to the side, tucking it behind her ear. My eyes never left hers.

"Good morning." She blushed and buried her head into the pillow with a groan.

"What's that for?"

"I was thinking about what we did last night." Her voice was muffled by the pillow.

I laughed. "I take it that you enjoyed it?"

She lifted her head. The twinkle in her eyes had returned. "Enjoyed, you could say that. It's more like I overindulged. I'm a little sore because someone used me well last night."

"I think I can finagle a cure that might help with that."

It was a sweltering day out again and even though we didn't feel up for an outing, I recommended the beach.

I ogled Alissa as she removed her sundress and revealed her curves in the purple bikini she wore underneath. The thing didn't leave much to the imagination, but enough I wanted to kiss, caress, and tantalize the silken golden skin that lay beneath.

What was up with me? It was as if I was some sex-crazed teenager all over again.

I groaned. "I'm starting to think that maybe the beach wasn't the smartest of ideas."

Her dress hit my face as she laughed. "Are you done perving?"

I caught the garment before it fell to the sand and let it drop onto the blanket we had spread.

"I'm just getting started," I said. "A man can't help himself to look when there's a gorgeous woman standing right in front of him." I took my sunglasses off, slipped my T-shirt over my head, popped my shades back on and pulled the rest of the shirt off of my arms. "And you're better?" I asked, and took the few steps to stop in front of her with her appraising gaze.

Her cheeks pinked. "You know you like it."

She shoved me back playfully before walking off toward the water, the sway of her hips accentuated to tease me.

Damn!

I ran toward her, picking her up like a sack of potatoes and threw her over my shoulder. Her shriek of surprise had me laughing.

I smacked her butt.

"Hey!"

"That'll teach you to walk away from me."

"Put me down, Pax." She pounded my behind and when I didn't relent, she pinched my cheeks, making me trip and both of us fell into the knee-high water.

I surfaced first and didn't see her in the water beside me. She jumped on my back and wrapped her legs around my waist. I started to drop but recovered in time. We laughed as I walked us into deeper waters.

I shook her off, making her topple backward. She was still chuckling when she surfaced. I stopped laughing, captivated by the water beading off of her like jewels sparkling under the sun.

Next thing I knew, she ducked under the water, grabbed onto my hips, brushing her body up against the front of me as she resurfaced. Her face stopped mere inches from mine, filled with unbridled satisfaction.

"You little minx," I said. I was hard again. Hell, I don't know if I had even fallen out of my state of arousal since waking.

She grinned. "Me?" Her hip nudged my pelvis.

"I think you know exactly what you just did. That innocent façade of yours doesn't fool me one bit."

"And I think you need to cool off," she said and jumped up to dunk me.

We played like that for a while. As simple and childish as it was, it had been the most fun I'd had with a woman in years. The entire visit had been like that so far. It baffled me that something so simple made me happy, and the look of enjoyment on her face made it all the better.

Alissa was doing the starfish, floating on her back when I crept between her legs. She jumped and her head nearly sank underwater as I grabbed hold of her thighs, securing her legs around my waist. I grabbed her arms and pulled her up so she could wrap them around my neck. My hands held and squeezed her butt.

"You're beautiful," I said.

"You're not so bad yourself, you know." She laughed and let her forehead fall onto my shoulder as I rubbed her core through her bottoms. I couldn't help myself.

"Mmm." She squirmed. "Not here?"

She pulled away to look around before looking me in the eyes.

"Was that a question or a statement of preference?"

I figured I'd test the proverbial waters when she didn't answer right away.

My eyes locked on her lips and I went for it.

She sighed into my mouth when I opened for her.

We took our time.

It was nice.

Fuck the water, I was swimming in all things Alissa.

Her arms wrapped around me and she pressed her front as close as possible to mine. The feel of her peaked nipples over my bare chest heated me up more than the sun ever could. My hands left her derrière and rubbed up her back and settled on either side of her neck, with my thumbs rubbing just below her jaw. She nuzzled my nose.

I stood there with her wrapped around me, trapped in our moment.

"What are you thinking about?" I asked.

"How wonderful this is. How happy, comfortable, and relaxed I feel."

"How are those muscles doing?" I asked. "Better?"

She nodded.

If there was something I appreciated more than Alissa's physical attributes and her sense of humor, it was her blunt honesty and her willingness to speak her mind.

"I'm glad," I said. "What do you say we get out of here?"

❧ <u>CHAPTER 9</u> ☙

Bocconcino, although slightly upscale, was a favourite dinnertime haunt of mine that served the best Italian food. It was also where I planned on taking Alissa for dinner if she'd hurry up.

I sat in the living room, waiting.

Before I could check up on her, I turned to find the woman standing before me in a strapless fire-engine red number that could make a blind man turn his head and claim his vision had returned.

One word came to mind: hot.

She grinned. "I guess this'll do."

I had yet to say anything.

Collecting my thoughts and closing my mouth, I walked up and kissed her on the cheek. "You look gorgeous," I said in her ear.

Her warm breath fanned up my neck. "Oh good. I thought it wouldn't meet your standards." She pulled away with a small laugh and laced her arm around mine. "You ready?"

We were seated at the rear of the restaurant in a rounded sofa booth. After a bottle of wine and a few antipasti, we were served our main courses.

Opting to share a dessert, I let Alissa pick something: torta di ricotta.

As we waited for it, she shifted in her seat. Her thigh

pressed against mine, her elbow was propped on the back of the sofa, and she leaned forward as if studying me.

I set my goblet down and smiled, her eyes set on mine in an assessing way.

"Spill, what's going on in that sexy mind of yours?" I asked.

She grinned at my inquiry. "How there seems to be many sides to you that I don't know yet, but despite that, I feel like you're one of the simplest men I've ever met."

I draped an arm over the backrest and feathered my fingers over the bare skin of her shoulder. My eyes followed the lazy action before returning to her gaze.

"That's because I am a simple man," I said. "I live a quiet life ruled by my job and my son."

"*And* your writing."

I smiled. "That too."

The waiter came around and deposited the Italian cheesecake between us with two forks.

Alissa grabbed one and handed it back to the waiter. She winked at me. "We'll only need the one."

The man nodded and left.

I shook my head at her. "You manage to surprise me at every turn."

She dug into the cake and brought the fork to my lips. "You're just full of compliments today, aren't you?"

"I'm only stating what I've seen," I said. She looked down and her face darkened but for a short moment. "What was that look for?" I reached for her chin and tilted it. "Alissa, please don't hide from me. I don't know everything about your past, but I know enough. It seems like you've never been good at taking compliments."

"You could say that."

She tried to feed me another bite, but I took the fork from her and set it down.

She sighed at my forcing her to talk. "I'm used to the whistles, the cat-calls, the sexually overt comments." She rolled her eyes. "It's not that I can't take compliments, it's just that yours—"

"Aren't what you're used to," I finished for her and she nodded. "You've never heard anything sincere, huh?"

She acquiesced and looked past me. "Not from men I've dated, no. You're different than the others."

"Maybe that's what you need."

Her eyes came back to mine. "What do you mean?"

"Maybe you need someone who'll pay you a compliment with sincerity more often than not," I began. "Someone you can talk to, laugh, and cuddle with into the wee hours of the morning. Someone who cares how your day has gone and who's there to kiss and hug the stress of that day away or listen to you rant." I kissed her nose. "And I know, at the end of the week, you're not going to be able to let go of all of this like you think you will, because I sure as hell know I won't, and the week's not up yet."

I heard her breath catch and she shifted in her seat again. "Where is this coming from, Pax?"

"I heard you speaking with Julie before I came in to interrupt. Actually, I heard most of the argument," I confessed.

Her eyes grew in surprise and worry made its appearance. "So, that bit about me…" Her voice faltered.

"About you not giving up, that if things would end, it would be my call? Yeah, I heard it."

She huffed. "Well, that's just—"

"Wonderful," I said and tilted her averted face so I could get a better read on her. The back of my fingers grazed her jawbone before I trailed a gentle hand to the back of her neck. "Allie?"

Her gaze darted back and forth between my eyes and mouth. "Hmm?"

I leaned toward her, stopping right before our lips touched. "I'm not letting you go." I closed the distance, gently pressing my lips to hers for all too short a time. She kept her eyes closed and leaned forward, as if expecting more, but I pulled away.

"Here." I grabbed the fork to feed her a bite of the dessert. The sound she made when the flavor engulfed her taste buds was borderline orgasmic in nature. "Holy hell, Allie," I said and she blushed. "That was… Uh…"

"You like your women vocal," she said, and took the second bite I offered her.

I gave her a curt nod and leaned in to kiss her neck. "I never knew I would enjoy it this much, though. You do something to me when those sounds escape." Her hand gripped my thigh then rubbed up. I nuzzled her jaw. "I'm beginning to think that dessert would have been better in a to-go bag," I said.

"We should finish this." She took the fork out of my hand and scooped another bite to feed it to me. "It's too good to waste."

"And then what?" I asked.

"And then you can take me home. I need out of these god-awful heels."

"I don't know why you women bother with those torturous devices, but I do have to admit," I said, and began to rub my hand up from her knee to her inner thigh, inching higher, "I definitely appreciate the sacrifice."

She dropped the fork onto the tabletop. I heard its clang as it toppled onto the tiled floor beneath the table. She was the first to get up, straighten her dress's hemline from its high position, and raise her hand to be noticed. "Check, please!"

CHAPTER 10

After parking the car, I ran around to open the door and escorted Alissa out. She followed close behind me until we made it up the front steps. I was unlocking the door when I felt her arms come from behind with a hug.

"What's that for?" I asked, as I pushed the door inward, urging her ahead of me.

"Just because."

She turned to face me as I turned the deadbolt. "You're a sweetheart," I said. "You do things without thinking, like its effortless for you. It's like you know how the small things matter most to me."

"Really?" she said and I nodded. "Most men would call that overbearing and clingy." She shrugged her shoulders.

"There're a few more things I like about you too," I said, as I approached her stilled frame and held her hips so she stayed put. I kissed her cheek. "I like the way you ramble on when you get nervous." I kissed her other cheek. "How you bite that lower lip of yours when you get flustered." I kissed her nose. "How you wrinkle this," I flicked her nose, "when you think I'm full of shit like you did just now." She laughed. I grabbed her face in my hands and looked into her eyes. "And I particularly love the way you look at me when you discover something new about me, or when I do something that gets you all hot and bothered." I kissed the side of her mouth.

She arched into me and put her hands on my chest. "Is that all?"

"Nope." I brushed her lips with mine. "My list could go

on. A week wouldn't ever be long enough to convince you that I'm being honest about what I see, but I sure as hell won't stop trying with the few days we have left."

"Is there anything you don't like?" She took me off guard with her question.

I pondered for a short moment. "A couple of things come to mind," I said. "I dislike the fact you don't seem to believe me when I pay you a compliment. I despise the fact that your exes have made you feel less than deserving when you should have been treated like gold. You're perfect, Allie. And I hate the fact you have to go away at the end of this week."

I could tell she didn't quite know what to say to my purge but I needed to know. "Allie, say something."

Her voice came out with a quiver. "That's three things."

My hands dropped to my sides and my lips tried to quirk up in a smile, but I was sure they had formed something akin to a grimace. The woman hid her emotions quite well when it came to matters of the heart, and I couldn't quite get a read on her and her thoughts right then.

"Allie." I wanted to apologize for possibly spooking her.

Just when I thought she would bolt, she did the opposite.

She closed the gap between our bodies, making me succumb to her feverish kiss. Words didn't seem to cut it for her and her speechless state, but her actions conveyed more than enough to appease me.

W hat might have started off as a demanding kiss soon became one filled with gentility. With passion and sensuality, she conveyed more than I ever could imagine. Each of her kisses I returned with as much urgency, adding to the proof of what I saw in her, of how she made me feel.

I pulled away first and she said, "You're too good for me." She pecked my lips.

"I think it's the other way around, but I'd like to say I bring a certain *je ne sais quoi*."

The light danced in her eyes. "I suppose," she said, and the next thing I knew, she was running upstairs toward my bedroom, giggling.

"Why you little…" I gave chase to find her barefoot, standing at the foot of my bed, waiting for me with a smile, and looking flushed from her mad dash. I arched my brow as I walked up to her. "Screw the next few days." I stalked her. "I'll make sure you believe how beautiful you are, inside and out, before the night's end, and maybe I can prove my worth while I'm at it."

"Impossible," she declared and bit down on her lip.

Was she taunting me?

I grabbed her hips and pulled her into me. Her arms wrapped themselves around my neck.

I nuzzled her nose. "Nothing's impossible, sweetheart." I trailed kisses along her jaw to her neck and up to the tender skin below her ear. "Just wait and see." I took her lobe between my teeth and sucked on it, her breath getting caught in her throat.

"Pax?"

"Hmm?"

"Prove it," she said with sincerity.

"What's that? My worth or—"

"Paxton," she interrupted and held my eyes. "I already know your worth, and Fort Knox couldn't hold your weight in gold."

She undid the buttons to my black dress shirt, trailing kisses down my chest as she revealed the skin.

I kissed her, one hand clasping the side of her face, the other unzipping the back of her dress. The material pooled at her feet, and I guided her until the back of her knees hit the edge of the mattress. I stepped back and unbuckled my pants, admiring her appearance. She was wearing nothing more than a red lace thong.

"You mentioned sweet and slow for tonight," she began. "I figured I'd bring a little naughty since I know you like it so much."

I smiled down at her as she stepped up to me. "That you did. And I like it very much."

I took her lips with mine and laid her down. I covered her body with my own, kissing, tasting, and caressing down her chest before taking her nipple to savor her sweetness. I switched to the other and inflicted the same bit of tender attention as the first.

I basked in the sweet melody of her sighs, whimpers, and moans. Tucking my fingers beneath the sides of her underwear, I pulled them down. I kissed down one side, ridding her of the tiny bit of lace once I'd reached one foot, and began my ascent on the other.

"Alissa, you have no clue how special you are," I said when I reached her knee. "You know just what to say and do when I'm down and out." I climbed to her thigh, my hand rubbing the inner portion of it, and I felt her tremble as my lips made contact with the sensitive flesh in the crease where her leg met her hips. "You're smart, sweet, forgiving, and affectionate," I said as I reached her core. "You're the sexiest creature I've ever had the pleasure of being with." I kissed the top of her mound. She arched her hips up to me in presentation and I pushed them down. I indulged her for a bit and took her bud into my mouth, sucking and running my tongue over it as her moans grew desperate for release. "When you're in the room, there isn't anything else I want to do but be with you." I pulled away. She groaned from the absence of my mouth, my breath on her core. "And when I think of you going back home, I find myself wanting to be selfish and keep you for myself." I kissed around her navel and kept moving up.

Alissa's breathing became laboured. I moved my kisses to the hollow between her breasts and looked up at her face. "Most of all, I love the way you look at me. The whole world fades away and my troubles disappear." I grabbed her right hand, kissing the inside of its palm while keeping her gaze. "You're compassionate." I brought those hands above her head, interlacing our fingers. I grabbed her left hand with my other and administered the same infliction as I had to her right. "You're accepting." I covered her body, her face inches from mine. "We might have just met in person, but we've known each other for nearly a year. I know there's a lot more to know about each other but I want that opportunity, Alissa." Her eyes watered. "I can't see myself saying goodbye without knowing that you're mine. Not now, not two days from now, not yet."

Without even batting an eyelash, I had put my entire heart on the line. Never with Julie had I ever bared my soul to this degree. She hadn't been one for romance and heartfelt anything. Perhaps that's where the divide was that caused the eventual break in our relationship.

What happened with Julie was simply the natural evolution of a relationship.

What we thought we'd both wanted.

What others had wanted.

What felt comfortable.

But how Alissa made me feel was out of my control, and I welcomed it with open arms, never actually having felt like this before.

"Please don't cry," I said against her lips. "I didn't mean to upset you."

I let my forehead fall to her shoulder and sighed.

Had I gotten it all wrong?

Was it too quick?

Had I just ruined it all between us?

What if she didn't feel the same?

Part of me whispered. *What if she does?*

I felt her lips on my shoulder. She let go of one of my hands, reached for my chin, and tilted my head up to look at her.

"And you thought you had no worth?" The tears she had tried to contain had overflowed but she was smiling. "I'm not going anywhere, Paxton. I'd be crazy to let you go."

She flipped me over and began to kiss my chest in all her naked glory. With a trail down to my stomach, the feel of her lips combined with her soft hands drove me wild.

I arched my hips up to help her slide my boxers off. I caught her licking her lips as she eyed my erection. The want in her eyes told me she was a woman on a mission.

Alissa took me into her hand, kissed the tip, and licked the rim before I wrapped my hand around her wrist to stop her. "Allie?" I gulped. "This isn't what I planned."

"Shh," she said. "Let me take care of you."

I felt her tongue graze my entire length and all inhibition almost left me. "Not yet. I need to be in you."

She must have been feeling the same sense of urgency as I was, because with a sly smile, she grabbed the condom and sheathed me.

I grabbed her arms and pulled so she covered my body, and with a swift thrust of my leg between hers, I flipped us so she lay on her back beneath me again.

"This is supposed to be about you," I said before briefly plundering her mouth with my tongue.

"Who said it wasn't?" Her hand reached up to stroke my cheek. "I wanted to do that."

Without wasting any more time, I positioned myself at her entrance and rubbed my length through her slit, teasing her swollen nub, and feeling the wetness of her folds.

I pushed into her slowly. Her eyes widened with the feel of me stretching her tight channel. I withdrew, leaving only the tip inside and stayed there. Cradling her cheek with one hand, I let my other slide the length of her body, down to her leg, and wrapped it around my waist. I plunged into her again, our eyes never straying from the other's.

Our bodies rocked with a rhythm in time only meant for us. I stroked through her, felt her tension build around me. Her slight internal tremors told me she was near her peak.

She arched, her core squeezing me in a begging act for release. Her nails dug into my shoulders before moving to massage the nape of my neck. She pulled back on my hair and covered my mouth with hers as her moans grew louder.

When her climax hit, her insides wrung mine out of me, the room being filled with our combined cries of ecstasy.

I thrust slowly, letting Alissa come down from her heights, her hands stroking my hair as I nuzzled her cheek.

"That was…" She swallowed as she tried to regain her breath. "Oh hell! I can't put words to what just happened."

I smirked. "Way to go to boost my ego, baby, but we're not done yet."

She gave me a wry smile. "I was hoping you'd say that."

She had me up against the cold tile wall but I wasn't feeling much of the temperature difference.

My body overheated.

The feel of her scalding mouth over my cock, her ministrations as she stroked, licked, and slurped had my head tilted back in ecstasy.

I was at Alissa's mercy, and I wasn't about to complain, either. The woman had a fierce hunger, one she had never let on about. Then again, apparently neither had I.

I came hard and fast into the back of her throat.

She slowed her strokes and continued to milk me with that devil mouth of hers as she swallowed every last drop of my essence.

When the feel of her velvety tongue and lips had disappeared, I looked down and met her eyes. Her smile said it all as she got up to her feet.

"The way you do that—" She pulled my head down to hers and kissed me with hungry abandon. I could taste myself on her lips, something I had grown accustomed to and rather enjoyed. The woman sure knew how to take care of me.

"I'm glad you enjoyed it," she said between quick pecks. "Now, let's get out of here."

She made a move for the stall's door but I yanked her back hard against my chest. "Not so fast, my little vixen." I bit her earlobe. "It's my turn now."

I turned her around to face me and pressed her back into the wall before dropping to my knees.

I pressed my face into her core, guided her leg over my shoulder, further opening her treasure to me. She pressed herself into my face as I reached for her other leg, my hands and shoulders bearing her weight. I dipped my tongue into her depths, as far as it would go.

"Mmm… Pax."

I felt the grip of her hands in my wet hair grow tighter as her hips rotated in a circular motion, my hands latched to her ass as she ground herself into my face.

As her momentum built, she tilted her head forward and opened her eyes. Her climax was like seeing fireworks go off in those irises.

"Beautiful. You're absolutely breathtaking." I got to my feet and kissed her while reaching to turn the water off, and helping her out of the shower.

I grabbed and wrapped a towel around her body, licking away the beads of water that remained on her shoulders from behind. She leaned back into me and I folded my arms around her torso.

"Tired?" I asked.

"Not really, I think that shower woke me up." She winked at me in the vanity mirror. Her towel fell to the floor as she walked out of my grasp. "Come to bed, I want to cuddle."

That drew a short laugh from me. "You know damn well that won't happen with you naked."

"Are we having a hard time controlling ourselves?" She threw me a heavy-lidded smirk over her shoulder.

"It's not me I'm worried about, sweetheart, it's you," I said before dropping my own terry cloth sheet and following her.

I sat with her between my legs, wrapped in the sheets as we watched some TV. Alissa had grown silent, her laughter at the sitcom that was on had halted altogether. I looked down to find her sound asleep. Leaning my head onto the padded headboard, I closed my eyes.

CHAPTER 11

Morning had come and I realized I was alone in my room. A listening ear was all it took to know that Alissa was in the bathroom, taking a shower. The smell in the air told me she had also made coffee.

I rushed downstairs, grabbed two cups, and added her cream and sugar, just like I'd watched her do over the last few days.

By the time I had returned, she stood in the bathroom doorway with nothing on but my black dress shirt from last night, her tresses damp.

"I love seeing you in my clothes." I smiled. "That shirt looks better on you than me."

I put the coffee mugs down on the bedside table and sat down on the edge of the bed.

"Good morning," she said and came to a stop between my legs. She gave me a chaste kiss before wrapping her arms around me. My hands rubbed up the back of her thighs and made contact with her bare bottom. I arched my brow at her. "Don't you get any ideas, mister." She giggled into the top of my head, her fingers entangled in my messy hair, as she deposited a kiss to the crown.

The phone rang, breaking us out of our moment. One look at the caller ID and I set the cordless back down with a grunt.

"What's the matter?"

"It's Julie," I said.

"Answer it."

Picking up the phone, I hit 'talk.'

If I only knew how I'd wish I hadn't.

"Hello."

"I need you to look after Jasper," Julie said without a word of greeting.

"Okay."

"You're sure?"

"I said I'm fine with it, so yeah, I'm sure."

"Is *she* there?" she asked.

"Yes, why?"

"I want her gone, Pax."

"It's not happening," I said.

I remained short with my ex for the remainder of our conversation.

"Forget the papers then," she said. "And I've told you I don't want her around my son, and if you refuse—"

"Then you'll be hearing from my lawyer."

After I slammed the phone down on its charging base, the good mood I had woken up in had evaporated, being replaced with anger, worry, and stress, not to mention loss.

"Damn her!"

"What's wrong?" Alissa asked and kneeled onto the floor in front of me. "What'd she say?"

"How do I tell you this?" I debated where to start and rubbed one hand down my face.

"It's obviously not pretty, so just say it. I'm not going anywhere."

I took a deep breath and nodded. "She's still refusing to sign the papers."

Her jaw dropped, but just as quickly, she closed her mouth and her lips formed a thin line. "I'm sorry."

"I wish she would just give up, for once," I said.

"You know as well as I do, you'll most likely have to force

the issue, so why do I get the feeling that there's more to all of this?"

"'Cause there is. She wanted me to look after Jasper again. When she found out that you were still around, she flipped and told me I wouldn't be seeing my son, so I told her that I'd be calling my lawyer."

"Maybe I should go." She got up and I could see the hurt in her eyes. I hated I had been part of putting such a look there when all I wanted was to see her smile, hear her laugh, have her close. My subconscious reminded me that Julie was really the one at fault.

I grabbed her wrists and pulled her back to me. "No," I said and leaned my cheek into her stomach with my arms holding her in place. "I'm not letting you go."

"But what about Jasper?"

I pulled back and looked up at her. "He's my life, yes, but I still want to see where this, between us, can go," I said. "Julie's being unreasonable. This'll all blow up in her face once I get my lawyer involved."

Her hand caressed the side of my face. "I don't want to be mixed into this more than I already am, Pax. I don't want to cause trouble."

"You're not," I said, rubbing my face into her palm. "You're not an issue in all of this, Allie."

"Julie made me an issue whether you're willing to admit it or not," she said. "I'm the one who's standing between you having a relationship with your son, and I can't have that kind of guilt on my conscience. Maybe it's best if I go."

"Any judge will see through Julie's façade," I said, and pulled her down so she straddled my thighs. Our faces were mere inches away from one another. "I need you to understand that I can't let Jasper go, but I'm not letting you go either. I think I'm entitled to my happiness in this mess, and you make me happy, Alissa." I grabbed her face and crashed my lips to hers.

She didn't hesitate to open up and let me in.

We tumbled back onto the bed.

When I reached up to remove my shirt from her body, she covered my hands with hers and took over with the striptease.

Her glossy eyes never left mine.

Something about our joining felt different than all the others.

This time, it was rough.

It was needy.

It was filled with unspoken emotion.

Carnal.

Need won over want.

My hands glided up the sides of her torso and grasped her breasts. The way she rode me was like she was trying to quench a thirst she had been cursed with. She was beautiful with her head arched back, her hips moving in a sensual circular rhythm while she satisfied herself with a little up and down bobbing.

Her hands rubbed up my chest and I took that opportunity to pull her down so our bodies were pressed together in length. Her eyes had come back to mine as I rocked my hips in time to hers, slowing our rhythm.

The heat building up between us began to take its toll. I felt her insides spasm around me as she reached the edge of her climax. I could tell she fought the urge to explode, as if she didn't want it to end.

"Come for me, baby," I told her as I suckled her bottom lip. I felt her clamp down. "That's right, baby, give it all to me."

As her fit of bliss calmed, I flipped her onto her back. I wasn't quite done with her yet. I doubted I'd ever have enough of this woman.

I thrust as deep as possible into her a few times, extending the end of her release before almost pulling out of her. I teased her a few times, massaging her clit with my thumb simultaneously.

I felt her flex her muscles around my engorged girth; squeezing, yet pulling me further into her depths. I groaned. "God, Allie," I said. "You feel better every time."

I struggled to maintain the slow pace I was carrying as the arching of her hips into each of my thrusts, combined with her tremors, was inching me closer to detonation.

Her moans got louder and my hips sped up. Her hands found the sides of my face. She kissed my lips as if in need of air and ran her hands down to leave them on my chest while she pulled back to look at me. Her emotions weren't hard to read: lust, sadness, joy, something that looked like regret? Our release taking over, I slowed as our worlds imploded, forgetting about that last flicker of emotion I had seen. All I saw were white spots cross my field of vision, Alissa staring back at me at their epicenter.

Basking in the afterglow, lying over her, still sheathed by her warmth as we exchanged sweet kisses I said, "How about you get ready for the day? I'll go make us some breakfast."

CHAPTER 12

I was looking forward to spending a quiet day with Alissa. After my call with Julie, she had been amazing with making me forget about the resulting conversation. Hell, my mood had done a complete one-eighty for the second time that day.

Something bothered me about our last coupling though. As into it as Alissa had been, her mind seemed like it was off somewhere else.

You're overthinking things.

The woman in question came down and joined me in the kitchen. We ate with minimal conversation and I got up to collect her plate.

She turned me around at the sink. "Go do your thing, I'll handle the dishes."

"Back in fifteen," I said.

With a long hug and a chaste kiss, I headed upstairs. The feeling something was amiss continued to hover about. My gut churned and I knew it hadn't been the food we had eaten.

When I got downstairs, I noticed how quiet the house had fallen.

Too quiet.

Thinking Alissa would be sitting in the living room, on her laptop, I smiled at the thought of seeing what she looked like in a writing spree. But just as I'd found the living room to be empty, so was the kitchen as I entered it next.

What the hell?

The piece of paper, folded on the kitchen table grasped my attention. Picking it up, I began to read…

My dearest Paxton,

You are, by far, the most incredible man I've ever met. It's why I couldn't bring myself to do this in person, and for that I'll forever be sorry.

I've gone home.

I know you've said to stay and to be honest, I almost did, but for selfish reasons. I'm leaving because right now, Jasper needs a father more than I need a man.

I know you said you would fight and that everything would work itself out, but I feel that by being here, I might hinder progress, and I can't have that on my conscience—not if there could be an 'us'—and God do I hope there still will be.

Please know this isn't goodbye, not unless you want it to be. You don't need the added stress with Julie, and if me being out of the picture for now works best, then so be it.

I have nothing to regret about our time together, with the exception of what I'm doing right now.

Paxton, you are an amazing man, a man I've always dreamt of having, and that's what makes this so hard. I hope you find it in your heart to forgive me for leaving this way, taking the cowardly way out. Please know that I'll still be around. I may not be there in person, but I'm always there for you, and as we've resolved, you'll have to get rid of me yourself.

What you've managed to make me feel in these few days together, and over the last ten months at a distance, those are memories I'll always hold dear to my heart. I will never let go of those, and I'm terrified I'll be the only one to hold on to it all in the end.

That's a risk I'm willing to take.

You're worth it.

Always yours with love,

Your woman,
Allie

 My heart sank farther into the pit of my stomach with each subsequent time I read her letter.

I couldn't breathe.

I knew why she'd left, and I understood as much as it hurt like hell.

For the first time in my life, I had someone I felt I couldn't live without. Sure, you're thinking I would feel that way about my son, and you're right. But this thing with Alissa was different on so many levels. She held the potential for being my partner, my equal. I'd be lying if I said I hadn't already started to see her in that light.

I knew I couldn't chase her to the airport. Leaving hadn't been easy for her and I wanted to honor her decision. I knew it was for the best. For now. It took her leaving that letter to convince me. With Alissa gone, I would be able to concentrate fully on seeking a resolution to end my marriage and ensure I didn't lose Jasper. If I were lucky enough, I wouldn't lose Alissa either. I cursed Julie for putting me in this predicament.

Enough is enough.

I fished out my cell and searched my contacts for the number I needed. If it was a war Julie wanted, it was one she would soon regret bringing to light. Jake would make sure of it, and if I knew my best friend as well as I knew I did, he'd be putting a rush on things.

I walked out of Jake's office with a sense of confidence that I would soon see an end to all this. The courts had been called and we had a date set for next Wednesday. Of course I had paid a premium for Jake to pull in a few favors and rush things, but I was done waiting. Having a lawyer as a best friend sure as hell helped. Jake knew his stuff, and he was a force to be reckoned with in the courtroom when it came down to family matters. I had no doubt Julie would regret pushing me this far.

I had the urge to share my good news with someone who would appreciate it, but the only person I wanted to inform was no longer around.

A knock on my door tore me away from my plan.

I pocketed my phone and answered it. I groaned at my disruption.

"How could you?" Julie asked with tears streaming down her face.

"I'll see you in court on Wednesday. Anything you have to say you can say to my lawyer. We're done here unless your visit concerns our son."

I looked around to see Jasper wasn't anywhere to be seen. With that, I slammed the door in her face.

I spent the better part of the weekend hanging out with Jasper after Julie dropped him off on Saturday afternoon, but not without searching my place high and low for the woman she despised.

By Sunday morning, my little man was going on and on about Alissa and her blueberry pancakes. With how things were left, I hadn't gotten her recipe and so I indulged him and his wants by purchasing a box of the instant stuff and grabbed some fresh blueberries to mix in with them.

He shook his head as he stared down at the plate. "Those'll taste like poo, Daddy."

"I promise you that I'll get Allie's special recipe for next time, buddy, but you have to eat something."

"Can I have toast?"

I grabbed his plate. "Sure."

I sat down in front of him and attempted to eat my portion of pancakes to prove to him that they weren't that bad. One bite was all it took for me to realize that Jasper had been right. My culinary skills gone to waste, I gagged at the consistency of sawdust rolling about in my mouth.

"I told you."

I grumbled, "So you've said."

Over the course of the next few days since Alissa's departure, I found myself missing her presence, haunted with visions of her in every nook and cranny, the subtle scent of her perfume that still lingered in my car and on my pillow.

And the dreams.

I'd wake up feeling her all over me until I realized she was no longer there.

I had tried calling, sent her a few emails.

I even logged on to the writing site we met through and still, there had been no sign of life from her, aside from one thing. She had posted a new story, which I had read right away, leaving my thoughts on the comment board.

Despite the story, however, Tuesday had arrived, four days since her departure, and I ached to know what she was up to and how she was doing. I needed to let her know I was okay with her decision and hear her voice on the other end of the line, and not that pesky voice mail system of hers. For more than ten months, she had been by my side—despite our geographical positioning—and now, when I was looking for her, I couldn't seem to be able to reach her.

More like she's not reaching back. I grumbled for what must have been the tenth time that day.

I was snapped out of my reverie by Jasper tugging on my hand. "Daddy?"

"Yeah, buddy?" I ruffled his hair as we started to walk home from the park. Spending the day outside hadn't done much to lighten my mood.

My son looked up at me and said, "Why are you sad?"

"What do you mean?" I forced a smile.

"You look sad. Is it because Allie's gone?"

"It's complicated, Jasp," I said. I didn't want to overcrowd that tiny yet too-smart-for-his-own-good brain of his with complex adult issues.

"Why'd she have to go?" he asked.

"She doesn't live here, Son." I elaborated. "She had to go back to work."

"So she can come back and see us?" he asked with an air of hope.

His expression garnered a short laugh on my part. "Sure thing." It seemed to put his mind at ease, and I wish it did the same to mine.

Would I ever see her again?

"I know what I want for my birthday," he said after a short moment of silence between us.

I looked down and eyed him on the sidewalk before crossing the street. "What's that?"

"Can we go see Allie?"

"I don't think Mom would like that very much," I said, being cautious with my choice of words and tone. He didn't need to know about the current hostility that festered between his parents. "She might miss you too much."

"But Allie is missing me longest. I know she is, Daddy," he said. "Maybe we can have her visit again and then we can make more pancakes."

It's all about the pancakes, but then again, I knew there was more to it than that. I shook my head at his persistence. "I'll see what I can do."

Today was the day.

Not knowing how the week would play out, I had taken most of it off, spending as much time with Jasper as I could, seeing as I wouldn't have him for the entire week. I didn't like it, especially with not knowing how this whole court thing was going to work out.

With my son's sitter being ill, Todd would be looking after him while we were occupied with our respective lawyers.

Showered, shaved, and ready to get going, I chose to check my email before heading out for the courthouse. My heart leapt out of my chest when I saw Alissa's name in my inbox.

I paused before clicking on it though.

It had been nearly a week since I had last heard from her,

seen her. My over-analytical brain began to turn at breakneck speed. I worried that she'd have some bad news or worse, a change of heart.

I missed her more than I ever believed I could and that fact alone swayed me. After all, if she'd changed her mind about us, she wouldn't be doing anything to end things over an email. It wasn't like her. Deep in my subconscious, I knew her avoidance wasn't based on the way things had been left either.

I closed my eyes, took a deep breath, clicked to open the email, and began to read.

Paxton,

I'm sorry I haven't been available like I normally am.

Since coming back early, my boss saw it fit to send me off to deal with preparations for this conference we're handling and I haven't had much time to breathe since.

I'm glad you enjoyed the new piece. I had it sitting on my laptop and after I got back, I felt inspired to finish and post it.

I've received all of your messages and I would have replied but somehow, it didn't seem right to do over email. After being in the same room with you, emails almost feel too impersonal.

So today's the day, huh? Good luck, stud. I'll be home tonight, please call me. I miss your voice and I want to hear all about how things went. I have a sneaking suspicion that emails will fade and long distance phone bills will sky-rocket, but as I've said before, you're worth it.

Yours with hugs and kisses,

Alissa

I couldn't believe that I had thought her message would have been one filled with anything negative.

After what seemed like minutes of staring at my computer screen with a goofy smile, I turned off the contraption and got up to leave. The fate of my dilapidated marriage hung in the balance, and I hoped to walk away a free man when all was said and done. Would today be the day, or would I be spending the remainder of my week in and out of a judge's office?

We returned from a brief lunch break and sat down alongside our legal counsels in the judge's chambers.

The room hung in silence as we waited for the man to speak.

"I've listened to both parties and based on the facts before me, I have no choice but to side with Mr. Lowell," the man said.

"But, Your Honor," Julie said. "I—"

The man held up his hand, ceasing her speech. "Before you continue on protesting my decision, I will let you know that I am not pleased with your latest conduct. This isn't my first rodeo, and I cannot allow a failed marriage to remain intact because of some vendetta or unjust jealousy. Your case has no validity whatsoever, and I have no choice but to rule your marriage as null and void." He looked at my soon-to-be ex-wife, pinning her down with a disapproving parental-like gaze. "I suggest you continue on with the lives you've been living and the custodial rights will remain unchanged," he said. "However, what I don't want to see is you two back in here for something as petty as withholding a child from his parent." He arched his brow at Julie, making it known that he knew of her former threats. "Children are not pawns, Mrs. Lowell. Don't make me regret my decision on equal parental rights. You won't like my ruling."

"But—" Julie said.

Her legal representative hushed her with a pat on the hand.

The judge ignored her whiny plea and pushed papers in front of us. "These need your signatures. Once they're complete, your marriage will be legally dissolved," he said.

I watched like a hawk as Julie accepted the pen with somber resolve from her lawyer and signed on the dotted lines.

It shouldn't have been that difficult in the first place but it was official; I was a single man by the time the judge had put ink to paper with his final signature and stamped it with his official seal.

Jake walked with me to my car and asked, "How about a beer? It's been a while."

Nodding. "Sure."

"Dude, it's finally done! It's time to get you back on the market." Jake slapped my back, grinning.

"Don't think so, buddy."

"Who's this chick that Julie was ranting about in the hall when we walked in, anyway?"

"Long story," I sighed.

Three hours and a couple of beers later, I had filled Jake in on what had been going on in my life. As per usual, the guy sat, listened, and advised all the while scoping out the scene at *Fairfax,* the pub we were at.

Feeling like I had purged more than enough, I said, "So, when are you planning on settling down?"

"As soon as divorce stops making me a wealthy man," he said. We laughed at his statement but after some of what he'd been through, I understood his skepticism.

"You're welcome." Jake's gaze had locked on a redhead who sat at the bar. "Old habits die hard, huh?"

"The least I could do for being the one to introduce you both," he mumbled and turned his full attention back on me. "What a head case she turned out to be. I'm sorry man."

"Not like you knew."

"Yeah." He paused to ponder something and proceeded to push the subject of Alissa further. "About that chick. I sense that there's something you're not telling me. Let's hear it."

She's got you hooked…

You've got it bad…

Those lines played over and over in my mind. I wasn't going to deny it. I knew it to be true. She had me hook, line, and sinker after five days spent with her.

With my divorce being official, I was free to do with my life as I saw fit and it felt amazing.

That's when Jasper entered my thoughts.

I knew that Julie couldn't hold him from me. Not without landing in court again. But I had little faith she wouldn't try to cause trouble if I were to start something up with Alissa and that was disconcerting.

Who am I kidding? It's already started.

I saw the notice about a parcel delivery attempt from the postman.

Must be a gift for the kid. I figured I'd pick it up tomorrow as I peeled the sticker off my door knocker.

When I walked through the threshold, the flashing light on my house phone beckoned me.

I checked my messages.

You've got to be kidding me, I grumbled.

A proverbial fire at the office needed my immediate attention. After all, manuscripts don't edit themselves and a man has got to work for a living.

CHAPTER 14

The rest of the week went by without a hitch.

I had spoken to Alissa every night since my divorce had become official. My heart broke to deliver the news that Jasper's wish to have Alissa around for his birthday wasn't going to be realized.

"Is it because she doesn't miss me?" The sight of his quivering bottom lip and tear-glossed eyes broke my heart.

"No, Son," I said. "But she did say she wanted to talk to you. What do you say we get together on Skype on Sunday? I think she's been waiting all this time to cook her pancakes with you again and it's kind of like seeing her, only she's on the computer."

Jasper beamed. "Really?"

"Really." I handed over the parcel I had picked up earlier in the week. "And in the meantime."

"Another present!"

On Sunday, before I brought Jasper back to his mother, we logged on and I set up the laptop on the kitchen table for our Skype date with Alissa.

Needless to say, where the pancakes were concerned, I ended up doing everything since Jasper was stuck in front of the computer, talking away about all the neat things he had received for his birthday, including the parcel Alissa had sent him.

I think her gift meant more to me than it did to him, but I'd never let him know that since he was over the moon about his unexpected surprise.

The woman had taken off with the memory card from my camera and had made Jasper an album of him and me.

Since I had allowed him to open up his gift from her on the day I delivered him the news that Alissa wouldn't be around for his birthday, Jasper had refused any kind of bedtime story and had demanded to look at the photo book instead. She had topped the gift off with the photo of her and him and their ice creams and a *Happy Birthday, Handsome* note on the back of it.

"That was yummy, Allie," Jasper said.

She giggled. "I think you've got Daddy to thank on your end, buddy. He did all the work."

"I miss you," Jasper and I said together.

"I miss you both too," she said and sighed.

"I'll see you online later?"

"You bet."

The following month had been spent with me getting back into the swing of things.

Things had gotten busy and putting in time with my latest writing venture had become scarce since I was now bringing my editing work home at the end of each day. Hell, I was lucky to sit down for an hour and banter back and forth with Alissa. I preferred doing that to my writing anyway.

Tonight, Alissa hadn't seemed all that talkative during our online chat. She was withdrawn, what with her short and distracted responses.

Without hesitation, I rang her. It had been a week since we had spoken over the phone, and I needed to hear her say that everything was okay. I needed to hear the certainty in her voice.

"Hello?"

"You sound tired, sweetheart," I said.

"Pax!" She seemed to cheer up right away, what with the energy that her one word encompassed. "I wasn't expecting you to call."

"I missed your voice," I said. "And I had a feeling that things were a little rough."

"I miss you too." She sighed. "Work's been crazy but that's nothing new."

I know how that is. "Any plans for the weekend?"

"Aside from a few errands, not really," she said. "I planned on restocking my empty fridge and relaxing. Nothing really thrilling but definitely something I need."

I laughed. "I wish I was there to do just that with you."

"That would be nice," she said with so much longing that I smiled.

We talked about Jasper, my work, my writing, and then came the dreaded goodnight. As time went on, each telephone conversation was getting harder and harder to end.

"Pancake date on Skype this Sunday?" I asked.

"You bet."

"Goodnight, beautiful."

"Sweet dreams, handsome."

It was Friday and I sat at my desk, having my morning coffee as I stared at my computer screen.

I hadn't slept much last night.

Getting a call from Julie asking me if I was okay with her and Todd taking Jasper on an impromptu weekend getaway had left me feeling lost with what to do with myself, seeing as it had been my weekend with our son.

Still, my lack of sleep had more to do with last night's conversation with Alissa. I felt like there was something more than work taking its toll on her. Every day, chatting, emailing, calling, or Skypeing wasn't doing much to fill the void of her absence and keep me happy.

I missed her.

I needed her with me, and I was just as certain she felt the same way.

And so, I did what I had to…

CHAPTER 15

I rushed off the elevators to get to the reception desk. The woman who sat there looked like she was barely out of her teens. She bit onto a manicured nail as she spoke into her headset. Giving me a smile when she noticed me standing there, her eyes scanned me from top to bottom while she finished with her business.

"Can I help you, sir?" she asked with a quick lick of her bright red lips. Subtlety wasn't quite her forte, that much was evident.

"I'm looking for Ms. Hidgins," I said. "Can you tell me if she's here, or if she's left for the day?" I hadn't even thought on what I would do if she wasn't in her office. My efforts could have been pointless, for all intents and purposes.

Her smile faltered but remained slight. "Let me see." She typed a few beats on the keyboard and dialled what must have been an extension.

I stepped back, pacing the runner that was by the front of the desk as I chastised myself for not thinking my plan through. I wasn't the most spontaneous of men.

"Sir?"

My feet came to a dead stop and I turned to face her. "Yes?"

"She's in a meeting but I can show you to her office."

I nodded. "That would be great."

"Follow me." With an exaggerated sway to her hips, she led me to Ms. Hidgins' office. "Let me know if you need anything at all while you wait, the name's Lindsay."

"He'll be just fine in my capable hands, Lindsay," Hidgins' assistant said, as she remained seated behind her desk giving me a sympathetic look.

"Thanks," I said to Lindsay's back as the young woman walked away, clearly miffed at the middle-aged assistant who had dismissed her.

"My apologies about her," she said. "Can I get you something while you wait?"

Catherine, the assistant, had brought me a glass of water and a magazine before closing the door to the office. I waited, taking a glimpse around the workspace. There were a few photo frames of what looked like her and some girlfriend, as well as a few others. She had added her personal flair to the place with modern artwork and furniture, along with other decorative accents.

"Thank you, Catherine. Have a good…" She turned and the words left her for a moment as her jaw dropped. "Night. Holy shit!" She covered her mouth.

There, standing frozen in place was a very business-like, charcoal-dressed Alissa.

I grinned. "Hi."

As her shock wore off, she graced me with one of her best blushes, topped with one of her trademark shy smiles.

"Damn, I missed that look," I said gruffly.

She giggled. "What are you doing here? You are here, right? Please tell me it's not my imagination?"

"No, I'm really here." I laughed. "I had to see you."

She still hadn't moved so I took the few steps, then remembered we had an audience in the form of Catherine, who was smiling and nodding her approval at me.

I winked at the woman, shut the door, and wrapped a hand around Alissa's waist. I cradled the back of her head with the other and leaned in. She met me halfway for a tender kiss that neither of us was in a hurry to break.

"I hope you're okay with me hopping on a plane and just showing up," I said over her lips, then backed up to peck her forehead. "I mean, you did say you didn't have much to do over the weekend." I grinned.

"If I had anything on the agenda, I'd be clearing it, Mr. Presumptuous." She giggled before wrapping her arms around my neck and hugging me. A peaceful sigh made its way out from her when she snuggled into my chest. "You're a sight for sore eyes, Paxton Lowell."

I breathed in her distinct scent mixed with her light perfume. My arms squeezed her closer. "God, I've missed this," I said in her ear before kissing the side of her head.

"Me too."

Her apartment was much like her office: clean, organized, and modern in feel with crisp lines. We had stopped at the grocery store to grab some food, thanks to Alissa's insistence that she cook me a meal. I had agreed as long as she'd let me help her.

I noticed the picture of her and Jasper on one of the French doors as I began to stock the fridge with the perishables. I smiled at it and gazed at her from the corner of my eye. She looked peaceful, content, and the smile on her face still hadn't faded since I'd kissed her senseless in her office. It amazed me I was the one responsible for putting that look of happiness there, and I'd be damned if I'd see it falter in my presence.

I leaned on the counter to watch her cut up the vegetables for a stir-fry. We had music on in the background and I could hear her humming away to Breaking Benjamin's acoustic version of "Without You."

Suffice it to say, instead of helping her out, I was on a one-man mission; one to quench an urge I had been left with since the last time we had seen each other.

I snuck up behind her, brushed her silky tresses off to one side, and held on to her hips as I kissed the crook of her neck. A low rumble emerged from her throat when I nuzzled the soft skin below her ear.

"Paxton?" She dropped her knife onto the cutting board and braced her hands on the counter's edge.

"Keep your hands there," I whispered.

She leaned her head back onto my shoulder while my hands went to work on the buttons at the top of her dress, trailing my fingers on the swell of her breasts as I continued my downward assault.

"Pax."

Her breathing had hitched and the pinkish coloring to her cheeks gave her a glowing appearance.

"What is it?" I sucked her earlobe into my mouth, she groaned.

"I…" she started. "We should…"

I pinched her nipples through her thin bra and smirked into her neck when she yipped at the pleasurable sting.

"Tell me," I said in a husky voice.

Her body felt hot to the touch, as if an inferno had begun, and I wanted nothing more than to fan those flames until she was out of control.

She whimpered when I slid a hand inside her bra to cup one of her breasts and rubbed my thumb against her taut nipple, while the other wrapped around her stomach and pulled her tight against my body.

I licked down her neck and said, "What do you want, baby?"

She shivered.

I took my hand away from her breast and ran it down her smooth stomach, heading south. She moaned when I cupped her sex over the skirt of her dress. Her ass arched into my growing erection.

"Fuck me, please," she said, as her hands tightened on the cool granite countertop. "I need you inside me."

"I would love to, baby, but we have dinner to prepare." I tried to keep the laughter that wanted to escape at bay, but the teasing smile on my face was far from erasable.

I got the exact response I figured I'd end up with.

"Why you—" Alissa turned to face me and smacked me across the chest. When she readied herself to push me away, lustful want and sexual frustration in her eyes, I grabbed her wrist. With my free hand, I grabbed her jaw in a firm grip, my thumb spreading and feeling her thumping pulse, and looked into her eyes. "A little game or two never hurt anyone. Plus, I love it when you're this needy," I said before crashing my mouth to hers.

I bit her lower lip and licked it to ease the sting. Her cry indicated she enjoyed the way I was manhandling her.

I grabbed her hips, turned us so her rear faced the kitchen island and backed her up until she was barricaded between my arms. Her arms bent at the elbows as she used her forearms to pull my head closer to her face while she devoured my mouth. My hands rubbed down her sides until I had reached the hem of her skirt. I began to hoist the garment up and around her hips, and then squeezed her ass tight.

She hissed at my roughness and I pulled away long enough to see the surprised look on her face, which faded into pure animalistic lust. Sitting her on the counter's edge, I kissed her hard and fierce, supporting the back of her neck as I lay her down on its surface.

Now this is a buffet.

I reached for her lacy gray thong and pulled it down her legs, kissing, licking, and nipping the inside of her thighs, feeling her muscles tense.

I peered up at her, lost and enjoying the erotic sensations I had brought forth.

Reaching for the barstool, I sat myself down, lifting her legs over my shoulders to marvel at the sight of that glistening core of hers. "Your pussy is begging me to taste it, baby," I said my voice hoarse with lust.

"I need you, Pax."

I blew on her heated core and watched her lower lips tense up at the feel of the cool air. I gave her a long lick from bottom to top and felt her hips twitch under my hands.

"Undo the rest of that dress, sweetheart. I want to see those tits."

She did as I told her and I was glad to see it was a front-clasped bra. I reached up and tackled it with one hand as it snapped open to either side of her, her speed insufficient for my liking.

"Mmm." I let my fingers skim over their perked tips before pinching one and twisting it, causing her to arch her back. The motion caused her to jam those juicy folds of hers into my face.

No longer able to resist, I grabbed onto her outer thighs, stuffed my face in that wet and swollen haven and began to feast.

My lips sucked her clit, while I plunged a finger into her, arching it so it hit the sweet spot that seemed to make her detonate twice as hard. Her hands reached down to grip the edge of the countertop in an effort to brace herself.

Her moans grew louder and when I looked up next, her hands were pinching, tweaking, and rubbing those pebbled peaks of hers as I lapped up every ounce of her juices. I added a second finger and then a thought hit me.

I continued to suck on her nub before removing my fingers from her core and proceeded to that tight puckering of skin in the folds of her ass cheeks. She was so far gone, and the pulsating of her muscles was telling me she was near eruption. I rubbed some of her juices around the tight hole before adding gentle pressure.

She moaned loudly, her knuckles, back to gripping the

counter, had turned white. She shocked me further when I felt her push onto my hand as if to pull me in faster, as this new area I was exploring gave way with slight resistance.

I thrust my finger in a gentle manner and felt the tension in that area ease, allowing me smoother movement. I now had a finger in both holes and my mouth was clamped down on her protruding bud. The sounds coming out of her would have brought me to my knees had I not been sitting.

"Oh, God!"

I hummed into her heat. Her body shuddered at the same time and both holes began to tighten and pulse in a rhythm around each digit. With a few additional thrusts, her body bucked off the counter and I heard the most amazing guttural cry of passion, followed by the sight of the largest squirt of juices I'd ever witnessed.

I was so hard, it hurt.

Withdrawing my hand from her dripping mound, I kissed up her bare stomach, past the valley of silken skin between her breasts, up to her neck and jaw. I captured her parted and swollen mouth in a slow sensual kiss. Her chest rose and fell heavily as she grabbed my face to hold me there.

Alissa wrapped her legs around my waist and dug her high-heels into my ass. The pain from their jabbing me made me want to rut against her like some wild beast.

I nuzzled her jaw. "Damn, baby, that's got to have been the hottest thing I've ever seen."

"What was that all about?"

I sat her up and pecked her mouth. "Something new, and by the looks of things, I'd say you enjoyed it."

She traced my jaw with the tip of her index. "Mmm. Now," she gave me one of her mischievous smiles, "let me take care of you."

I groaned as she cupped me through my pants. "As much as I'd like that, I think maybe we should get a start on dinner," I said. Her bold touch, if she kept it up any longer, would cause me to embarrass myself.

She eyed me with a knowing grin. "Are you sure?" I would cave if I allowed her to continue, but her firm rubbing felt so damn good.

"You devil woman. It's damn well near impossible to resist you." I shook out my sex-addled brain and grabbed her wrist to still her hand and pulled it away. She gave me a disappointed look. I'd be lying if I said I wasn't going to be sore for resisting her. My dick was hard enough to knock nails into a board if I had the notion to do so. "There'll be hell to pay later."

I groaned as I turned and walked to the sink to wash my hands, deciding that I already regretted my decision.

"I'm counting on it," she said.

I heard her rustling in the background and assumed she was straightening herself out. Footsteps stopped directly behind me and she hugged me from behind as I dried my hands off. Turning around in her arms, I was shocked that all she had on were her heels.

Her hands went to work on my buttoned shirt and opened it.

I growled, "Alissa."

She gave me a not so innocent pout. "What? I can't wait for dessert and you can't tell me that is comfortable." Her eyes moved downward. "Besides, you're the only thing I'm hungry for right now." She gave me a sloppy kiss as she started to unfasten my pants.

Before she could drop them and fall to her knees, I wrapped my hands around her upper arms to stop her. "Not here," I said. "I don't want that, sweetheart." She eyed me as if I had rejected her. "Not right now at least. I want you under me." I kissed her. "No foreplay, baby. I need to be buried deep inside you and watch those eyes of yours darken and glaze over as I make you come."

"Well I never!" She started doing up the button to my pants.

I picked her up. She wrapped her legs around my waist in her naked glory and I allowed her to direct me toward her bedroom.

As I stepped inside her room, I was engulfed with all scents that comprised the woman in my arms.

Her nimble fingers undid the button that sent my pants tumbling to the floor, while I pulled my shirt over my head.

I laid her down on top of the covers and removed my underwear, towering above her. I rolled on the condom I had in my pocket and met her gaze and held it. She extended her hand and I took it, crawling upright on both knees between her legs, using my free hand to rub up the bare skin of her side.

I released her hand and came to a hover above her.

"You're beautiful," I said, and dipped my head to take her lips softly with mine.

Her hands trailed down my front, leaving a trail of fire that made me shudder when she reached my throbbing cock. She took it in her hand, guided me to her entrance, and with her legs wrapped around me, she squeezed them, forcing me inside her.

I moaned in her mouth at her directed invasion to her swollen core.

I stayed there, unmoving, while we indulged in each other's mouths. Her legs slid off my hips and rubbed down the back of my calves. She smiled against my lips, contracting those internal muscles of hers. I got the hint and pulled back to thrust in hard, causing her to grunt from my force.

"I've missed this," I said. "I've missed you so much."

"Show me. Please, Pax."

We found a slow and sensual rhythm, enjoying the feel of one another, getting reacquainted. She kissed my chest as I looked down, revelling in her softer side and I felt the tug at my heart. I brought my face down into the juncture between her neck and shoulder. I could feel her small spasms as my balls tightened.

And then she cried out my name.

Aiming to take us over the edge and leaving us in a puddle of spent energy, I thrust with purpose until I shattered with completion and joined her in postcoital bliss.

"Alissa," I said, my face sinking into the pillow next to her head.

That satisfied sigh she let out made me want to give her a repeat performance and then some.

I pulled out, Alissa groaning her displeasure. My shaft was still hard and as I wiped myself up and proceeded to pump myself as she watched, I made the call. "Sweetheart, I don't think we'll be making dinner tonight."

"Damn." Her eyes rolled and she smirked up at me. "What do you have in mind?"

"All fours. Now."

The woman moved as if my word was law. "I love it when you're demanding."

CHAPTER 16

The rest of the evening was perfect, except for the incessant ringing of Alissa's cell phone. After the fifth time her office had called, and she'd pushed them to voice mail, she apologized and turned the device off, leaving it on the kitchen counter.

Alissa handed me a drink before sitting herself down and cuddling into my side to relax after eating.

I looked down to find her eyes closed and asked, "Tired?"

"I'm just comfortable," she said.

She opened her eyes and looked up at me. Those doe eyes of hers had me captivated. I kissed her forehead before smiling down at her.

"I should bring you back with me," I said and tightened my hold on her.

She smiled. "Why's that?"

"You could clearly use some time away. And there's the fact Jasper asked that I bring him back something, and I think the only thing he'd be happy with right now is you," I said. "I'd have to say that having you nearby would make things easier."

I couldn't be any more honest about that statement.

Over the last month, our weekly pancake Skype dates had become something of a staple for the three of us. I loved the interaction between Alissa and Jasper about as much as I loved being with her.

The woman was incredible with my son. She'd even taken him on when Jasper had refused my methods to put him to bed one night. He'd been upset we'd had to miss our regular pan-cake date with Alissa, due to her being out of town on busi-ness. I didn't know the tyke could miss someone that much with such a short stent of knowing them, and it cut me. When the boy let me know that the only way he'd sleep was if he spoke to her, I gave in. Since then, every so often, I'd call her just so Jasper and she could talk. The weekly Skype dates were no longer enough for my four-year-old boy either.

"I love that boy." She absentmindedly rubbed a hand over my chest.

"I think I might have some competition." I clasped her wandering hand.

"Poor guy. " She looked up at me. "How will you ever move on?"

I laughed. "Move on?" I pushed her back onto the couch and covered her body with mine as I began tickling her sides. Her playful giggle was contagious and I found myself laugh-ing about as loud as she was.

"P-Pax!" she said. "S-stop! I c-can't breathe!"

"I don't have to move on. You're mine and I'm staking my claim right here, right now," I said laughing.

"What?" she said between winded giggles.

My tickles stopped and I pulled back. "You heard me. You know Jasper. The boy never quits until he gets what he wants. Where do you suppose he gets that from?"

"Are you asking me to break a four-year-old's heart by telling him he can't have me because I love his daddy?" Just as quick as she'd said it, she slapped a hand to her mouth. "Oh, God!" Her face turned a bright crimson. She rushed to push me back and get out from under me.

"Oh, no you don't," I said.

First, I grabbed her thighs and pulled her back down so we were face-to-face.

The second thing I did was grab her wrist to pull her hand away from her mouth, and then used my other hand to pin them both on either side of her head so she couldn't escape me.

"Pax," she said, her head shaking from side to side, "I'm—"

"Don't say it," I warned. I knew she was going to try and take it back.

"It's too soon. Dammit, why did I have to—"

I kissed her hard, that cute scrunching of her nose she did to go along with her flustered ramblings had been too much.

"Shut up," I said against her lips. I nuzzled her nose.

"I—"

"Alissa." I pulled away so I could see her face, and I sighed. "Sweetheart, calm down."

I released her wrists and framed her face with my hands.

"But—" I hushed her up with my lips again. I poured every ounce of what I felt for this woman into my kiss as her lips moved in sync with mine.

When I pulled away from her, her eyes were hazed and a shaky breath fanned over my face.

I smiled.

"Please don't take it back," I said, my fingers brushed her cheek as I stared into her eyes. "You have no idea how relieved I am."

"Why?"

"Because I feel the same way," I said. "How couldn't I? It took you being around Jasper for what, less than five minutes, before he adopted you as his new best friend? Watching you two together…" I swallowed the lump in my throat. "I never thought he would bond with any other woman but his own mother. I think it was impossible not to fall for you. I never asked for this to happen, nor did you, but it did, Allie." I took a deep breath. "You have the largest heart out of anyone I know, excluding my mother of course." She laughed. "You've been there for me when most would have run. You faced off with Julie, without knowing how you truly felt about me. You have no idea how you affect people with—"

Her hand stopped me before our lips collided in a short kiss.

"Shh," she said. "I get it."

"Damn, I love you."

She grinned. "I think we've established that." She pushed me back so she could sit down facing me. I pulled her so she was back into the crook of my arm and smiled at her before kissing her forehead.

"How about that movie?" I asked.

"I think I'd rather go to bed and have you hold me."

My smile broadened into a grin. "I think that can be arranged."

CHAPTER 17

I was on fire. Everything burned. As the fog subsided from my mind, I knew for a fact that whatever was happening right now was far from a dream.

Fucking hell!

My ears picked up the slightest slurping sound. She hummed around me and then when she grazed her teeth along the length of my shaft, my hips shot up off the mattress.

"Oh, God." I gasped. "Alissa!"

She increased her rhythm once I spoke, her fingernails scraping my abs, adding to the quickly overwhelming sensations.

I cursed the sheets that she was hidden under. I would have appreciated watching her please me.

My mind set itself to work, conjuring up the scene. I pictured her blonde hair, wild as if a hurricane had swooped in, her lips swollen from the friction against my length, her face flushed from her efforts. The more I thought about it, the more the image became vivid, taking a life of its own. The overwhelming urge to explode grew with her every stroke.

"Oh," I drawled out. I tried to hold off on my release, wanting to prolong the bliss if only for a little while, but the woman knew what she was doing. With one last hum, a few lashes of her tongue, and some suction around the tip. "Fuck, Allie!" I shot off like a rocket.

She made her way back up, trailing kisses from my stomach, to my chest, my neck, and nibbled on my jaw. I was aching for a taste of her seductive mouth.

"That's one hell of a wake-up call," I said huskily when she zoned in for my lips.

"I thought you'd appreciate it," she said. "Breakfast?"

I kissed her hard and quick. "Yeah."

She made her way to the bathroom, shoving a satin baby blue nightie over her head.

We hadn't been halfway through our morning meal when my cell's shrilling ring-tone filled the air.

I gave Alissa an apologetic look, got up, and kissed her on the top of her head. "I'll be right back." She nodded and I rushed to take the call. I didn't recognize the number. "Hello?"

"Paxton, it's Julie."

One word summed her tone: panic.

"What's happened?"

The woman broke down.

Worry overwhelmed me.

Had something happened to Jasper, to her, maybe it was about the baby?

My empathic nature was wreaking havoc on my reasoning and sense couldn't be made with the lack of information.

I gave the woman a minute to get her bearings and then repeated myself. "Julie, I can't guess. What's going on, what's wrong?"

"It's Jasper, Paxton. He's in the hospital."

My butt hit the couch's armrest. "What? When, what happened?"

"We had to come back home last night because he wasn't feeling well, and then he started acting weird, and complained of a headache. He could barely walk, Pax. I gave him medicine for the fever but it didn't work. There was nothing I could do. The doctors don't seem to know anything right now either. They're running tests to see what it could be, but it's all they're telling me."

"And you're just calling me now?" I asked with fury. "I'm coming back."

"Back? Back from where? Where are you Paxton?"

"It doesn't matter. Why'd you wait until now to call me?" I asked again. "I'm on my way."

"Okay," she said.

Silence filled the line for a few beats. "Julie, he's going to be fine, right?"

"Paxton, just get here." She sniffled. "I've got to go."

I ended the call and let my phone drop to the floor.

I had to get back home and fast.

"Is everything all right?" Alissa asked, making me jump at the sound of her voice. I'd been sitting there with my head hanging in my hands as I tried to make sense of what Julie had told me.

"Sorry," I mumbled and lifted my head to face her.

"Oh my, God, Paxton! What's wrong?" She rushed to me. I hadn't realized that I'd been crying until her fingers swept across my cheeks and came away glistening.

My mind was playing tricks on me, causing me to presume the worst of everything.

Alissa cradled my head into her chest and wrapped her arms around me. A gentle hand rubbed my back, as I clutched onto her for support I hadn't a clue I needed so desperately.

"That was Julie. It's Jasper, Allie," I said, and I felt her tense up in my arms. "He's in the hospital and he's very sick. The doctors don't know what it is yet."

"You have to go back, Pax."

I nodded. "He's never been this sick. He's never been inside a hospital since he was born."

"I'm sure he'll be fine in no time," she said, but I could hear the fear in her voice.

"I'm sorry," I said again, pulling away with my head bowed.

"For what, for loving your son and being man enough to be there for him? I can find worse reasons to leave, honey," she said, and tilted my head so she could look me in the eyes. "If you didn't go, I would question the man you are."

"Thank you," I said. "I promise I'll make it up to you."

"There's no making up needed. Jasper comes first," she said, and she grabbed my hand to pull me toward the kitchen. I stood rooted to the spot my feet were in and pulled her back to me.

"I think I love you more this morning," I said, and smiled solemnly before kissing her forehead.

She rolled her eyes. "Just when I thought it was impossible. Now, let's get you fed and to the airport, mister."

∿ <u>CHAPTER 18</u> ∿

Five hours later, I entered the hospital lobby with my carry-on bag and the determination to locate my son.

I spotted the reception desk and rushed to it. "Excuse me," I said. "My son was admitted last night and—"

"Name please." I don't think I'd ever heard someone so detached before.

"Lowell. Jasper Lowell."

The woman typed in the information in her computer and ran a quick scan. I bit my tongue, the urge to tell her to hurry up a little too potent, and then she looked up. "He's in the pediatric unit. Just go down this hall, take the elevator on your right to the third floor, and the nurse at the desk will be able to help you from there," she said, pointing in the direction I should take.

Nodding my appreciation, I took off as quick as my feet could take me without breaking into a run.

Jasper was sleeping. His tiny four-year-old form was as white as the sheets that covered him. If it weren't for the shiny gleam of sweat glistening on his forehead, and the beeping of the monitoring devices, he looked like death had warmed over. Todd had his arms wrapped around Julie by the room's window, their backs to me. I cleared my throat as I approached.

"Where the hell have you been? You said you'd be right

over," Julie accused. Her eyes were puffy and her makeup had run down her face.

"Now's not the time, Jewels," Todd said, rubbing her shoulders.

"No, I want to know." She crossed her arms.

"I agree with Todd. It doesn't matter where I was. All that matters is that I'm here," I said and looked at Jasper.

My eyes stung for the third time today as tears threatened to spill over.

I made my way to him. I grabbed his clammy hand while I sat on the stool beside the bed. Kissing the top of it, my head hit the edge of the mattress.

After a silent minute, pregnant with far too much despair and whirling thoughts, none too pleasant or positive, I looked up and over to the other side of the gurney where Todd and Julie were now standing. "Any news since you called me?"

Julie shook her head.

"The doctor should be in soon with the latest test results," Todd said.

I pointed to the electrodes hooked up to my son's now shaved head. "What are all these?"

"They're running neurological tests," Todd said, and Julie began to cry again.

I looked from Todd to Julie. "Am I missing something here? This is worse than you made it seem. This is not just a fever and odd behaviour, is it?"

Before I could be granted an explanation, I heard a throat clearing.

I turned to face a young doctor and got up to shake his hand.

"Mr. Lowell, I presume?" he asked. I nodded. "I'm Dr. Messing. I'm the lead on your son's case."

"Doctor, what's going on?"

"I'm afraid it's not good news," he said, and my heart sunk along with my butt, which happened to hit the stool I had just vacated. "Based on our current treatment regimen, nothing seems to be working. We can control his fever for the most part, but we needed to run a battery of tests to find out why this fever has sprung up and why it's been so resistant to the medicines we've been giving him. We initially thought that Jasper might have dementia but we've since ruled it out. I suspected meningitis, and with the help of our neurological testing, and an extensive review of the basic blood work, we've proven that it is, but I—"

"Then what's the problem?" I asked.

"I've never seen a case like this before, and before I give you an outright answer, I'd like to confer with my colleagues about my suspicions," he said.

"What are your suspicions, Doc?" I asked.

"I don't think Jasper is suffering from meningitis alone. His symptoms are too broad and don't fall in with the disease's historical findings. I think we're dealing with multiple diseases, here," he said. "Give me until the end of the day, twenty-four hours at the most. We'd like to run an MRI, as well as perform a spinal tap to help us along with my suspected conclusions. Those results should be in by the time they finish running the rest of the bloods we've collected within the last hour, provided the lab isn't overrun. I assure you that we're being as thorough as we possibly can be."

"Do what you have to," I said, but the doctor's words hadn't made me feel any better.

Meningitis was bad enough on its own.

But two diseases?

Fuck!

Answers were better than nothing, but there were still too many holes to really relax and feel reassured that Jasper would be okay. He sure as hell didn't look it.

The day had come to pass and Dr. Messing walked through Jasper's room's door.

I had watched as multiple medical personnel had come and

gone, jotting short notes in his chart, adjusting his fluids, switching parameters on the machines, pushing, poking, prodding at my son like he was some sort of pincushion. No one had anything to say about his progress or a definitive diagnosis, and it wore me to the last of my frayed nerves.

Inept.

The thought of the word, the reality that the definition suited me to a "T" drove me insane. To not be able to do anything to help Jasper had always been but a blip on my radar where realities were concerned. It was my job as his father to mend all the wounds, to kiss and wipe those tears away, and make sure that he smiled. Now, he was just a small mass atop a hospital bed, looking like the Reaper was well on his way to fetch him, and all of us were completely at the mercy of an outsider's professional expertise.

"So?" Todd asked, as Julie and I got up to stand beside him and face the facts.

Ashen-faced, that's when I knew the young doctor's think tank hadn't panned out so well.

We did get a name to what was plaguing Jasper, in conjunction to his meningitis: Juvenile Myelomonocytic Leukemia or JMML.

All I heard was 'leukemia.'

That was enough.

"Cancer?" My voice cracked.

Messing nodded. "It's a disease that is hard to cure and affects children between birth to the age of four, not like the types you most often hear about," he said. "I'm afraid that things are a bit more complicated with the fact that Jasper here has meningitis, which is why his symptoms pointed to so many possibilities." In mere minutes, he'd managed to twist and stomp on my heart as he went on about prognosis, treatment plans, even handing us a pamphlet each to leaf through in order to know more about what to expect as a parent of a child with JMML. "I'm sorry. I'll be here throughout the night, should you need me to answer any more questions. I know this is a lot to digest and so I suggest—"

"Doctor?" Messing turned to face me. "How long does he…" *God, I can't even say the words.*

"With meningitis as a major player here, I won't lie," he said. "We need to treat that and get rid of it as soon as possible. The good news is that your son seems to be responding well to the treatment so far. If it were strictly the JMML, as rare as this type of leukemia can be for a kid Jasper's age, because he's at the top of the age cusp, your son can be around for another few years, but that also depends on the aggressiveness of his disease, barring any other complications. I'm presenting you with the average life expectancy, but know that time can be longer like it can be shorter. No two patients are alike, sir. The important thing to know is that you have options for treatment. There's still hope."

I nodded. "And what about quality of life, will he be stuck here the whole time?"

"We'll talk more about it when we get him stabilized on his meds and his meningitis is no longer a threat." Spoken like a true optimist, which I appreciated. "With JMML, Jasper will be more susceptible to infections, as like with most cancer and immuno-challenged patients, which could compromise his progress. I know the reality of having Jasper remain in the hospital is tough to swallow, but if it ensures his survival, wouldn't you want to take that chance? Then again, I've seen patients respond incredibly well by being surrounded with what's familiar to them, especially in the younger age groups, so I'll be sure to let you know when and if he can go home." Dr. Messing looked at each and every one of us. He knew he wasn't painting the best of pictures. "Again, I'm truly sorry, but as the days go on, we'll know more about what to expect for your little guy."

The man walked out and I walked toward the window.

I turned and peered at my son's sleeping form and fought the lump in my throat.

I couldn't believe it. I was possibly going to lose my son—my life, my *raison d'être*—in the worst possible way. He was the little miracle that had always managed to put a smile on my face, no matter how grim life could get at times, and I might have an accelerated expiration date to the time I can spend with him. Parents should never be able to lose their kids. It's just not natural.

"I need some air," I said to Julie, that lump in my throat rapidly growing into a thick ball, threatening to choke me altogether. "Will you be okay?"

She nodded and for the first time since before our separation, she hugged me. We might not have agreed on much, but there was no dispute as to the one person we both loved unconditionally. It was the little boy lying in that bed, losing his life before us. We clutched at each other, no words needed as we soaked every bit of comfort that we could from the other.

Julie sniffled. "I think you should call her." I backed away, shock all too evident on my face, as I knew she meant Alissa. "Don't look at me like that. Jasper talks about her all the time lately. She needs to know too, Pax. And as much as you'll probably say you don't, you need the support right now. That's where you were, wasn't it?"

I hadn't known what to say.

Nodding, I left the room and headed for the nearest exit.

Reaching for my phone, I dialed Alissa's number.

CHAPTER 19

Much like over a month ago, I stood in the airport waiting for Alissa's arrival. After we spoke the previous night, she refused to stay home—despite my numerous protests that I was able to deal—choosing to jump on the first flight available. Thinking of it now however, I know my protests hadn't been strong-willed.

"Everyone has someone but you," she'd said.

I had pondered that for a few minutes while on the line with her. She did have a point, and as much as I hated to say it, so did my ex. Despite that, I had argued against it until I thought of Jasper and what he would want. The meningitis could be what claimed him before the cancer ever had a chance to do so, and as much as I claimed to be strong enough, this wasn't the time to assert my pride and display my strength. It was about doing what was right for my son, and what was right was to have everyone he cared about surrounding him.

I looked up and there she was running toward me with her purse and bag in hand. If I said the embrace I had with Julie yesterday was comforting, it had nothing on the emotional release brought forth by Alissa's arms. I finally felt as if it was okay to let go somewhat, but I chose to wait until we had found some privacy.

"Has he woken up yet?"

I held on to her. "Not yet," I said into her hair. "Julie said she'd give me a call if he did."

She backed away, palmed and studied my face. "You haven't slept at all, have you?"

"No." Declaring I couldn't bring myself to leave Jasper didn't need to be said, she knew why. "I stayed behind so Todd and Julie could go home and get a bit of rest."

"I think we should go home and get you a few winks before you go back," she said.

"I won't be able to sleep."

She rubbed the sides of my upper arms. "How about you try? I'll be right there."

I nodded, too exhausted to protest anymore.

I walked out of the bathroom after a quick shower and found her sitting on my bed waiting for me. She pushed the blankets to the side and motioned for me to get in beside her.

I laid my head on top of her breasts and she wrapped her arms around me; that's when the first sob racked my body. For the first time since I had been a child, I realized that showing weakness wasn't all that bad.

I felt her fingers brush through my hair and listened to the calm rhythm of her heartbeats before she pressed her lips to the crown of my head, whispering assurances that she was there for me every so often, but remained mostly quiet until the surge had passed.

"Close your eyes, honey," she said.

I shimmied down so my head lay on her stomach and wrapped my arms around her torso.

Soon enough, I felt myself drift off.

I came to in the same position I had fallen asleep in. Alissa was rubbing my back.

Despite the trauma of the last two days, I managed a smile at the comfort she offered.

"What time is it?" I asked with a sleepy voice.

"A little before one." I bolted, sitting upright. I felt like I had slept the day away. "Relax, Julie hasn't called." She proceeded to scoot out of the bed, but I grabbed her and pulled her down so she lay on her back and I towered over her from her side.

"Thank you," I said, and kissed her before pulling away so I could look into her face. "I know I said I would've been fine without you here but honestly—"

"There's no way I would have let you deal with this alone. I would have shown up on your doorstep whether you agreed to me coming or not," she said. "Now get dressed so you can go back there and see your son."

"You're coming," I said with finality that brokered no argument.

"I don't think that's a good idea. What will Julie say?"

I hadn't told her that Julie had been the one who recommended I call her in the first place. I saw it as a test my ex was issuing. She wanted validation as to what kind of woman Alissa was, and I was hell-bent on making sure my woman passed that exam with flying colors.

"I have a sneaking suspicion that she'll be fine."

She eyed with suspicion. "Please elaborate."

"It seems Jasper has been dropping your name at Julie and Todd's," I said. "Julie recommended I call you before I left the room to do just that." I chuckled dryly at her look of incredulity and pulled her into my arms when her eyes grew watery, despite her smile.

Forty minutes later, we were walking through the hospital doors. I escorted her to Jasper's room but she insisted I go in alone at first. She wanted to ready herself before going in.

Julie's eyes held a questioning gaze.

"She's out in the hall," I said. And I honestly can't blame her for her hesitance.

My ex sighed, "I owe her an apology." Todd gave her shoulder a squeeze. "I've said some awful things, and it wasn't until Jasper started talking about her all the time that I realized she was more than just a fling to you."

"Julie—"

She held up her hand. "I know that you don't sleep around. I've always known that, Paxton," she said. "She was right when she said I was terrified. I was trying to hold on to a family I no longer had, and I was the one to blame for it. I had no right. I wanted to be the only woman in Jasper's life but—"

"Jasper will always be your son and you, his mother."

We all turned to see Alissa standing in the doorway.

Julie walked up to grab her in a tight hug. Alissa looked at me, her eyes bulging out of her skull at Julie's actions, while she patted her on the back with awkwardness.

"Thanks for coming," Julie said and let go of her to grab Todd's outstretched hand. "We'll give you some time. Be back later."

I was coming back with coffee for Allie and me when I heard Alissa's voice. She was talking to Jasper and so I leaned onto the room's threshold and kept vigil on the pair.

"…so Jasper, honey, I need you to wake up for me," she said. "Mommy and Daddy would like to see those beautiful bright green eyes of yours. We miss you and that smile, sweetie. What about our pancake dates?" Her voice cracked, sending a jolt of pain to my heart. "I need someone to pour those blueberries for me. And who else would help me make a big mess?" She began to sob softly into the edge of the mattress. "We all need you, Jasper."

I walked over to her, set down our cups and turned her to face me. I cradled her cheek and she buried her face in my chest, clutching at my shirt. I couldn't help the tears filling my eyes as we held on tight to each other.

"Allie?"

My head snapped toward the bed. "Jasper!" My heart thumped like crazy.

I was quick to let go of Alissa and page the doctor before rushing back to my son's bedside.

"Hi, handsome," Alissa said, and cupped his pale cheek and pulled her hand back to wipe at her tear-stained cheeks. "I've missed you."

My little boy smiled weakly. "You came back," he said and coughed a few times.

"Of course I did. No one can keep me away from you, silly."

I smiled at their exchange before hugging her with one arm and kissing her temple.

"How are you feeling, Son?" I asked.

"My head hurts, but I'm okay," he said.

"You scared me, champ," I said and leaned over to kiss his forehead. "I love you."

Saying those three little words was no longer enough now that I felt as if I had a deadline for reminding him of how I've felt about him since before he was born.

"I love you too, Daddy."

Dr. Messing came in and ran a variety of cognitive and diagnostic tests. After a lengthy waiting period, he announced that Jasper's meningitis was losing strength and his antibiotics were working. I couldn't have been more relieved, other than if Messing had divulged that Jasper's JMML had been cured, but it wasn't the case.

Armed with a variety of prescription medications for him, Jasper would be able to head home in a few days, provided he fared well throughout his time in the hospital, and we brought him back every day for an assessment. It was a small price to pay to have him at home with us if you asked me.

Jasper was to be put on oral chemotherapy, despite being informed the treatment would most likely not cure him. It rarely did with JMML. If anything, it would help stall the progression until a suitable treatment plan was decided upon for him while we weighed our options. There weren't many, but more than enough to make one's head spin.

CHAPTER 20

The drive home had been one filled with silence. I couldn't get past the fact that out of all of us, Alissa had been the one to bring Jasper out of that frightening sleep.

I grabbed Alissa's hand and kissed her knuckles. "You're amazing."

She looked over at me and offered a bright smile. "So I keep hearing," she said and winked. "If you guys keep praising me as this miracle healer, I swear I'll develop a complex."

"I never asked. When are you here until?"

Her nose scrunched up. "I have to go back tomorrow. That conference I've been working on starts on Wednesday and runs until the end of next week."

I nodded. "We'll have to make sure Jasper gets his pancakes in before you leave," I said and smiled.

She giggled. "That we can definitely arrange. Maybe I'll even make extras to bring to the nurses."

The moon and stars were out and peeked through the darkness. I remembered I still had a blanket in the back of the SUV from my picnic with Jasper last week.

Last week.

When everything was perfect and normal.

Sure, it was a little after eleven, but I wasn't in a rush to get home just yet.

With a quick right turn, I headed toward the beach.

"I thought we were going home." She turned to me with an inquiring gaze. "Why are we at the beach?"

"I was thinking we'd make a pit stop here first." I parked the car. "I'm not ready to go home yet."

I allowed her to exit the car while I grabbed the blanket from the back.

We made it to the sand, me holding her hand as we found my favourite spot: the one I had taken her to a month ago.

"I never pictured you for one to stargaze," she said with a hint of humor.

"It's one of Jasper's favourite things to do," I explained, as I spread the blanket down and we lay on our backs looking at the sky. I sighed. *How many more times will I be able to do this with him?*

I hadn't noticed the melancholy lacing my being, but Alissa sure did. She perched herself up on her elbow and turned her body toward mine.

"He's not gone yet, Pax." I looked at her. "You'll have many more nights like this before that happens. *If* it happens. I'll make sure you do."

"I know, baby." I reached up and ran my fingers through her hair. "I'm still digesting all of this, I guess. My mind won't stop going back to yesterday when the doctor told us. It's a lot to take in."

She hummed her agreement and put a hand on my chest. "Anything I can do to make it better?"

I eyed her. "Maybe."

I fisted her hair and pulled her down to me, kissing her hard, drowning in the feel of her lips against mine, the sweet taste of her velvet tongue, the pure scent of her. I revelled in her flavor and the comfort she offered.

"Pax…"

"I need you right now," I said, as I pressed my forehead to hers.

She smiled down at me. "I'm not going anywhere,

handsome." She pecked my nose. "At least not until to-morrow night."

I groaned in remembrance and rolled her onto her back, towering above her.

"I'm glad I have you for that long at least," I said against her lips and gave her a chaste kiss. "Next time, I might not let you leave."

"If it was up to me, I wouldn't be leaving," she said, and brushed her lips to mine in that tender way that always made my heart soar.

I traced her lips with the tip of my index finger. "I know, sweetheart."

Her jaw went slack and her eyes darkened. She grasped my wrist, turned her head, and kissed the palm of my hand. I shuddered.

"Baby?" she said.

My emotions were swirling, making me dizzy with the subtle ache of death when all I wanted was a moment of respite, a break from reality, a brief time to feel alive. And a thought popped into my head.

Alissa needs this too.

"I love you." I pecked her lips.

Before she could reciprocate, I gave her a smile, pushed up to my feet and removed my shirt.

She laughed at me as she sat up. "What are you doing?"

I smirked down at her. "Haven't you heard of a midnight swim?"

"But we have no suits," she said, and my smirk broadened into a wide grin when I threw down my shirt and reached for my pants, my hands stalling on its button. "Oh! You have got to be kidding me? Have you lost your ever-loving mind?"

"I'm not kidding, and to answer your second question, no. I'm sane, baby. You saw how there's barely anyone here during the day. We're all alone," I said, as I undid my pants, let them drop, and winked at her.

"It's a public place," she argued, but her eyes betrayed her with the amusement and hunger burning inside them.

"Live a little." I dropped my underwear and she gawked. "You coming?"

"We have no towels," she persisted.

"We have a blanket." I pointed to it. "Now get naked with me. You know you want to," I cajoled.

She opened her mouth as if to say something else and then shut it.

I took off running toward the water and dove in once I got up to my waist.

I heard the splash from behind me when I surfaced. Alissa was keeping beneath the surface of the water as she made her way toward me. I chuckled at how cute she looked, trying to keep any wandering eyes from seeing her goods. I grabbed her arm and pulled her to me when she got close enough.

"Glad you could join me." I smiled down at her, our naked forms pressed together.

She smiled. "Anything to make you happy." She wrapped her arms around my neck.

I arched my brow. "Anything?" My hands grabbed onto her bare bottom, making her clutch onto my shoulders to maintain her balance. She nodded. "Then make love to me, right here, right now."

"Not here," she said with a playful swat on the shoulder, and I cursed the darkness for engulfing her blush.

"Why not?" I asked and began to pepper her face with kisses. "I want to know what it would be like to do it under the stars." I sucked on the skin below her ear. She shivered under my grasp.

"B-but…" she said and stopped when I thrust a finger into her heated core. "Mmm. Pax? Okay…beach."

I kissed her senseless and began to walk us out of the water toward the blanket, while she held on with her legs wrapped around my waist.

I lowered us to the blanket, sitting on my legs with her

perched on my lap. She shivered beneath my touch as I kissed down her neck, letting my fingers trail up her back.

When she reached down between us and began to guide me to her entrance, I stopped her. "Wait, I'm not—"

Her kiss was soft and sweet but all too brief. "It's okay, I'm on the pill."

"Are you sure?"

"I want all of you, Paxton," she said, holding my eyes as I released her wrist and let her position me so she could slide down the length of my shaft.

Never having gone bareback with any woman, other than Julie, I revelled in the silken feel of Alissa's swollen core, the rightness of the moment. "You feel amazing," I said as I found myself seated completely within her depths.

"You too."

She began to rock her hips. The sensation was pure heaven as we bonded closer than we ever have.

She was utopia.

Alissa arched her head back and I began to kiss down the column of her neck, to the valley between her breasts. She was intoxicating under the bright moonlight, which seemed to illuminate the spot we were in enough so that all we could see was the shimmering waters in the background and each other. It was nothing but us and nature as we stroked our respective heats into the highest of tensions. Our moans merged into a sensual song of pleasure, carried away by the night's breeze.

I'd loved only three women in my life: my mother, Julie, and now Alissa. Each had been loved in very different manners, but I can tell you this for a fact: none of them but Alissa had made me feel like I wouldn't be able to survive without them in my life.

What started as an evening of fun and distraction from life had turned into something beautiful and heartfelt. It killed me to think Jasper could possibly never live to see how beautiful the love for a woman, other than his mother, could be. How possible it was I would never see his first day of high school, his first date, his first broken heart, and all that would follow. Life was fragile and filled with so many unexpected surprises, both good and bad.

"Come back to me, Pax," she said, and pulled back enough to look me in the eyes and palm my face with both her hands. "I love you."

"I love you too," I said.

To say Alissa took the pain away would be giving her too much credit. No one was that capable. What Alissa did for me was lessen the blow of it all without much effort. She made it so this downward spiral that was my family life was bearable. I was able to keep breathing, be the strong person in all of this for my son, and keep one foot in front of the other as each day rolled by. I wanted to know I was the best damn father and man I could ever be for everyone in my life.

Lost in the sweet and blissful moment with Alissa, I felt our impending releases coming blindingly fast. She was looking at me, and I at her. Her beautiful face was flushed. Her lips were a deeper pink as we took each other over the edge. I could have sworn I saw a life with her flash inside those cerulean pools of hers the moment we had hit the pinnacle of our climax.

Spent, our bodies glistened with a cooling sweat from our lovemaking.

I showered her with soft, lazy kisses.

"I love you," she said into the skin of my neck and kissed me in that spot.

"And I, you," I said. "More than you'll ever know."

I held Alissa tight to me, as if letting go would cause her to disappear, and all of these emotions I held for her, and what had just transpired between us, would wash away with the cresting waves behind us and become nothing but a dream.

CHAPTER 21

A month had passed since Jasper's diagnosis. I was dealing with the conflicting reality on a day-to-day basis. Daily conversations over the phone with Alissa were about the only thing keeping me sane. She seemed to have developed a sixth sense about when things were going the roughest with me. We hadn't seen each other again since her departure a few days after Jasper's diagnosis, her job being the culprit. Things had been busy for the woman, and it didn't seem like there was going to be any respite for her in the near future.

"The joys of doing a good job," she had told me once.

In fact, she had done such a great job organizing that conference, she had landed a coveted promotion, one she thought she had wanted. It hadn't taken long for her to voice her dislike for her new role, despising the fact she was at her boss's beck and call around the clock. Neither was I, since our conversations had grown shorter and more sporadic as time went on.

Jasper's health was deteriorating despite the chemotherapy. On some days, he was his old self with so much rambunctiousness that my energy was drained dry by the time my boy went to bed. On others, he was so dead to the world, pale and sickly, that we'd stay in. Those days typically ended with me falling into bed, mentally exhausted with additional worry.

There had been two instances where Jasper had ended up in the hospital for testing, only to find out he'd come down with another infection of some sort that could compromise him further. Those days had sent me to bed crying and praying it would all just go away. I wanted my son back, and not for a day. I wanted him to be the healthy little four-year-old he should have always been. On those days, I cursed Dr. Messing and his diagnosis. On those days, I ached to feel Allie wrapped around me to soften the blows. Our calls, although soothing in nature, weren't completely cutting it for me anymore. I wanted to see my woman in the flesh with a desperation I never imagined feeling.

A second month had come and gone and I still hadn't seen Alissa. As a matter of fact, I hadn't heard from her except for the one email three days ago that assured me everything was going well, that she loved me, and should I need her, she was reachable through her assistant. I hadn't bothered calling as I knew she had more than enough on her plate with her latest project, and there hadn't been any emergencies. I could wait.

Jasper was in bed after a long day of treatment at the hospital. My son was now in need of regular blood transfusions in conjunction with his chemotherapy.

After all my procrastinating, I had painted and decorated my son's bedroom as I should have six months ago, when I had first moved into my townhouse. I felt horrible for not doing it sooner so he could enjoy it more.

I was sitting on the couch, perusing channels in order to find something that would strike my fancy.

Taking a drink from the bottle of beer I had decided to indulge in, my phone rang. One look at the caller ID and I smiled.

Alissa.

"Hello, beautiful," I said.

"Hey, handsome." I could hear the smile in her voice.

"How've you been, honey? I miss you."

"I miss you too," I said. "How's your week been so far?"

"Pure hell. I need out. A change," she said. "Listen, do you think Jasper would be up to a blueberry pancakefest tomorrow?"

"I'm sure he'd be open to it every morning, sweetheart, but why can't it wait until the weekend? Did something come up?"

"Yeah," she said. "It's been too long."

"I hear you," I said.

I heard a knock. "Someone's at the door. Can you hold on for a second?"

"Expecting someone?"

"No," I said, and wondered who it could be at this time of night.

"Go answer. I'll wait."

Walking to the door, my phone still in my hand, I opened. The device dropped to the floor, the battery cover went flying, as I stood there shell-shocked.

I stared. "What are you doing here?"

"I believe we have a pancake date in the morning." Alissa grinned. "And I doubt Jasper would appreciate me missing it, even if he doesn't know he's got one yet." She stuffed her phone in her purse.

I pulled Alissa in and gave her a bone-crushing hug. She had floored me with this unexpected surprise visit.

I kissed her and asked, "What about that project?"

"What about it? Someone else can handle it, I'm not going back," she said into my chest.

"What?"

"You heard me, Paxton Lowell. I'm. Not. Going. Back. I've been sick of that place since before the promotion. The money may be phenomenal, but it also gave me the push to leave. I thought I would have been happier with the change, but I'm miserable."

"So what are you going to do when you go back?" I closed

the door, locked it, and dragged her to the sofa.

"You're not listening, Pax," she said. "I'm. Not. Going. Back. Period. I've been here for a full day and I've already found the perfect place to rent, but I wanted to know how you felt about me being closer before I signed the lease. I was thinking of staying and seeing where things went with us." She kissed me.

"You did what?"

"I thought you'd be happy." She eyed me, searching for the answer I would provide next as she pulled back, but I didn't let her move away.

"Truth is I'm ecstatic," I said. "But are you sure about this?"

"I already have a job lined up," she said. "This little event planning place that handles local stuff was looking for someone with my experience. They practically begged me to partner up with them."

"Are you serious?" I asked and she nodded. "That's fantastic!" I grabbed her face between my palms before kissing her like nothing else mattered. I heard her giggle into our kiss before her arms came around, pulling us closer.

W hen I brought her luggage to my bedroom, what had started as a simple kiss of appreciation had evolved into one filled with pure carnal desire.

Her soft hands ran up my chest as mine ran down to her tight bottom. She pulled away and reached for her shirt, stripping it up and over her head, making her hair cascade down on either side of her face and shoulders. I caught on to her obvious hint, pulling mine off and chucked it to the side. She made haste of her tight jeans while I looked her over, licking my lips. She rubbed her hands down my bare chest, kissed me as her hands trailed lower to my belt buckle, and undid it.

"I think I need to remind you that Jasper is in the other room."

"As hungry as I am to fuck your brains out, stud, I want this to be nice and slow. I've missed you too much for a rough romp," she said. "Besides, now we have all the time in the world to explore that kinky side of yours." She winked, pushed me back onto the bed, and pulled my jeans off.

As she straddled my waist, she laid kisses over the heated skin of my chest, her fingers trailing not too far behind the wetness her lips and tongue were leaving behind. I felt the tension of the day melt away.

"Why does my man seem to be wound so tight?" She pecked my lips.

"It's been a rough week. Hell, it's been a rough couple of months," I said.

She laid her body over the length of mine. "I'm sorry, honey," she said against my ear. "We need to do something about that now that I'll be closer."

"I definitely agree." I kissed her shoulder while pulling down the strap of her bra. I reached around her and undid the clasp to slide the garment off. "You know, it would be easier if you stayed here with me."

She looked down at me. "Pax—"

I'm not sure why that had come out in the first place, but after a split second of thinking on it, I knew I had spoken from the heart.

I kissed her into silence before rolling us over so I lay over her. It was time to find out if she wanted the same thing.

"You have to admit," I said, and kissed her collarbone and trailed further up until I reached that sweet spot below her ear I knew sent shivers through her body whenever I nibbled it. "It would make what we're doing right now, a hell of a lot easier."

"Yes, but—"

"And coming home to you every night would make it even better," I said with a nip at her earlobe.

"True."

"I cook, I clean, I'm self-sufficient and—"

She pushed me back so she could see my face, and I saw her arched brow. "Paxton Lowell, are you trying to seduce me into moving in with you?"

I grinned. "Is it working?"

"Hmm." Her head tilted to show her amusement. "Maybe."

"Let me see if I can convince you then." My smile widened to a full grin, causing her to laugh.

I kissed down to one of her breasts and took a nipple into my mouth. I made her gasp as my tongue twirled around her erect peak, giving it enough attention before I switched to the other.

Her breathing picked up.

"You," I said between kisses, as I headed south, "can have this," I paused, wrapping my fingers around the waistband of her underwear and pulling them down, "every night." I hovered above her core and blew hot air before giving her a quick flick of my tongue, causing her hips to arch up in want, and a whimper to escape her parted lips.

"Oh…" she said, her face flushed from her arousal, its scent permeating the valley of her legs.

"Say you'll stay with me, Alissa," I said before sucking on her clit.

"Oh, my God! I-I…" I nipped at her clit this time around and she jumped. "Ah! Pax, what's gotten into you?"

"Say it," I growled, as I slid two fingers into her heated core and felt her clamp down on them. "Say it, Allie. I love you, let's be together. I want to wake up to you in the morning, hear about how your day was, share meals, hang out with Jasper together."

I could tell she was overwhelmed by the sensations I was inflicting on her, and maybe even my words; maybe too much for her to answer. I stopped the thrusting of my fingers.

She whimpered at the loss of movement. "Fine," she said.

"Tell me what I want to hear," I said, and resumed the thrusting of my fingers and clamping down on her swollen bud with my lips.

"I-I'll stay with you, Paxton," she said, as I followed through and sent her over the edge with her first orgasm.

Not wasting any time, I pushed my boxers down and plunged myself into her hot sheath. She was still riding out the high from her release and the feel of those tremors was amazing as they circled my bare shaft.

I engulfed her mouth with mine and began to thrust.

She held me close as I buried my face into her fragrant hair, its scent one of my favorites.

Surrounded with nothing but our deep-seated emotions, I showed her how I loved her, much like she had showed me that night on the beach.

I felt her tremble under me as our passions heightened and the world collapsed all around, leaving us both in a haze of carnal bliss.

I fell asleep with the largest feeling of happiness, which I hadn't felt in a long time. I had my woman by my side, and it was no longer for a few days or a week at the most. It was for however how long we dictated it to be.

CHAPTER 22

"Allie!" Jasper squealed, waking me with a jump.

I heard his light-weighted footsteps make their way to my bedside.

Had I not grabbed on to Alissa, I would have had a lot to explain to my four-year-old about the birds and the bees, and the fact *Daddy's friend* was lying in his arms, naked as the day she was born. She looked up at me and clutched the sheets, wrapping them around herself as a slight blush overtook her exposed skin.

"Why hello there, handsome," she said with a smile, and extended a hand to ruffle his hair as he giggled. "Glad to see your gorgeous hair is growing back."

I grabbed my underwear and shoved them on under the sheets before standing up.

"Hey, buddy, why don't you come and help me out in the kitchen?" I asked.

"But I want to stay here with Allie," he said.

Alissa and I laughed at his pouting expression.

"It's okay, Jasper," she said. "I'll be right out in a minute. I just have to go to the little girls' room, and then, what do you say we have ourselves some pancake fun?"

"Okay," he said excitedly, and as he escorted me out of the room, he turned to me and asked, "Daddy, what's a little girls' room?"

I could hear Alissa's giggle in the background.

"How about I let her tell you all about it?"

When Alissa had come to join us moments later, Jasper didn't hesitate to jump on her about the topic.

"It's another way of meaning the bathroom, sweetie," she explained.

"Is it because you paint your face in there when you stay here?" he asked.

Neither Alissa nor I were able to keep a straight face.

"Sure." She decided to leave it at that.

Blueberry pancakefest was a hit, as always, and seeing as Jasper was beginning to show signs of difficulty breathing and joint weakness, we opted for a quiet day in.

I popped a movie in while Jasper weaseled himself between us. Instead of doing what he normally did, which was cuddle into me, he cradled himself under Alissa's arm.

Alissa looked at me and gave me the largest satisfied grin.

I laughed. "Traitor." I poked at Jasper.

"Hey," Alissa said. "It's his turn. I'll make sure you have yours later."

"Yeah, Daddy, she's my girlfriend," Jasper said with a loud wheeze.

"What?" I held a hand in mock shock in front of my mouth. "Where did you learn all about that?"

"Todd told me," he paused to take a breath, "that Mommy and he were boyfriend and girlfriend until he asked her to marry him." He took another breath and grimaced. Well the engagement, although not a surprise, was news. "Then he explained that after," another wheezing pause, "the wedding, she'll be his wife." And out came a wheezing cough.

Alissa looked at me worried. I shook my head to let her know it was normal, but his coloring kept me on guard.

"Is that so, handsome?" Alissa asked and gave him a small squeeze.

He nodded. "You're Daddy's friend, right?" he asked and sucked in hard-earned air as she nodded. "And you're a girl too. Does that make you his girlfriend?"

"You got it, buddy," I said while looking at Alissa and smiling. She beamed.

"Does it mean that Allie will be your wife someday?" He coughed a bit more and took the glass of water I offered him.

"I don't know, sweetie," she said before kissing the top of his head. I could tell her emotions were getting the better of her.

"If Todd will be my other daddy, you could be my other mommy," he said. My heart beat wildly, as if a stampede was going on behind my rib cage.

"Oh, Jasper," Alissa said choked up.

She wasn't meeting my eyes, and I couldn't blame her because the lump was growing in my throat as I tried to fight the tears too. The wisdom this four-year-old possessed was beyond what he comprehended, but he knew of the basics. He understood that I loved her because I had told him so, and he knew from love, things could evolve to something greater.

Alissa excused herself and headed toward the kitchen. Jasper looked confused for a slight moment and he lay down in the spot Alissa had been sitting in. Within minutes, he was out like a light and his color was back, despite the subtle wheeze that popped up every couple of breaths. The morning's events had taken their toll on his ailing body more than I wanted to see.

When Alissa hadn't returned after five minutes, I covered Jasper with the couch's throw and headed to find her.

She was bent over the sink, her hands braced on its edge, breathing deeply.

The tightness in my chest came back and I struggled to find the words. Instead, I walked to her, touched her shoulder. She turned around and buried her face in my chest.

My arms wrapped around her as her body was racked with sobs. "He's okay, Allie," I said against her hair and rubbed her back, fighting my own tears.

"I'm sorry. I don't know what's wrong with me," she said. "I should be the strong one here," she sniffled.

"You don't have to be strong all the time, sweetheart," I said.

She took a deep breath and I felt her relax more in my arms, conceding to her weakness.

"I didn't expect it to have gotten that bad," she said. "You said he was getting worse but it's a shock when you haven't seen any of it. He's so frail looking, but it wasn't until—"

"It's one of Jasper's bad days," I said. "He's normally not like this."

"I know. I wasn't prepared for that," she said and backed away. "It's scary." She lifted her eyes to mine and held them as I leaned her back against the counter.

I grabbed her face between my palms and let my thumbs wipe the remainder of her tears away. "Are you sure that's all that was about?" I asked while watching her, attentive for any signs of withdrawal.

Instead, I was met with her lips against mine, which bore sweet conviction. "Yeah, that's all," she said and gave me a sad smile. "I can't believe that son of yours." I gave her a curious look. "I knew he was a smart cookie, but when did he get that wise and all-knowing about relationships?"

"I don't know, but it scares me. I guess I have Todd to thank for that, huh?"

I took in her puffy eyes, her flushed face, and parted lips. No matter what state she was in, her beauty always shone through.

"Will you be okay with all of this?" I asked.

"Why wouldn't I be?" she said defensively. "I love that boy in there." She pointed toward the living room. "It doesn't matter if he's healthy or sick; if he has a good day or a bad one. I can't explain it. It's…it's like he's my own, Pax." She tried to push past me.

"Hey! Hey! Sweetheart, calm down," I said, as I grabbed her arm and pulled her back to face me.

"Don't you tell me to calm down, Paxton Lowell," she said, trying to keep her voice low so she wouldn't be overheard, and punctuated her words with a shove at my chest, but I didn't move.

"I was only making sure that this wouldn't be too much for you," I said, and held on to her shoulders to prevent her from pulling back more.

"And it's not for you?" she asked and her body relaxed. "Pax—"

"Sometimes it is, and that's why I needed to ask you," I said. "Promise me if it gets to be too much, you'll let me know."

"And I expect the same," she said. "You're not in this alone."

I smiled. "You've got it, gorgeous."

"Now kiss me," she said, returning my smile.

I brushed the strands of hair that had fallen from her ponytail, tucking them behind her ear, before cupping her cheek and indulging her in her request.

"Daddy," Jasper said with a loud wheeze as he came into the room while our lips were fused in passion.

I pulled away and looked at Jasper, who now stood in the kitchen entrance watching us and rubbing at his tired eyes. His color had a definite blue tint, and it looked as if it was progressing to a deeper shade of the latter.

This isn't good.

I rushed to his side and bent down to feel his forehead and inspect him closer. "He's burning up," I said to Alissa. "Are you okay, Son?" He shook his head indicating the negative, but the rumbling sound from his chest combined with his loud wheeze just about made me lose my cool. This wasn't like the other times at all. *God help me.* "We need to get you to the hospital, sport," I said. Alissa nodded frantically with wide eyes when I looked at her. "Let's go."

When I had Jasper settled in the car, with Alissa at his side in the back seat, I knew I had one more difficult task at hand. I had to call Julie. For the first time, it was I who had to deliver the news about the negative progression of our son's fatal disease. I now understood how Julie had felt every time she'd picked up the phone to make the call I was about to make.

CHAPTER 23

The week had gone by in a flash. Jasper had been hospitalized with a severe case of pneumonia and had nearly ended up on a ventilator to assist his breathing.

I came home alone from a meeting with Messing to find Alissa on her laptop with a bit of music in the background.

I smiled at the look of concentration on her face.

She was so lost in her work, she failed to notice my arrival. "What is it you're working on that's got all of your attention?" I asked, as I came to a stop in front of her.

She jumped and gave me a concerned look. "How'd it go?"

"As good as could be expected." She nodded in understanding. Her eyes averted themselves from me and flew to her computer screen. "You never answered my question."

"What?" Her eyes snapped back to mine. It was clear she was preoccupied with whatever she was working on.

"Must have been some decent writing spree you're on if your head is up in the clouds." I let myself fall back on the couch and leaned over to kiss her cheek.

"I wasn't writing," she said.

"You weren't?" She shook her head, and then I noticed the look of guilt cross her features. "What—"

"I know you think that I've been writing all week long because that's what I let you believe, but I haven't. Truth is, I haven't written a word in a month."

"Sweetheart, you're scaring me," I said and turned my body toward her as I sat up straighter. I could see she was conflicted. "What is it? Should I be worried?"

"I've been doing some research."

Then she showed me.

Baffled at what I was seeing on her laptop screen, I couldn't help but wonder why she felt so guilty, but more than that, why she felt she had to keep something like this hidden until now.

Before me, there were oodles of information on stem-cell research. It looked like there might just be hope after all.

"I can't believe this," I said, as I scrolled down from one screen to the next, having highjacked her laptop. I turned to her. "Why didn't you say you were looking into this?"

"Because I didn't want to give you false hope," she said. "I wanted to be sure before I brought it to you and Julie. Your hearts have been broken once already. There's no way I'd be the one to break them a second time."

"This is so much better than a marrow harvest and transplant." I smiled. "I'm calling Julie and then Messing right now to tell them about this. If anything, I know we've kept Jasper's cord blood so they can get right to it."

Alissa left me alone and went to the kitchen to start dinner.

I left a message on Julie's voice mail and then put a call in with Messing. He agreed to meet with us tomorrow to discuss what Alissa had found, as well as our next course of action as soon as Jasper was cleared of his pneumonia. Time was no longer a luxury we could afford.

I followed my nose to the wonderful aroma of spices and meat, and found Alissa stirring a rather sizeable pot of what I presumed to be spaghetti sauce.

I wrapped my arms around her and smiled into the side of her neck. "Thank you," I said. God, those two words weren't anywhere near enough.

"It's nothing," she said and squeezed her cheek into the side of my face while keeping up with the stirring.

"Nothing?" I asked, as I kissed the inside of her neck before turning her to face me and pulling her away from the stove. "Allie, do you not realize what you've done?"

"I did what anyone else would do," she said, as if her actions were insignificant.

"No, you didn't," I said. "No one would have done what you did, sweetheart. We've all been sitting here worried out of our minds, caring for Jasper, and while you were doing the same, you held hope that maybe there was something we had overlooked." My hand cupped her cheek. "Allie, whether this works out or not, we'll know we've done everything we could. This stem-cell thing… The success rates are higher than the old-school methods." I wiped the single tear that had fallen from her eye.

"It's not like it's a new thing, Pax," she said. "Messing told you he wanted to discuss further options. For all we know, he was going to mention what I found."

"But you mentioned it first." I brushed my lips against hers. "And that means more."

That night, I found myself watching over a sleeping Alissa. This woman who lay in peaceful slumber beside me had managed to worm her way into my head, then warm me physically beyond a boiling point, and fill my heart with love and joy.

I was bewitched.

If I had to choose words to describe her, I would need an entire thesaurus, and then some, to give anyone a true glimpse of what I saw when I looked at her.

"You're really beginning to freak me out with that staring," she said with a sleep-hazed voice, before opening her eyes and smiling up at me. "Why aren't you sleeping?"

"I can't." I yawned. "I've got too much going on in my head."

"Come here." She pulled me so my head lay on her shoulder by her breast. "Just close your eyes. You need your rest, honey. You'll know more about things in a few hours."

Her fingers played with the hair at the nape of my neck and within seconds, I felt sleep take me, and the faint feel of her warm lips on my forehead.

CHAPTER 24

Wesat in the office waiting for Dr. Messing to join us. I refused to let Alissa stay home. She deserved to be part of this whole thing. As far as I was concerned, she was family too.

"I understand that you've beat me to the punch about stem cells?" Dr. Messing said and looked down at the stack of papers I had printed out and brought with Alissa and me that morning. "Judging by your reactions, it seems like you're all in accord with going through with the procedure. Mr. Lowell, I understand by yesterday's conversation over the phone, you've told me when Jasper was born, you had his cord blood stored?"

I nodded.

Julie flinched from the corner of my eye.

I turned toward her. "Are you all right?"

"I did something," she said and a guilty look crossed her face.

"What?" I asked, and I knew it wasn't going to be good. Not good at all.

"I had the bank release it," she said.

I shot up to my feet. "What?"

"Well, he was always so healthy and the place charged so much—"

"Julie, that was a joint decision," I said. "Why didn't I know about this? He's my child too!"

"Because I knew how you'd react!"

"And—"

"Hold on, folks." Dr. Messing put up his hand to diffuse the tension. "It's not at all uncommon for parents to do what Julie's done. I agree; the fees are astronomical. I suggest we put this to rest, and you two can deal with it in your own time. What's important is not losing sight of what we're all here for. Regardless, it's not a lost cause." Nodding, I took a breath and sat back down.

The man was right.

Alissa grabbed my hand and squeezed it, and my frustration eased slightly.

"I can look through the databases and see if we can find something that way with our research programs. If not, then I'm afraid we have one last resort, and it's spinal marrow, which means you'll need to be tested to see if you're suitable matches for Jasper. If you fail to be, Jasper will have to be added to our recipient waiting list. Unfortunately, we don't have research programs for regular marrow donations. Now, if you'll all excuse me, I have a patient assessment I need to be looking into and thanks to you folks, a fair bit of calls to make. I'm thinking I should have an answer to you by the end of this week, if all goes well, and we'll be able to move forward from there."

CHAPTER 25

The week passed and I found myself pacing the living room after dinner on Thursday.

Alissa had started her new job on Monday and as luck would have it, she ended up having to stay behind for a team meeting and was running late. I was waiting on her to get home so I could tell her the news.

When the door to my townhouse opened, I pounced. I had her back pinned to the door and kissed her like a man starved of oxygen. She smiled into my kiss and wrapped her arms around my neck, while I trailed my lips down to savor the soft skin that peeked through the top of her light pink camisole.

"Now that's a welcome home I can get used to." She giggled before I nipped the skin above one of her breasts, causing her to moan. "What's gotten into you?"

"I owe you a lifetime of welcomes like this one," I said against her heated flesh before capturing her mouth with mine again, and spun her around before setting her back down.

"Mind telling me why I've been mauled walking through the door? You keep evading my question." She grinned. "I'd like to know what I did so I can do it again."

"We got the call," I said and saw the disbelief, the relief, and the overwhelming joy cross her features. "They're going with a marrow harvest if the blood work proves that either Julie or I are a match. First thing tomorrow we're getting tested."

She looked at me in shock. "What? That quick?"

"Yeah." I said and smiled. "They couldn't find anything in the database."

She pulled my face into hers and kissed me hard.

"That's our last resort, but it's great news that we can finally move ahead."

I kissed her tenderly. "I love it that you're referring to everything that's going on as *our* dilemma and not mine."

I explained everything to Alissa as she sat and ate the plate I had made and kept warm for her. Tomorrow was the day where things could change for the better. First thing in the morning, Julie, Jasper, and I would be heading in to the hospital to run a battery of tests and discover if we were donor matches to save our son. If it worked out, they would schedule a marrow harvest, and get to work on synthesizing the latter so it could be transplanted into Jasper.

Alissa had called her boss, notifying her of the great news. Now that she was involved, she refused to leave my side. The minute she ended the call, I wrapped my arms around her waist and pulled her into me.

I grabbed her phone from her, set it on the kitchen countertop and leaned in for a kiss. "Get that sweet ass of yours up those stairs and to the bedroom." I pulled away and looked at her face before continuing, "I want some dessert and you, gorgeous, are on the menu."

She laughed but didn't move. "Have you used that line on anyone where it's worked?"

A growl formed in my throat and I picked her up and wrapped her legs around me, her skirt riding up her thighs, as I proceeded to rush us toward the bedroom.

I hadn't expected the sudden bout of clumsiness that hit me, or the sultry assault Alissa would bring on to cause such an event. With a long swoop of her tongue from my collarbone to my jaw and a pinching nip to the skin below my earlobe, my knees buckled on the third step from the bottom of the staircase.

"Fuck," I said under my breath, but one look at Alissa told me that she hadn't been hurt; quite the opposite, really. She wore a smirk and seemed to be amused with our unexpected tumbling. "You just couldn't wait, could you?" She shook her head.

Her hands went to work straightaway as I watched her rip my button-down, its buttons spilling everywhere. Her nimble fingers tackled my pants and before I knew it, she had managed to push them down to my knees with her. I hiked her skirt up farther and attempted to get rid of her underwear only to realize that there were none. I looked up.

"Someone got them all wet earlier so I figured I'd lose them," she said with a mischievous gleam in her eyes.

"Damn, baby." I groaned and kissed her nice and fierce before reaching for her camisole.

With a hand on her lower back, I arched her butt up off the step and plowed into her, generating a sensual cry. She wrapped her legs around my hips, arching into me as I propelled into her. Her arms were at her sides, preventing her from sliding down the step. Her heels dug into my rear as I turned up the heat.

The sound of skin slapping filled the air. The sight of her spread out under me made me want to take her to heights unknown.

When the urge to explode hit me, I buried my face in her neck and bit down on her shoulder. Her tight heat clamped down harder than it ever had on my length and with a guttural cry we both came. Hard.

"Mmm." She nuzzled my cheek as I pulled away to look at her. I loved it when I turned her into a mumbling mess of satiated flesh and bones.

I smirked. "So much for the bedroom."

She laughed as she tilted her head back and rested it on the carpeted stair to catch her breath. Lifting her head up for a quick glance at me, she said, "Tuckered out already, handsome?" and ran her hands up and down my chest, sporting a sly grin.

"Hardly," I said, and flexed a certain appendage that was still buried deep inside her, far from flaccid. Her eyes grew wide at the feel of me. "The more I have you, the more I want you."

"With that said, I suggest you get me up there real quick, stud." With that, she leaned in to lick my bottom lip, while tightening the muscles that were still wrapped around my still needful shaft.

I came out of the bathroom to find my woman turning down the bed, dressed in a short satin bathrobe, her dampened hair curtained to one side. She noticed my staring as she removed her robe and settled herself under the covers.

She smiled. "Is everything okay?"

"Perfect," I said and crawled in beside her. I gave her a peck. Her hand lifted and cupped my cheek before she gave me another quick kiss in return.

Contrary to a week ago, I fell asleep right away. My anxieties for the next day were replaced with a sense of relief that it was a huge possibility I would have Jasper back as the normal four-year-old he should have always been.

CHAPTER 26

We awaited news from Dr. Messing while Todd was consoling a rather depressed Julie, who was worried about the news that had already been delivered prior to our testing.

Given the high-risk nature of Julie's pregnancy, her donating marrow was no longer an option, seeing as the procedure would put her and the baby at risk.

Regardless, Julie had gotten her blood tested. It might have been a shot in the dark but if she were a match, we'd have to bide our time until the baby was born and her own health issues stabilized before the procedure could be done.

All wasn't at a loss, but according to Julie, it was.

As I paced the room, Alissa got up from her silent ponderous state and grabbed my arm when I walked by her.

"Pax, you're driving yourself and everyone else crazy. Sit down," she said. "The doctor should be in soon. It's already been two hours since they've done the blood work."

And sure enough, as I settled in the chair next to her, Messing walked through the doors.

With that sombre look on his face, I presumed he wasn't the bearer of good news. I was trying to convince myself that I was reading too much into things, but I couldn't move past that soul-numbing, heart-thumping, gut-wrenching feeling that overwhelmed me.

"Guys, I'm afraid it's not good," he said. "Neither of you are a match. I'm sorry."

My world began to crumble around me again as my back fell against the back of my chair from the blow of the bad news. Dr. Messing stood in front of us in silence, allowing the facts to sink in.

"But," Alissa said.

"Yes, Ms. Hidgins?" he asked.

"Can't anyone be deemed a match?"

"Of course," Dr. Messing said. "A familial match is always the easiest and best with regards to donor rejections, but not everyone has the resources to find those donors, and not everyone is willing to be a donor either. I'm sorry, but unless you find a suitable match on your own, there's nothing else that can be done aside from adding Jasper to our recipient list. Rest assured, I made sure he got on the list the instant we discovered the results."

I heard Alissa gulp. "Thank you," she whispered.

I sat in the SUV waiting for Alissa who had left her cell phone in the room we had congregated in earlier. It had taken her a while, but when I was about to get out and go find her, there she was.

"Found it?" I asked when she got in and buckled herself up.

She nodded and waved the device in her hand.

"I was thinking," she said, and I turned to look at her with my hand on the ignition. "What if we pooled all willing relatives and friends of yours and Julie's together to see if they're a match? I mean, it could work, right?"

"Alissa," I sighed. I didn't want to take away her hope, but I wasn't about to feed her any beyond measure.

"No!" she said, stubborn as ever. "I'm not giving up on this, Pax. You heard what Messing said. The statistics of finding a compatible match in time for Jasper through the lists is a draw. Why wouldn't you try? Just *try*, dammit! Then you can say you've done everything. There's no shame in asking for help."

I should have known she wouldn't give up easily. If she

hadn't given up on anything else that she'd worked on—our relationship included—then she wasn't giving up on Jasper.

"I love you so much," I said, and cradled her cheek before kissing her forehead.

"I love you too, but I don't want to see you with that defeated look again until it's time, and now isn't it."

I nodded.

I dreaded the day that perhaps we were all going to face; the one that bore the ugly reality of Jasper's mortality. I feared Alissa was putting too much faith in the goodwill of people, and she was choosing to ignore the real possibility that my son may not make it through, with or without a donor. Still, I couldn't help but admire and respect her tenacity in the matter.

CHAPTER 27

The next day, I was unlocking the front door after running a few errands with Alissa when I heard a car's engine cut from behind us. I looked back and saw none other than my parents.

"This is not how I planned it," I said more to myself than anyone else.

"Paxton?" Alissa looked at me with a questioning gaze.

I wrapped my arm around her waist and pulled her into me. "My parents," I said and she smiled at me. "Hey, guys." I smiled and moved from Alissa to greet them each with a hug.

"Is this the Alissa we've been hearing Jasper bragging about?" my mother asked and smiled at my girlfriend.

"The one and only," I said. My mother attacked her in one of her hugs while my father patted my shoulder. "What are you guys doing here?"

"We were out and figured we'd stop in to see how things are this morning," my father said.

Alissa's cell rang and she excused herself to the kitchen after the four of us had gone inside.

I had just entered the kitchen to fetch refreshments for all of us when I overheard the tail end of her conversation.

"Thank you! Thank you! Thank you!" she said, and was laughing as she put down her phone. When she turned, I saw the tears coming down her cheeks.

"Sweetheart," I said when our eyes met. "Is everything okay?"

"Of course," she said and wiped at her cheeks.

She gave me a bright smile before walking to me, wrapping a hand around the back of my neck and pulling my face down to hers. She kissed me quick and hard. Her eyes twinkled when she backed away and all of my questions were lost. Her tears were genuine, but then again, so was her joy.

"Need any help?" she asked, as she headed for the fridge before I could get there. Forgetting what I was in there to do in the first place, I watched her as she took out the pitcher of lemonade, a tray of ice cubes, and walked over to the counter where I'd laid the glasses with what seemed to be an added bounce to her step. That smile of hers never faded as she filled the cups and put everything else away. "Help me bring these out," she said.

I couldn't resist. "Come here," I said and took the few steps toward her. I pushed the tendrils away from her face and tucked them behind her ear. "I don't know what's made you this happy, but that smile of yours is amazing. I didn't think anyone else but us Lowell men could put a smile like that on there." I kissed her cheek and proceeded to grab two glasses, and she grabbed the others.

"Ah, but it indirectly has something to do with you both, so I guess you really did manage to put it there," she said, as I followed her out to the living room where my parents waited.

"Really?" I asked. "I wouldn't mind knowing what we've done, considering I don't recall doing anything for that kind of a reaction. Or are you still riding on that high from last night?"

"Oh, I'm ready for the boost, stud, but as for your other answer, you'll know in time," she said, and winked at me as she set the two beverages in front of my parents.

My father and I sat there for the better part of an hour

as we watched the two women interact as if they were age-old friends.

If I were being honest, I wasn't terrified at all for Mom and Dad to meet Alissa. I found myself wondering why I had waited so long to begin with. If she were similar to Julie's character, I knew I would have been facing an uphill battle, but then again, had she been like Julie, I wouldn't have been with her. It's not that Julie was a bad person; it's just she was all wrong for me.

And then the conversation floated to Jasper and his deteriorating health.

"We went and got tested," my father announced. Mom nodded and I found myself reaching for Alissa's hand. She squeezed it tight. I hadn't even asked them to do that after my call with them yesterday, to let them know how everything had gone.

Submersed in our sombre thoughts, the phone rang.

"Mr. Lowell?" the woman asked when I answered.

"This is."

"This is Dr. Messing's office calling."

"Yes?"

"We're calling because it appears that we've found a match," she said, and for the second time that day, I lost my footing as my ass hit the armrest of the sofa. Alissa grabbed on to my free arm and put a hand on my knee to balance me out.

"How's that possible? Messing told us that it would take a considerable amount of time for Jasper to climb up the recipient list?" I asked. Could this be real, or was this a huge mistake? I looked between my parents wondering if it would be possible so soon to have their results?

"Well, what can I say? We do have a match here who's been tested specifically for your son's case. We'd like to get started with Jasper's pre-op consultation. How does next Wednesday morning sound?"

"Thank you. We'll be there," I said and cleared the ever growing lump in my throat. "What time?"

"Ten o'clock, sir," she said.

"Thank you," I said again.

I hadn't realized the room had grown silent as everyone's attention was focused on me. I put down the receiver and looked around at the three concerned faces. "Pax," Alissa said. "Honey?" I hadn't responded but the movement of her hand on my thigh snapped me back to the present and I blankly stared at her.

"They've found a donor," I said, sounding detached, and then I repeated that statement to myself a few times as reality sank in. "They've found a donor!" I laughed and got up, grabbed Alissa and pulled her in for a tight hug while I spun her around. She giggled into my neck.

"But how?" my father asked and I stopped our spinning. "They told us that we wouldn't know until tomorrow."

I shook my head and ran a hand through my hair, still trying to make sense of it all. "I don't know. If it's not you guys, someone came in and got tested and they're a match."

I found myself hoping there'd be a way to thank this potential lifesaver in person for the sacrifice they were making. If Jasper survived, I wanted them to know the face of the person they had saved. I wanted my son to know his hero. This person had no clue as to the difference they were making in my life. I now understood the hope Alissa had been holding on to. Someone out there was selfless enough to give a stranger an attempt at a new lease on life.

My mother rushed over to me the minute I let go of Alissa, and I found myself cuddled in the tiny woman's arms as she cradled me to her. "Oh, Mama," I said, and the tears of relief hit and I felt another set of arms, large ones, engulf the two of us, knowing it was my father.

After what felt like a short eternity of being sandwiched between my parents, my reeling emotions stabilized and we pulled away from one another. I looked over to Alissa, who giggled with a bright smile while she wiped her tears away.

Mom and Dad left before dinner, despite our inviting them to stay.

Alissa had made her way to the kitchen and could be heard chopping away at whatever food she was preparing.

I headed in there to join her.

A glass of wine waited for me at the breakfast bar. She looked up and smiled at me as she continued with what looked like a garden salad and extra veggies that she had left to the side. Judging by the wok on the stovetop, she was planning a stir-fry. "Need any help?"

"It depends," she said. "Do you plan on helping out or helping yourself?" She smirked, and I couldn't help but laugh remembering the last time she had attempted a stir-fry in my presence.

"How about I help you and then we help ourselves?" I asked in an amused tone.

I came around and took the knife from her hand while kissing the side of her neck. I caught her biting down on her lower lip again and felt the silent purr in her throat through my lips. I smiled against her skin and nuzzled her cheek.

We managed to get through dinner, and Alissa seemed quiet; a little more than usual throughout the evening.

When we made it to bed, I kissed her head as she cuddled into my side and asked, "Is everything okay?"

"Perfect. Why?" She followed with that sweet smile of hers.

"You just seem like your mind is somewhere else."

"Wednesday's going to be a big day," she said. "I hope this works, Pax."

"Me too."

CHAPTER 28

Wednesday came around quick.

Alissa wasn't able to come along with us, but I had voiced my understanding that her new job needed her and I would keep her updated on the day's progress as it went on. With a few tears and a supportive smile from her, I sent her off at eight thirty.

We arrived at the hospital half an hour early. I asked Julie if she had any idea how the hell we'd managed to get a donor so quickly, and one who knew about our case at that. She confessed she hadn't even spoken to her parents, friends, or other family members about our appointment when her phone had rung with the great news.

Dr. Messing came in with a smile on his face. "How's everyone doing this morning?"

"Pretty great," I said and shook his hand. "I still can't wrap my head around it." I shook my head in amazement.

"I can imagine. Hell, I don't think we've had this quick of a turnaround by using the stem-cell database to be honest with you," he said. "You truly have an angel looking out for that son of yours."

"That we do," I said and smiled at Jasper, who was busy playing with a few of his toy cars in his hospital bed. He hadn't come back home after his bout with pneumonia. Dr. Messing thought it prudent to keep him in a more sterile environment so complications were less likely whenever the time arose for his marrow transplant. The man had stated the sooner we were able to go through with the procedure, the greater the likelihood for success. I wasn't about to mess with that.

"I do have one question for the lot of you before we get to the business at hand," Messing said. "Normally, we try to keep things confidential until the procedure is finalized and the necessary paperwork is filed, but the donor has requested to meet with the recipient and his family beforehand."

"What should we do?" Julie asked me.

"It's a little unorthodox and not exactly protocol, and I understand if you would rather wait until after the procedure is done, but I figured I'd put it out there since it came as a personal request from the donor, and in this case, I've chosen to bend the rules if you're interested," he said.

"I think I'd be okay with that," I said and Julie nodded her assent. "Jasper?" My boy looked up at me. "Would you like to meet your hero now instead of later?"

"You mean the one that'll make me all better?" he asked.

"That's right," I said.

He nodded with vigor and I looked at Julie, who nodded her approval.

I turned to look at Messing. "Let's do this."

The man escorted us down a maze of halls and stopped outside the door to the room we were meant to walk through.

"Are you ready?" he asked.

"Let's do this," Jasper copied my earlier statement and Julie, Todd, and I nodded.

"I'll let them know that you've agreed," he said and left us to wait in the hall.

After a few minutes, he came back out and gestured for us to go ahead.

Hand in hand, Julie, Jasper, and I walked on as a family unit with Todd and Messing bringing up the rear. I first saw the linen covered feet as the curtain was half-drawn. The smell of disinfectant assaulted my nostrils and the low and steady beeping emanating from a heart monitor was going strong. I could hear the rhythmic ticking of an IV drip and my feet continued their progress.

"Hi." I was met with as I peered around the curtain and was greeted with the warmest smile.

Everything began to spin.

CHAPTER 29

I no longer knew up from down as my knees threatened to give out from under me. My eyes registered one thing, my head another, and before long, so did my heart. I felt fear, shame, pride, elation, amongst many other reeling emotions.

"You," Julie said. "It's you?"

I registered the anger in her voice. My ex was livid and if smoke could physiologically manifest itself from her ears, she'd be a dead ringer for a steam train. Myself, I was confused as all get out.

"Julie, I can explain everything," the patient in the bed said.

"Allie!" Jasper said, far more enthusiastic than his mother clearly felt, and took a running leap toward the hospital bed, only to be stopped by his mother.

"Alissa," I managed.

She'd said she had to head in to work. I saw her dressed and ready with my own two eyes. I saw her off with a kiss. Her tears. What is she doing lying in that hospital bed?

As I pondered, a short answer formulated itself.

I knew why.

"Paxton. Jasper. Julie?" Alissa said, and her eyes stayed locked on Julie's face. I turned to look at what Alissa was being faced with, seeing as Julie had yet to say anything and from experience, silence was about as bad as her coming to blows with my ex's words. "Let me explain."

Julie kept hold of Jasper's shoulders and tapped her foot. "Please," Julie said, impatient and clearly vexed.

My gaze trained itself on Alissa, who had wires and tubes dangling from her left arm. She was prepped and ready to go. Before long, it was going to be Jasper's turn. Speaking of which, the little monster had managed to free himself from his mother, climbed up onto the bed, and now sat on Alissa's lap.

"I thought Daddy said we were meeting my hero," Jasper said. "Are you sick too?"

"No, buddy, I'm not sick," she said and gave him her best smile, which never reached her eyes. The uneasiness to her voice told me she was nervous. "I hope you're okay with me helping you get better."

The boy nodded.

"Explain," Julie said. "Now!"

I saw my son jump at the venomous anger in his mother's tone, and I didn't appreciate it one bit.

Before I risked stoking the fire, Todd beat me to the punch with better results than I probably would have yielded. "Julie, calm down, and give her a chance to do just that."

Alissa nodded her appreciation and looked at me quickly before finally settling her gaze on the fiery resistance in the room. "I honestly thought that you'd be thrilled," she said. "I never once expected for you to be mad. Disappointed, sure…and envious, maybe."

"I'm not mad. I'm fucking furious," Julie said.

Jasper gasped. "Mommy, that's a bad word."

Julie didn't bother to react to Jasper's scolding. In fact, I was shocked she had forgotten he was even in the room, and had paid him no never mind despite that he was still perched on Allie's lap.

One look at the intensity in the woman's face told me that she was trapped between this surprise of sorts and her raging pregnancy hormones.

"I'm sorry," she said to my ex-wife.

"How?" I asked. "I mean, when did you get tested?" Then I began to clue in. There had only been one moment where she could have done this without us knowing. Messing's secretary had mentioned someone had specifically stated that their sample was for Jasper's case. "You never left your phone behind that day, did you?" I asked.

She shook her head. "No."

Alissa had gone through the motions of explaining that after we had found out about Julie's and my test results, she had feigned leaving her cell phone behind. It turns out she had run in to make an appointment to get tested and was lucky enough to bump into Dr. Messing before he had left for his rounds.

"He didn't want to run the blood work because he thought I was in all of this too deep already," she said.

"I was adamant that she speak with you both beforehand," Dr. Messing said and came up from behind. "And for good reason." The man looked at my ex-wife.

"But I persisted and I told him that if there were issues, we could all deal with them after we got this going for Jasper. If I was a match that is." I watched as she eyed Julie with sternness and tilted her chin up with pride, and that stubbornness of hers I had grown to love in all of our time together. "I realize this is a shock to you all, but I figured if there was the slightest chance, that you two as parents should take it."

"She's right," Dr. Messing said and looked between Julie and me. "There's no way of knowing when another matching donor could come around, and Alissa is one of the best matches I've seen in my history of donor and recipient matching. You need to take this chance while it's available. You know that the chemo hasn't been working as well as it should, and platelet therapy can only help so much, and he'll need more of that after the transplant—"

"You just like to steal the show, don't you?" Julie accused more than asked. "You waltz in here and—"

"Julie! You have to calm down, honey," Todd said, and

took hold of her arm as the woman attempted to move toward Alissa. "This isn't the end of the world. I find what she's doing incredibly valiant."

"It's not about bravery or valor," Alissa said and reached out to Julie who, with reluctance, Todd released, and by some unseen force, Julie moved forward, but never gave the woman her hand. "It's about what's right for that boy of yours." Alissa paused to smile at Jasper. "He's your world and I know that, and I know what it is to love him, Julie. Let me do this for you. I can't bear thinking that you could lose him over the simple fact that we have our differences. Do it for Jasper?"

After a moment of silence, which felt like an eternity, Julie gave in and reached her hand out to cover the top of Alissa's. Without another word the woman picked Jasper up from my girlfriend's lap and nodded. With that unspoken acknowledgement, Julie made to exit the room with our son in her arms and Todd followed them out of the room.

She paused at the door. "Good luck," she said before she disappeared altogether.

"I'll give you two a minute," Dr. Messing said and bowed out.

I teetered on my feet as I studied Alissa from head to her covered toes. She looked nervous, worried, relieved. What made me feel a slight semblance of comfort was that she also looked strong, proud, and determined.

"I can't believe you didn't tell me," I said. "Is that why you were crying the other day when I walked in on you thanking someone on the phone?"

She nodded. "Yes. I'm sor—" she said, but I rushed to her side, and cradling her neck in my hand, I kissed her with such desperation that even a glutton would still be hungry after overeating.

I pulled my lips from hers and leaned our foreheads against each other's.

"Are you okay with this?" she asked, and I could tell that she was forcing back her emotions. "I know it's not the greatest. I know I probably should have gone about it—"

I shook my head and pecked her. "You're crazy for doing this all on your own, you know that?" I kissed her again, keeping her face between the palms of my hands. "I wish you would have told me. Did you think about how the hell you were going to get home after all of this?"

She shrugged her shoulders, her smile sheepishly. "Not really."

"You're hopeless. For what it's worth, I'm not happy you chose to do this alone, but I love you all the more for it, sweetheart. And now that I know, I'm not leaving your side."

"I'm not hopeless." She nuzzled my nose. "Anything but. I'm saving a life."

"And you'll never know how much that means to me, to any of us," I said. "I love you so much, you crazy woman."

"You know I do too."

CHAPTER 30

Dr. Messing came in and asked Alissa if she was ready to go. With a quick kiss to her hand, I let the two nurses wheel her away, promising I'd be there when she woke up.

"Jasper is being prepped as we speak, if you'd like to see him before we take him away," he said.

"I would," I said. "And, Doc?"

"Yes?"

"You make sure those two come back to me." I swallowed the ball of emotion in my throat. "They're both my world."

"Got it," the man said, and put a hand on my shoulder as if a father would his son. The irony was that we were both about the same age. "They'll be fine. You'll see Alissa within the hour. Jasper, however, will take a little while longer."

"How much longer?"

"We'll be running his blood again to make sure everything is still a go, despite the fact we did it less than a week ago. From there, we'll take Alissa's marrow and synthesize it into the serum we need, and make the transfer," he said. "Jasper's procedure will be nearly three hours from the beginning of Alissa's aspiration, the synthesising, and transplantation. Basically, he'll be out for about an hour, if that."

I must have had a look of horror strewn on my face because Messing chuckled and patted me on the back as he urged me forward and out of Alissa's room.

"Don't worry," Messing said again. "It sounds worse than what it is. It'll reflect more on Alissa than Jasper, believe it or not."

"Why's that?"

"Transplants are typically harder on the donors, because they lose something their body is still using. She'll be sore, particularly in her hips and lower back. She might be a little extra tired as well. Her soreness will most likely last several days, but it can be up to a few weeks after the procedure," the doctor said. "We'll be keeping Jasper in here for the foreseeable future, but depending on how well Alissa fairs with the anesthesia, she should be fine to go home tonight, provided she keeps off her feet as much as possible for the remainder of the day and has someone to look after her, help her exercise her legs from tomorrow on."

"God, she's crazy," I mumbled under my breath, dragging my hands through my hair.

Dr. Messing chuckled. "Not crazy, but honestly, the most determined woman I've ever met."

"She is that. Thank you, Doc." I shook his hand and realized we had walked all the way down the hall to what was Jasper's room without my being aware.

"Go ahead," he said, and gestured for me to move forward.

"Daddy, Nurse Jackie said I'll be going to sleep and dream of all my favorite things," he said. "She said I can dream about ice cream and going to the park for as long as I want. When can we go to the park again, Daddy?"

Julie kept silent but I noticed the tears welling up in her eyes. I looked down at our son and fought the resilient lump I couldn't quite manage to clear in my throat. "As soon as this is all over and you're better, we'll all go play at the park. Why don't we make a *Jasper Day* out of it?" I asked.

He perked up and said, "You mean like the day we had with you, me, and Allie?"

"Sure thing, tough guy," I said. "And we'll even get Mommy and Todd to come along with us too. How does that sound?"

He giggled and said, "Perfect! Does that mean I get two ice creams?"

"I doubt it, but we'll see. Let's get this show on the road," I said, and stuck my fist out so he could bump it with his free hand. "Are you ready?"

"Yeah, Daddy."

"I love you," I said. "I'll be waiting for you when you wake up. I promise."

"Okay, Daddy."

It had been nearly an hour and a half and Alissa hadn't been brought out yet. I began pacing the waiting area, wondering what the hell might have gone wrong, when a nurse walked our way.

"Mr. Lowell?" she asked.

I rushed to her and said, "Yeah?"

"Ms. Hidgins is ready to be seen, sir," she said. "We're sorry for the wait. We're a little busy today and it took the nurses a little longer to get her back to her room."

I breathed easier and turned to Julie. "Are you okay?"

She nodded. "We'll come get you or send someone when we hear about Jasper."

I gave a curt nod and turned to follow the nurse.

I walked into Alissa's room to that same beeping sound from the cardiac monitor from earlier.

She was sleeping.

I kissed her forehead, letting my fingers skim across her cheekbones as her eyelashes fluttered.

"I love you so much," I said to her. I sat down, laid my hand on her thigh, and let my head fall to the side of the mattress as I breathed my relief that she was okay. "I can't believe you've done this."

"And I would do it again," she said with a croaky voice before I felt her hand tangle itself in my messy hair. "Now kiss me like you did before they took me away."

I smiled at her loopy smirk and what else could I do? I indulged her. Hell, it was quite possible that she had saved my son's life. If all she wanted was a kiss, I was going to give it to her. She deserved the world in my opinion. Only, I was questioning if I would always be enough for this woman.

When I backed away, the look of clarity in her eyes told me everything I needed to know.

CHAPTER 31

A series of calls were made over the PA system and next thing I knew, hospital staff were running about the halls, rushing like ants to a piece of dropped fruit. By their frantic activity, things didn't look good for whoever the patient was.

It wasn't until I noticed Alissa was looking past me and toward her hospital room door that I filled with complete dread, and my son popped to the forefront of my mind.

Please, God, don't let that last mad rush be about Jasper.

"Mr. Lowell," the nurse said, and I turned toward the voice.

"Yes?"

Her sympathetic facial expression got my heart thumping and my blood to rush through my veins.

Oh God…

I felt Alissa grab my hand and squeeze it.

"It's your son, sir," she said. "I wanted to let you know they'll be a little longer than predicted."

The woman stood there, shifting on her feet. I could tell she hadn't been in the field for all that long and wasn't accustomed to bearing news to family members about their loved one.

"Is everything all right?" Alissa asked the nurse, as it seemed my attempts at composing myself were failing and my speech had left me.

"Jasper's had a reaction to the anesthesia, but we've got everything under control," she said. "I just figured that I would let you know of this now so you won't be surprised when he comes out."

"Surprised?" Alissa asked.

"Why would I be surprised?" I asked as relief took over, but only slightly.

"Well, sir," she began, "he won't be waking up right away. The doctor had to induce a coma due to his brain swelling after he threw a clot. It's a precaution he deemed necessary to use due to the nature of the procedure and your son's underlying condition."

"Are you telling me that my son had a stroke?" I asked. She nodded. "But he's only four!"

"I'm sorry, sir. These reactions rarely happen, but anesthesia does hold its own set of risks," she said and began to back away. "I just figured you would appreciate the information right away. The doctor will be available to answer any questions you may have when he's out of the OR."

I swallowed hard. "Thank you."

"And, sir," she said, and I looked her way once again to see a weary smile. "Everything else is going as planned. They should be done within the next half hour."

The air felt as if it had been knocked out of me. On one hand, I was relieved to know that Jasper was going to be okay, on the other, I was far from thrilled he had to suffer through yet another complication.

I felt helpless again, much like the day we had found out about his JMML. Despite knowing there was nothing I could have done about the clot, it was still a tough lump to swallow.

"Pax, stop it," Alissa said. "You're blaming yourself again."

"I'm that transparent, huh?"

"Even when I'm loopy I can read you like a book," she said. "Now go find Julie and make sure that she's—"

"We're here." I turned to the door to face my ex-wife. "How are you feeling?" she asked Alissa, as if their previous moment of hostility had never occurred.

"Sore, but I'll survive," she said. "How're you holding up?"

"The nurse came to let us know that everything is going smoothly and they're almost done," Julie said. "They're keeping him comatose for the day and they may try and wean him off over the next day or so, if there aren't any other complications."

"When can we see him?" I asked.

"That's why I'm here," Julie said. "Messing came out after I sent the nurse your way and said that we'd be able to see him in the next half hour. He seems optimistic, but mentioned that it would take some time. They're about to wheel him to his post-op room and then they'll come and get us."

Aside from evident exhaustion from the day's stress, Julie seemed quite controlled with her emotions. Instead of being just as solid on my feet as I'd been over the last few months, I felt a little off-kilter and emotionally drained. I doubted being able to support anyone but Alissa and myself. If anything, Alissa was the epitome of strength for both of us right now.

❧ CHAPTER 32 ☙

Before long, visiting hours were up and some middle-aged nurse rushed us out of Jasper's room. I wasn't the least bit impressed with her tact, but what was I to do? This was the Pediatric ICU we were talking about. Their protocols were a bit stricter, and when it came down to the fine line, I wasn't about to jeopardize my son's health, or that of anyone else's child.

I had made my way back to Alissa's room and found her chatting it up with Dr. Messing, glad to see her dressed and sitting up.

The tension in her jaw and the dullness in her eyes indicated she was having some discomfort.

She smiled the moment she saw me. "I've got the all-clear."

I walked to her side and kissed the crown of her head.

"I want you back here in two days' time so I can check up on everything," Dr. Messing said.

"I'll be here," she said. "I'll be going stir-crazy staying in until then."

I smirked at her. "I can think of a few things that don't require any or much effort on your part," I said, leaning into her ear so only she could hear.

She blushed, nudged me in my side, and then let her head fall onto my shoulder.

"Just remember the list of things to look out for. If any of them pop up, I want you back in here ASAP," Messing said.

"Let's get you home," I said when a nurse showed up with a wheelchair for her. "Riding in style, I see."

Alissa's nose scrunched up at my lame joke. "I'd rather walk, but I'm doing what I was told to do so I don't have to hurt as much."

"And I suppose hospital policy has nothing to do with it?" I asked, garnering a chuckle from the nurse.

"Are you kidding? It's got everything to do with it."

We got home and I had gone ahead, unlocked the door, and rushed back to her. I knew she could walk but I also knew that it hurt to do so. Enough proof of that was shown when Messing had gotten her up to help gauge if she was ready to leave.

"You're not carrying me," she said as if reading my mind.

I got close to her face and smiled. "Let me do this for you," I said. "You argued about me helping you into the Jeep and it hurt you. I don't need you hurting more than I know you already are."

She didn't put up a fight. Instead, she pecked my cheek, and studied my face before wrapping her arm around my neck, and letting me take charge.

I let her down on the bed, with her feet dangling off its side. She looked up at me and my gaze fused to hers.

"Are you okay?" I asked. "Do you need anything?"

She nodded and averted her eyes in a shy manner.

I grabbed her chin and tilted her face so her eyes came back to meet mine.

"What is it, sweetheart?"

"I need you to help me out of these clothes and into something more comfortable," she said.

I laughed because I knew she had help from the nurse earlier.

Like a gentleman, I catered to her needs.

She helped me shift her shirt up and over her head, revealing her bust.

My eyes never left hers except for the few seconds I needed to get to the buttons on her pants. I slid them down her body and got to my knees, where I helped her take her legs out of the garment, while she held on to my shoulders.

My hands trailed over her bare skin as I got back up to my feet and allowed my open palms to glide from her lower back, where I felt the edge of the bandage, to her shoulder-blades. She had closed her eyes, smiling as she melted into my chest. With her head tilted back, I took the opportunity to let my lips do the talking over the sensitive skin of her neck. "I love you," I said and finished with a nip to her ear. She whimpered. "Let's get you into bed."

CHAPTER 33

I woke to a still-sleeping Alissa. She had found slumber on her stomach, but hadn't strayed very far from me throughout the night. I ran my fingers down her bare back and stopped at the edge of the bandage.

How many people did I know would willingly put themselves through hell to save a life like she had? I groaned.

I recalled how she had woken up in the middle of the night in a heated sweat and ended up stripping down to her panties. It wasn't uncommon for a donor to come down with a fever after an extraction, but it was imperative that everything was done to keep the temperature down.

With nothing but a thin sheet covering her bottom and a light snore breaking the silence of the morning every so often, I watched over her.

That's when I heard her soft moan. "Pax."

Not sure if she was awake or sleeping, I kissed the back of her shoulder. Her breath picked up. I continued and kissed the back of her neck. I settled beside her and noticed her eyes were still shut but a smile on her face had appeared.

She was awake.

"Good morning," I said and nuzzled her cheek.

She rolled onto her back with a bit of effort. "What was that for?"

I hovered above her at her side. "The sight of you practically naked in my bed makes me want to do things, things I simply can't do right now." I pecked her on the lips. "How are you feeling?"

"Great so far," she said. "Not much pain, but I suppose I'll know more when I try to stand or walk." She kissed me hard on the mouth. "Now, about the things you so desperately want to do and can't."

"I've yet to show my appreciation for what you've done." I nuzzled her nose with mine.

She smiled. "There's no need for that."

"Oh," I brushed my lips over hers, "but there is."

She laughed.

I love that laugh of hers. It could cure anything and everything in my opinion. It turned the cloudiest day to nothing but sunshine and rainbows. She was able to make everyone around her happy. She made everything right. She showed me how genuine her feelings were, and that was simple, but most of all, it was enough. Alissa Hidgins had to laugh, it was that easy. It's all she had to do to make me happy; everything else, I could handle myself or would fall into place on its own.

"What's got you grinning like a goof?"

"You," I said. "Just you."

I left Alissa upstairs to relax while I fixed us some breakfast, and called the hospital to see how Jasper had faired overnight while I was at it. Nothing had changed, his vitals had remained strong.

Just finishing with the bacon and about to start with the eggs, I sat the crispy strips on the table when I heard a loud thud.

I rushed upstairs and heard Alissa cry out in pain.

I entered the bedroom but she wasn't where I had left her.

I followed the sound of the shower and let myself in.

"Alissa?" I found her in a rather interesting position; bent over naked with her heart-shaped bottom pointed right at me. "What the hell are you doing, gorgeous?" I asked but as I approached with admiration for the sight before me, she straightened herself up with the help of the shower stall wall.

"Need a little help?"

I bent over and picked up the bottle of bodywash she had knocked over onto the floor.

"Nice ass," I said with a smirk.

"Thank you." She took the bottle from me with a huff. "Now, get out."

"I don't think I can do that," I said. "What if you drop the shampoo bottle next, or maybe the conditioner?"

"Funny," she said, but couldn't remain serious as her lips quirked up. "Seeing as you're so worried about me, maybe I should take you up on your offer."

"Are you sure it's wise?" I asked. "I mean, what if you can't keep your hands off me? You know we'd be in trouble and I can't take you like I normally do."

Alissa looked like she pondered what I said and smiled back, mischief all too clear in her eyes.

"Come on, handsome," she said. "I can use someone to scrub my back and wash my hair. I think I can control my urges just fine, and you seemed to have done a good job with yours last night."

I stripped down while she stood in the shower, letting the water rain down on her. When I entered, I eyed her glistening body and groaned as I began to feel those familiar tingles heading down to my nether region.

God, have mercy.

I erred on the side of caution, choosing to start with her back and headed south from there. I didn't need her to see that the control over my urges was dwindling.

As I got to that firm tush of hers, she had removed the bandage, and I saw the bruising around the extraction site. I made a point to be gentle. When I ran my palm slightly over the area, I felt her flinch. Her butt flexed. I smiled at the sight and gave her a slight love nip on the opposite cheek.

"I'm not sure having you in here was such a good idea after all," she said through clenched teeth.

"I promise I'll behave," I said, having finished with her legs. I stood up, held up my index and middle fingers together and gave her a broad and overexaggerated smile. "Scout's honor."

She laughed at my shenanigans and leaned forward to kiss my lips with her hands resting on my chest. She gave me one of her classic endearing looks. "Thank you," she said. "Has anyone ever told you how sweet you can be?"

"Only once or twice." I winked.

Cleansed and fed, Alissa got up with another one of her winces.

"I didn't bring you down here for you to tidy up after my cooking," I scolded her, and got up to take our plates from her hands.

"Hey!"

"Don't you *hey* me," I said. "Now, get that cute butt of yours to the couch or better yet, to bed. Your out-of-bed privileges have been revoked. You've done enough walking for now."

She snorted. "What are you, my doctor?"

I put the rinsed plates into the dishwasher and wiped my hands on a tea towel. I turned, and my gaze softened when our eyes met as I faced her up close.

"No. I'm your man," I said, my hands on her hips. "I said I'd take care of you, and that's what I'm doing. So what'll it be?"

After a few seconds of internal deliberation, Alissa made her decision.

I scooped her up into my arms and carried her upstairs to our room. I set her up with the TV, a full glass of water, her pain medication, and cuddled her for what felt like too short of a while, but I had an important thing to do.

"Are you sure you'll be okay if I head off to the hospital to check on Jasper?"

"I'll be fine," she said and yawned. The pain meds had already begun to take effect. "I think I'll have a nap while you're away."

I kissed her forehead. "Sounds like a good idea."

"I wish I could go with you," she said with her eyes drooping.

"I know you do. I promise you can see him tomorrow when we go back to get you checked out," I said.

With a dreamlike sigh, I got an "Okay," and I was off.

I walked into the Pediatric ICU to find that Jasper's condition had remained the same as it had been earlier in the morning. My timing was impeccable. Dr. Messing walked in moments after my arrival.

"Mr. Lowell," he said. "It's good to see you. How's our donor doing?"

"She's quite sore, but I convinced her to take some pain medicine this morning. She's trying to sleep it off," I said. "She said it's not as bad as it was yesterday, but she didn't enjoy the walking I made her do this morning."

"That's normal," he said. "Mind if I recommend something? If you have access to a pool or you're near a body of water, she could always try a swim. She'd get the movement that she needs to avoid any clotting and cramping issues in her legs, and it makes it easier to bear the pain because of the weightlessness. Just make sure the procedural site is waterproofed and change the bandage afterward in case water got to it."

I nodded. "I'll have to mention it to her. So how's Jasper this morning?"

"I'm waiting on this morning's blood work results to help me out with that analysis. We'll be running an MRI to revisit the extent of his brain's swelling. If it's gone down, we'll wait another twenty-four hours before bringing him out of his coma," he said. "The good thing is that his electroencephalogram is showing optimistic readings. Jasper's brain activity is perfect, and he should recover and be as normal as he's always been, but we won't know about any glitches until he's awake."

"Thank God," I said, but I never questioned his mention of glitches. I wondered what they could possibly entail, but I figured it was pointless to worry until the situation called for it and if it ever did.

CHAPTER 34

By lunchtime, I had left the hospital and headed home.

Alissa was still sleeping when I made my way upstairs.

I sat beside her and attempted to rouse her as promised. Her head tilted to the side. I kissed her neck where it met her shoulder, smiling at her small whimper. Kissing beneath her ear, I trailed my fingers over the soft skin of her arm.

"Mmm…Pax." She was dreaming of me.

I nuzzled her cheekbone. She sighed in total contentment, her tensed body relaxing itself.

"Wake up, Sleeping Beauty," I said in her ear and gave her a soft kiss to the temple.

Alissa opened her eyes, and that's when I saw the fire in her irises. She grabbed on to my face and pulled me in for a scorcher of a kiss. Nipping my bottom lip, which caused me to gasp, she plundered my mouth with her tongue. I braced my arms on either side of her and groaned while she began to trail hot and wet kisses and nips down my jaw.

"Honey," I said, as I pulled away to look at her face. "That must have been one hell of a dream."

"That it was," she said. "Although the real thing is so much better." She winked and reached out for me again.

I shook my head at her and my eyes trailed lower only to realize that she was naked.

She smirked. "Like what you see?"

"Very much," I said. "But would you settle for some PG-13 fun instead?"

She laughed. "You mean make out like two horny teenagers? Why not?"

I leaned down and kissed her softly before she took over and things got heated quickly.

After our lengthy make out session, I had gotten up and walked to the dresser. I reached in and grabbed a few items and then threw them at her. "Put this on," I said. "We're going out."

She sat up in bed, the sheets draped over her naked figure and tucked under her arms. Holding up the two-piece bikini, she arched her brow and asked, "What are you up to?"

"Just put it on. I know you want to get out, so that's what we're going to do."

"What?" she said. "But I should be relaxing."

"And you should be walking around a bit more than you have been. I saw Dr. Messing when I visited Jasper this morning. He gave me a great idea."

"Okay, but what's it got to do with this?" She waved the tiny swimsuit as if it were a flag.

"You and I will spend the afternoon outdoors relaxing," I said. "Plus, I think the water will help alleviate some of the pain with the walking."

"I see," she said. "Sounds like my mind's been made up for me, hasn't it?"

"You need this," I said and kissed the crown of her head. "Now stop stalling, get dressed, and come downstairs. I'll go put something together for a picnic."

CHAPTER 35

We drove for a while before Alissa began to grasp where it was that I was bringing her. Her face brightened when she saw the large barn and country home, and her lips cracked a smile that suddenly disappeared and she groaned.

"What is it?" I asked.

"This is your parents' place. You expect me to parade around in a skimpy bikini at your parents'?" she asked with a blush that spread from her cheeks to her shoulders.

I laughed. "They're not here."

"You know we could have gone to the beach," she said. "It would have been closer."

"Yeah, we could have, but I didn't want to have to deal with people," I said. "Plus, you haven't seen this yet."

"Seen what? We're not taking the four-wheeler are we?"

"No," I said. "The thing would be too rough on you, same goes for the side-by-side. We'll take the Jeep there so sit tight."

She laughed. "You and your toys, you're truly a country boy at heart, aren't you?" She crooked her finger to beckon me closer. "I have to say that it's quite a sexy trait," she said over my lips before she brushed that pucker of hers lightly over mine.

The large manmade pond came into view, complete with the small dock and overgrown grass that surrounded it.

My father had built it for my mother when my brother and I were kids. As to what the exact story behind it was, Mom had told my brother and me that it was Dad's way of apologizing for working too much. Let's just say the man was a tough one to live up to when women came into my life in later years, especially from a romance standpoint.

"This was an apology?" Alissa asked as she looked around.

"Yeah. I don't remember much of him being around and doing stuff with us in my earlier years," I said. "After he built this thing for Mom, he changed a lot." I turned the ignition off.

"It's beautiful," she said. "The only thing that's missing is a large willow with a tire swing attached to it, and it would look like something out of the movies. It must have been a great place to party for you and your friends in high school."

I chuckled and remembered what had happened to the damn thing. "There was a tree." I pointed to the large stump decorated with a pot of flowers sitting atop it. "Dad, Theo, and I cut it down a while back, after we found it split down the middle after a bad storm."

"So no parties?"

"Oh, there were parties." I laughed and exited the vehicle. "This is where we kicked off the summer holidays."

My brother, Theo, and I had had some rather interesting get-togethers here back in high school. I smiled at the good memories and forced the dark ones back: the ones I'd never be able to relive with Theo again.

I rounded our ride and Alissa took my hand to be helped out. "How are you feeling?" I asked.

"My hips are achy but I'm fine," she said with a broad smile.

CHAPTER 36

I must have dozed off after our snack, caught up in the tranquility of our surroundings, because I woke up to the sound of a splash. I bolted upright and that's when I noticed that Alissa was no longer by my side.

Seconds later, she broke the water's surface. "You're right!" She giggled. "This does help."

I gave her a large grin. I was glad she was enjoying herself. As a matter-of-fact, I was becoming aware that no matter what it was that we did together, she always had the brightest of smiles and sunny disposition.

Something like this, I had never been able to do with Julie. She was a city-bred girl through and through. Come to think of it, the woman and I never had that much in common, and it wasn't until Alissa had come along that I realized I had brushed aside a lot more than just my writing over the years.

"Hey, daydreamer," she said. "Why don't you get off that lazy rump of yours and join me?"

"What's in it for me?"

She shrugged her shoulders and gave me an innocent look before dipping down so the water went up to her chin and lifted the tiny piece of material that had once covered her top. She chucked it onto the dock. My jaw dropped. "You did say your parents weren't here."

I jumped up to my feet and made a mad dash to cannonball

a few feet beside her. When I surfaced, she was facing me with a self-assured smile, and I watched as she pulled her bottoms up above the surface and held them up for me to see.

"Sweetheart," I said, as she chucked those onto the dock as well.

"This is nice, isn't it?" she asked with nonchalance. She approached me and wrapped her arms around my neck, pressing her naked breasts to my chest. We were in the shallow end by the pond's edge where my feet touched the sandy bottom. My arms surrounded her at the waist. She laughed into my neck, nipped my jaw. "Someone's a little overdressed for the occasion."

I felt myself harden. I wasn't used to this kind of overtness from her. I chuckled. "Are you drunk?"

"Must be the drugs."

She let her hands run from the back of my neck, down to my chest. When they had reached the waistband of my swimming trunks, I grabbed onto her hands to stop her. "You'll be the death of me. We shouldn't."

"You said exercise," she said, and I looked at her in confusion but nodded my response.

"That's not—"

She smiled, winked, and went underwater before I could finish talking.

Next thing I knew, my shorts were yanked down and I felt her hands on my length, her exhaled breath bubbling with gentle tickles up against my front as she surfaced from her underwater seduction. She reached one arm around my neck, pulled herself up, and kissed below my ear. I groaned at the havoc. "Devil woman," I said into her ear. "We can't."

She wrapped a leg around my hip. "We can."

My length was pulsing and nudged at her heated folds. She ground herself against me.

"You're unbelievable," I said, after I pulled away from her heated kiss. "It can't be helped that I give in to you so easily, but not this time, baby."

The look of rejection was too much. I captured her mouth, lowered her leg from my hip, and used my feet to widen her stance.

"What are you doing?"

"I'm not making love to you but I'll be damned if I leave you hanging like this."

I felt like a rebellious teenager, sneaking, bringing a girl home to fool around with in my parents' backyard. In reality, we were two consenting adults, and I really didn't care if we were caught while I loved on my woman.

I slid a finger into her and revelled in the feel of her slick internal muscles, clenching down on me.

"Oh, baby." My hand stilled when hers made contact with my erection.

I began to grind my hips into her grip.

Surrounded with only nature, away from civilization, we submersed each other into a world where only the two of us existed.

I watched Alissa as she held my gaze, her lips swollen from my kisses, her face flushed and her eyes blazing with the fires of passion.

When her neck arched back, I began feeling the tremors of her imminent orgasm surrounding my digits.

My balls tightened and I knew it wasn't going to be long before we took each other over the edge.

With a guttural moan, I felt her arch into my hand and clench my fingers tightly.

Her sounds set me off.

Our cries mixed and mingled, causing the birds that watched over us in the tree line to fly off as our erotic high descended onto us.

I buried my head into her neck as she caressed her cheek to mine, running her fingers through my hair and massaging my scalp. We just held each other without saying anything at all. Nothing seemed to need to be said.

"Are you okay?" I asked, as I rubbed the side of her face with my fingertips.

"I'm better than okay," she said and framed my face, depositing a tender kiss onto my lips. "You could never hurt me, handsome."

"I don't know about that, but I can tell you that I would never do it on purpose," I said. "What do you say we dry off, get dressed, and get out of here?"

"Do we have to?"

I chortled. "You sound like Jasper."

"I love this place," she said. "I always dreamed of an old house in the country, a few horses, and maybe some cattle. I'm a small-town country girl and I've never had the joy of living the full-blown country life."

"Hmm." I eyed her as we made our way to the ladder that was attached to the dock.

"What?" she asked, as I helped her out of the water.

Gravity pulled on her body and the weight of it caused her to wince as her hips and legs were once again forced to bear her true weight. I held her close as her knees showed signs of giving out. I thanked my lucky stars for putting my foot down earlier.

All I could do was smile down at her. "In pursuit of the simple life, are we?"

"It sure beats a complicated one."

Too right she was.

I felt bad for the pain Alissa ended up having tonight.

It was so bad that our relaxing movie session had taken a downward spiral and landed us in the bedroom, the lights turned off, her tears streaming down her face as it was scrunched up in that horrible expression of pain. It broke my heart to see her that way.

You only have yourself to blame.

"Pax, it's not your fault. You didn't hurt me. It's all that walking we did."

I knew she was right, but it was just easier for me to blame myself. I mean, I was the one to take us out, the one to suggest swimming which led to… Well, at least I put a stop to that. Mostly.

"Let me take you to the emergency room," I said still worried.

"I'll take the pain pills. If they don't work, then you can take me in, but I don't want to go."

Half an hour had passed and she had fallen asleep in my arms as I attempted to soothe her by rubbing gentle patterns up and down her upper back. Her face, a perfect picture of relaxation, with no signs of discomfort showing. Then I was able to relax.

CHAPTER 37

I swore loud enough to wake Alissa when I realized the alarm clock hadn't gone off.

We jumped out of bed to find ourselves with half an hour to get ready and hightail our asses to the hospital for her follow-up appointment with Dr. Messing.

I stood there in shock as I watched my woman run around at a frantic pace, pulling her pants on and make her way to the bathroom while shoving her arms into her shirt. She hadn't winced yet which had me smiling.

"Feeling better I see."

"It still hurts but it's not like last night or the day of the aspiration," she said. "I think I might be on the mend."

"I'm glad," I said and winked at her excited smile.

Alissa had been restless while we waited for Dr. Messing.

Fifteen minutes past our appointment time, the man walked in and closed the door to the examination room. "Alissa." He shook her hand. "How are you feeling?"

"The soreness seems to be fading," she said and looked at me. "I nearly broke Paxton's fingers last night from the pain, but today I'm barely feeling anything."

"That's good. Have you been walking around like I've asked you to, though you shouldn't have been in that much pain." He eyed the both of us. "What have you been doing?"

She gave me a shy look and blushed as she kept her eyes averted from the doctor's. "I may have overdone it yesterday when Pax got me out of the house," she said, leaving the most heated moments out.

"I see," he said. "The pain medication worked though?"

Alissa nodded. "I hate the stuff, but I had no choice but to take it. I thought I was going to go insane from the intensity of the pain."

"Something Mr. Lowell said yesterday tells me that you've not been taking the pills regularly." She shook her head. "That's fine. Now, can I get you to lie on your stomach? I'd like to see the procedural site and make sure that there isn't an infection, and please tell me you've at least been taking the antibiotics as prescribed."

She nodded. "Of course."

After his quick consultation and a few vials of blood to rule any issues like anemia or blood-borne infections, he dismissed us.

"If you're planning on sticking around to visit Jasper, I can let you know how your blood work came out," he said, as Alissa stood from the gurney.

I grabbed her hand and kissed its top before pulling her along the halls to Jasper's room. It's not like she'd have given me the choice to steer her away from the little guy anyway.

When we walked in, a nurse was there to adjust his IVs and make sure everything was right with the equipment that surrounded him at the head of his bed.

"How's my little man doing today?"

"Very well," she said and gave me a genuine smile. "I expect that Dr. Messing will be in shortly. He should be making the final decision on taking him off the barbiturates."

I nodded. "So does that mean that his scans came out clear yesterday?"

The nurse's smile brightened further. "Yes." I turned to look at Alissa, who squeezed my hand and smiled with about as much relief as I felt.

Thank God. "And what of the transplant?" I asked.

"That, you'll have to discuss with the doctor," she said and turned to Alissa. "Say, aren't you the donor?" The nurse sized her up, but in a kind manner.

Alissa blushed. "How'd you know?"

The woman beamed. "You guys have been the talk of the ward over the last few days." She looked between Allie and me. "How're you feeling?"

"I'm fine," she said. "It's this handsome boy here that I'm worried about."

I let go of Alissa's hand and wrapped my arm around her waist, kissing her temple as she melted into my side. The nurse's gaze stuck to us, and I could have sworn a look of envy had flashed across her face before she took her leave.

Julie and Todd arrived and Dr. Messing had come and gone, telling us about the good news.

Alissa was healthy, and Jasper's drug-induced coma was going to be discontinued. His basic blood work had come out clear of any secondary issues for the time being, but he would be monitored closely for quite some time.

As for his JMML, and if the transplant had worked, it still remained to be seen. We were looking at a very lengthy monitoring phase to make sure everything worked out, along with the continuation of anti-rejection medications and regular blood transfusions.

"Let's get you back home," I told Alissa.

"Sounds good. I wouldn't mind a do-over on our movie night."

"But it's barely lunchtime," I said. "You can't expect to watch movies for the rest of the day."

"Sure we can, but—" she said, and looked at me with an

arched brow that told me plenty. She wasn't planning on just movies.

"I should have known," I said in her ear and kissed her cheek. "But I think we should wait that out a little longer."

The woman gave me a pout. Something told me I'd have one hell of a time winning that battle, like I had with all the others.

As we said our goodbyes, Alissa made sure to whisper words in Jasper's ear that made Julie and I look at each other. I shrugged in response to my ex-wife's questioning gaze. Alissa kissed his forehead and ran her hand over his shaved head.

"What'd you tell him?" I asked, as we left the hospital room.

She smirked. "It's a secret between that prince of yours and me."

"I'll let you have that." I kissed her knuckles. "Just this once."

CHAPTER 38

"**G**od, Pax! Pax!" she said. I thought my eardrums would burst she was so loud.

I had her on her back, legs up in the air as I weaseled myself overtop of her. She thought my after-dinner misfortune to be a hoot.

"I'll show you how wearing ice cream is funny," I said. "It's your fault anyway."

"How is it my fault?" she asked. "You're the one with two left feet."

"You tripped me!"

She howled and I proceeded to rub my chest against hers and smear the melted treat I had on my hands onto her face.

She shocked me when she latched on to my wrist and sucked in one of my fingers. My eyes bulged out of my head, my manly appendage twitched as I felt her velvet tongue twirl and massage the digit clean. I guess tripping and landing flat on your face could always end worse.

"Allie." I gave her a warning groan.

"Shower?"

"Yeah," I said. "And you, my little vixen, are coming with, although I'm sure I'll regret that decision."

I got to my feet and picked her up off the floor in a bridal-style hold.

"Paxton Lowell, I can damn well walk!"

"I'm well aware of that, but I'm making sure you won't try anything funny on our way there."

Standing in her birthday suit, she leaned over into the stall and turned the water on. I groaned at the sight of those cheeks of hers that again, for the second day in a row, were presented to me, ripe for the taking.

"Are you trying to kill me?" I asked, my feet taking me to a stop right behind her, my erect shaft rubbing up against her heated core.

She hummed at my horny act and straightened up, melding her back into my chest as my hands found their place on her hips.

I groaned, "Get in."

She sure didn't waste much time. Once the shower stall door was closed, she turned and had me pressed to the cool tiled wall.

Her lips ate at mine as our bodies hit a fever pitch. If it were possible, the water beading on my skin would have sizzled and evaporated into steam, she had me so hot for her.

Her hands remained on my pecs as she slid herself down the front of my body until she found herself on her knees. Without missing a beat, her mouth was on my length, like it had lassoed her in. Taking me in deep, I felt my tip hit the back of her throat. My head tilted back and leaned against the wall as my eyes rolled to a close and my jaw went slack. "Damn, Allie, your mouth is pure sin."

Her tongue, teeth, and suction had me on the verge of collapsing to my knees in worship for her. I could tell she was enjoying her ministrations. The sure-fire confident shimmer in her eyes as she looked up at me and the amused hum she made around my shaft were perfect indicators.

My hands tangled into her wet hair in an effort to guide her to a more needful rhythm. I was throbbing and I felt the blazing heat in my balls as they began to constrict. I was going to blow between those swollen lips of hers if she kept going like that.

In a moment of clarity, I took charge. I didn't want to explode like that. Not this time. I pulled on a fistful of her hair and tilted her head back. Her flushed face made me want to give in and let her have her way with me. She looked up with confusion, as if she thought she had done something wrong.

"Goddamn, it's too bad you're sore," I said. "Get up."

"But—"

I pulled her up to her feet. My mouth covered hers. My hands held the sides of her face as if she was the most precious thing in the world to me. "There's only one place I want my release in right now and it's not your mouth," I said. "But first…"

I never finished with my words. I chose to show her instead.

As I lay Alissa onto the bed, the phone began to ring.

Instantly, Jasper popped into my thoughts. The doctors had taken him off of the drug that kept him in his coma earlier. Had something gone wrong?

I rose and reached for the cordless phone on my bedside table. I looked at the caller ID.

Julie.

Please let it be good news.

I looked at Alissa who gave me the small ounce of courage I needed to hit the button that would connect the call.

"Hello?"

CHAPTER 39

He's awake.

I kept repeating those words to myself as Julie kept talking on the other end of the line.

To be honest, I only registered her first statement, and the rest of what she'd said had pretty much fallen as mutterings much like that of Charlie Brown's teacher.

Alissa sat up as I stared off into space with the receiver stuck to my head. Her hand had been rubbing on my leg for who knows how long, as I sat there repeating Julie's first two words internally.

I grasped Alissa's hand and squeezed. The hand that held the receiver shook and when she realized I was in some sort of shock, she made a grab for it.

"Julie?" she asked.

I turned to look at her as she spoke to my ex-wife, barely registering what she was saying until she hung up the phone. "He's awake," I said, as I felt my emotions coming around. "He's awake!"

Elation had finally taken over.

Alissa sat there and watched me pace the room and ramble on in excitement, as if I were a child who had just found out he was headed to Disneyland.

I stopped dead in my tracks and looked at her when I heard her giggle.

"We've got to go," I said.

"I was just about to say that." She got up with the towel wrapped around her body. I eyed her with hunger. The memory of what we were about to do came back to me and I groaned. "You can show me how happy you are when we get back, stud." She walked by me, as I stood there naked, following her with my eyes. "Get dressed."

Forty minutes later, we were walking into Jasper's room. I saw him sitting up and telling Julie and Todd about something in that classically animated fashion of his. You could have sworn the little guy had only been napping and nothing had ever been wrong. Aside from the fact he looked like a human pincushion, and his pale complexion was still present, it was the best picture of him I'd seen in weeks.

"What's all this commotion about?" I asked, and couldn't help the boisterous laugh that rang out when everyone in the room jumped.

When my son looked up to beam in excitement at my presence, had it not been for the machines he still was connected to, I'm sure he would have jumped off the bed to leap into my arms.

"Daddy!"

I rushed to his bedside and held Jasper to my chest and kissed the top of his head for what must have felt like hours to the poor tyke, but he never complained.

When I released him, he turned to Alissa and began to bounce around in his seat.

"Boy they didn't lie when they said the recipients bounce back quicker than the donors," she said, as she made her way next to me and giggled.

Jasper had scooted over and demanded that Alissa sit beside him on the bed.

He recounted a dream about this angel who had come to visit him while he was sleeping and told him a story. Most of us were laughing except for Alissa. When I looked up, I noticed her eyes glistening.

"Why are you crying?" Jasper asked, when he looked up at her after she'd given him a quick squeeze. He was just as perceptive as he always had been.

"It's nothing, handsome," she said, and smiled while wiping her escaped tears and hugged him again, his tiny hand patting her arm.

"When do I go home? I want to go home, Daddy," Jasper said.

Soon I hope.

"It depends on Dr. Messing, sweetie," Julie said. "But I think you'll be here for a while yet."

My son grumbled his frustration at it all.

CHAPTER 40

Having to leave that night was one of the hardest things I'd ever done. It had been a great day and I didn't want it to end.

I paused before opening the car door for Alissa. Something begged me to ask her about her earlier display of emotion.

With a light grasp on her arm, I spun her around and backed her into the side of my car. I pecked her lips and pulled away. "About those tears. I sense that—"

"It wasn't an angel that Jasper heard," she began. "It was me. Those words…Well not those exactly, but—"

I laughed. "You told him that?" My hands rubbed up and down the sides of her arms.

"Well, not exactly. You know kids really only hear what they want to hear. Still… I'm shocked he actually heard me."

I nodded.

I waited until we were halfway home before I dared ask my next question. "So what exactly did you tell him?"

"I said we were worried about him, that he had lots of things left to do, and that if he didn't wake up soon, I would send him a tickle monster to wake him up. I told him we loved him and the princess needed her prince to make the king happy. I have no clue where the rest came from."

Jasper's version of the tale consisted of Alissa's said tickle monster kidnapping the princess, and Prince Jasper's blueberry pancakes had been poisoned with sleeping potion. Needless to say, he had to fight to come back to rescue the princess and bring her back to the king with the angel's help.

"Due to his obsession with your pancakes, I can figure why his favorite food got in there." I shook my head and laughed. "I'm not going to go anywhere near the rest of that story."

"The apple doesn't fall far from the tree." She reached for my hand. "He's got a great imagination, just like his father."

"He's always been smart, but this is the first time he's come up with something this wacky," I said. "Still, I'm wondering where he got the angel bit about you though."

"Hey!" She smacked me, but judging by the smirk on her face, she was far from insulted. "It's his dream, let him imagine what he wants. I'm kind of enjoying the fact he thinks of me as an angel. Then again, I enjoy being the devil woman of your dreams too." She winked.

I guffawed. "I love that you can have a little angel and devil in you, sweetheart." I kissed her palm. "I think I'll keep you, not just because you seem to be the only one to rouse my son when he's in a comatose state, but because I'm selfish."

She snickered. "I moved here, so you better. And I'll let you in on a little secret." She leaned in and whispered the next, "I want you to be selfish."

I squeezed her hand in mine as she leaned back in her seat and looked out the passenger side window. "Alissa, I'm not letting you go."

She turned and graced me with a sweet smile. "Good, because I wasn't planning on leaving anyhow."

That deserved a chuckle. "Glad we're on the same page."

We opted for some takeout to quench our ever-growing hunger and did one of my favorite things, which I'd done with Jasper too few times. I turned the lights down low, put the pizza box on the bedspread, stripped down to my boxers, and crawled in beside Alissa.

We munched on dinner and laughed at the latest rerun of *Friends*.

It was easy.

It was effortless.

Comfortable.

Once again, I found myself submerged in one of life's simple pleasures. I was in heaven. One look from Alissa and I knew she felt the same way.

Pizza box aside, drinks guzzled down, I had Alissa wrapped up in my arms with the TV long forgotten. Her breath fanned down my bare chest at a slow rhythm. She was asleep.

Looking down at her, I kissed the top of her head and smiled. The more I pondered about life, the more I wondered how I could have ever thought that Julie had been the one for me. In retrospect, I deduced that she might not have been the one to make me happy, but she had been the one to give me the most precious of gifts life could bring: Jasper. It was unfortunate that I had to work my way through heartbreak in order to find what Alissa and I have, but I had found it nonetheless.

In such a short amount of time, Alissa had come into my life when I least expected to find my luck changing. She made everything better. Her words offered comfort and smiles. Her voice rang about in my head like music. Her laughter, though melodious as it is, made all the grays and blacks in the world fade and shine through with more color. Alissa was the missing ingredient in this intricate recipe that I call my life.

"What are you thinking so hard about?" she asked against my chest, before she left a lazy kiss on my skin and snuggled closer.

"You…us," I said and squeezed her closer to me.

"I love you," she said, and lifted her head to look at me with those sleepy doe eyes of hers.

"I love you too."

CHAPTER 41

The following morning, I was called into the office due to some client emergency.

At Alissa's request, I dropped her off at the hospital and called Julie to let her know that if she felt comfortable, she should sit back and take some time for herself and Todd instead of rushing to Jasper's bedside.

It was a little after two in the afternoon when I was able to pull myself away from work, a day I shouldn't have been in at all, considering it was a weekend. I was en route to find the two most important people in my world when an idea struck me.

When I arrived, I took my surprise along with me. I was hoping Julie wasn't there, or else I knew I'd never hear the end of it.

I came to a stop right outside of Jasper's room door. A smile broke across my face when I heard the giggling.

"How about you ask Daddy about that? I don't think I should be the one telling you anything about that stuff," Alissa said.

"But—" Jasper said.

"No *but,* mister." Her voice held sternness to it, but I could hear the smile in her voice.

"Daddy should know," Jasper said with a slight lisp.

My heart raced. I felt like I was a car and someone had

double-started me. What the heck were those two talking about?

"Daddy should know what?" I asked before I realized my feet had walked me into the room, and I held up my brown paper bag.

I kissed Alissa on the cheek and then hugged my son.

"What do you have there, handsome?" She tried to sneak in behind me and reach for the parcel.

I was too quick for her and kept my surprise out of her reach. "If I didn't know you better I'd say you were evading my question."

She blushed immediately.

"Allie said—" Jasper started, but Alissa rushed him and started tickling him.

"I told you not to say anything. Now the tickle monster is going to get you."

Jasper squealed. "No fair! Daddy, make Allie s-stop!"

This went on for a few more minutes until Jasper swore he wouldn't say anything, and when Alissa backed up, he blurted it all out in one breath anyway.

That's my boy! Hold on… What?

"Daddy, she wants to be my mommy." His next few words were what nearly caused me to fall flat onto my ass. "You have to marry her, Daddy. I want Allie as a mommy too."

Alissa, bless her soul, steered me to the nearby chair and sat me down. She reached for the brown bag that I clutched in my hand and opened it up.

"Ooh!" Jasper clapped with excitement when he saw Alissa pull out the small tub of ice cream I had purchased for all of us to share.

"Chocolate chip cookie dough," Alissa said and handed a spoon to both of us, keeping one for her as she popped the lid and seal off of the container. "Great choice. Let's dig in."

A few minutes later, I was snapped out of my shocked reverie by a spoon filled with the dessert being held to my lips. I jumped back, looked up at a smiling Alissa, who winked and nodded for me to take a bite.

When I had done just that, she bent over and kissed me on the forehead and turned to go back to sit beside Jasper, who seemed to be going to town on the treat.

"Hurry, Daddy, there might not be any left for you by the time you get over here," Alissa said, as if what Jasper had blurted out hadn't even occurred.

I smiled and shook my head at her, got up, and jumped on to sit on my son's other side. I rubbed his bare head and kissed the crown of it as I started digging in.

One thought came to mind when I peered over Jasper's head and found Alissa smiling back at me.

This was home.

Home wasn't about where I was. Home was about whom I was with.

And I was home.

CHAPTER 42

That night, Alissa walked out of the bathroom, clad in nothing but a small towel. I lay on my bed, taking in the sight before me with my fingers interlaced and tucked behind my head.

She grabbed her bottle of lotion and walked over to the bed and sat down on its edge with her back to me. She poured a small amount into the palm of her hand and proceeded to rub it into her arm. There was something sensual and erotic in the way her fingers glided across her skin.

I had watched her over the last few weeks performing this same ritual after her showers, but for some reason, this time was different.

I found myself knelt behind her, brushing her damp hair over her shoulder and kissing the nape of her neck.

A small tremor ran through her body. "What are you doing?" I could hear the smile in her voice.

"Need help with that?" I asked, as I trailed my kisses outward to her shoulder. Before she could answer, I had her bottle of lotion in my hands and began pouring a small amount to rub into her other arm. "Why don't you lie down while I do this?"

"Why, Mr. Lowell. " She turned enough so I could see the flirtatious look on her face. "If I didn't know better, I'd say you were trying to start something."

"Me? Never."

"M-hmm."

I worked her entire backside all the way down to her legs. She was so submersed in her own peaceful little world that she hadn't noticed her towel come undone, or the fact I had pulled it away from her, leaving it on the floor beside the bed.

"You're killing me with those low moans of yours," I said.

"It's not my fault." Another moan. "You're so good at this."

"I had no idea." I kissed her mid-back up to one of her shoulders and positioned my lips right at her ear to whisper, "Flip over." I felt the shiver pass through her body and the almost inaudible whimper that she emitted.

She turned for me and I had to fight my urges in order to even get started on applying the lotion to her front. My member swelled larger, and the pain from the tightness in my jeans had caused me to reach down and adjust myself.

"Take them off." It's as if she'd read my thoughts.

I didn't have to be told twice. Stripped down to my boxers, I assumed the position I had been in prior to shedding my clothes.

I started with the front of her legs. Her eyes never wavered from my face, which made this whole experience even more intimate. Whenever I looked up at her, our eyes would connect and heat would surge.

The more my hands climbed toward her core, the heavier her breathing became. Her eyes darkened to that classic bright blue. Her lids looked heavy and her mouth parted as she licked her bottom lip before biting down on it.

I worked lotion up from her belly, to her breasts, avoiding her nipples to which the peaks had hardened.

When I finished, my hands may have left her body but my lips joined in the fun. I kissed up her neck, nibbled her earlobe and gave her a deep kiss on the mouth. Her eyes were glazed with sheer relaxation and her body lacked any and all tension that it previously had carried.

I pulled back and ran a questing finger over her cheek, down her jawbone and to her lips. "Come out to dinner with me tomorrow night," I said before depositing a chaste kiss.

She nodded her head before nuzzling my nose. "Paxton?"

"Hmm?" I kissed a trail down to her collarbone before I settled my body over hers.

"Roll over," she said and leaned up to kiss me softly. "It's my turn to have my hands all over you."

By the time she was done with her rubbing, my entire body felt like a pile of jelly.

She crawled her body back up over mine and I grabbed her forearms, pulling her down.

My lips collided with hers in a slow lazy kiss that made her sigh into my mouth. I smiled up at her when she pulled away, my fingers tucking a loose piece of her hair behind her ear. "That was amazing." I tilted her head down to kiss her forehead. "I don't know why I've never contemplated a massage therapist before, but I doubt they'd be as effective as you."

Alissa gave me a perplexed look. "You mean you've never had a full-body rub from your women before?"

I shook my head. "You're the first and only to grace my entire body with your hands."

"You've been missing out," she said. "Then again, I'm glad I'm the only one who's had the pleasure of touching every square inch of you."

Her fingertips created electrical currents over my upper chest as she traced an indiscernible pattern.

My curiosity won over. "So you've been rubbed before?"

"Only once," she said. "There's this parlor the girls brought me to once. They had the most wonderful hands." I groaned at her dream-like sounding voice. Yes, I was jealous about another man having his hands all over her. It didn't matter that it was his profession or it was in the past. "I mean, big hands." She demonstrated how large they were with gestures. "Hands that knew where to touch me to make me—"

I kissed her hard and fast to shut her up, laughing into her mouth. "Bullshit."

She giggled and sat up over my hips. "Whatever do you mean?"

That exaggerated aloof look of hers made me laugh harder. "You had me fooled at first, until you got to the hands bit." I mimicked her descriptive actions. "Then there was the mischievous glint in your eyes and the upward quirking of your lips that gave you away."

"You're right. It was a massage therapist and she was a very manly looking lady named Gretta," she said before grinning and laying her head on my chest. "Can I say it's scary how well you know me?"

"I'm glad you're easy to read. Not having to guess is one of the things I love about you, sweetheart." And I hugged her closer.

CHAPTER 43

In the mood to celebrate, I managed to make a quick pit stop.

Glad to see that Alissa had gone out when I arrived home from meeting up with my parents, I headed up to our room and placed my fancy packages at the foot of the bed, where I knew she'd see them when she got home.

I wondered what she'd have to say when she saw my surprise, and wished I could be there to see her face when she saw my gifts, but my fatherly duties beckoned me.

I headed to the hospital and stopped in to spend some quality time with Jasper. Julie and Todd were there and a few minutes after my arrival, Dr. Messing walked in.

"How're you feeling, Jasper?" he asked, as he made notes inside the chart he had gathered from the foot of Jasper's bed.

"Good," Jasper said, and seemed to look like he had a bunch of ants in his pants. "Can I go home now?"

"I think we might be able to manage that eventually, but it's important to keep you here until we're sure that you can stay healthy at home. The medicine, we're giving you to make sure you get better, can make you feel sick most of the time," the doctor said. Jasper nodded with a grimace on his face.

After a bit of whining, he conceded. It took a few promises on my part to get him there, but it worked, and the fact Dr. Messing had brought in a boy about Jasper's age who was a long-term patient helped too. The two boys decided they'd have sleepovers and seemed to be excited at building forts in their joint room.

"Can I speak with you two for a moment?" Messing asked Julie and me.

We followed the man into the hall where he led us to a small conference room a few doors down. He gestured for us to take a seat as he closed the door to give us some privacy.

"Is everything okay, Doctor?" Julie asked.

"I've observed Jasper closely since he's woken, and I have to say that I like his sudden boost of energy. His color seems good and his vitals are strong and getting stronger each day. His speech is still slurred from time to time, and I can confirm it's because of the clot he threw in surgery and not because of the medications we've given him, since those have long since been flushed out of his system. With that said, I don't think it'll be a permanent issue," he said. "All in all, it doesn't seem like he's getting worse."

"That's great though, isn't it?" I eyed him carefully, expecting more bad news, since so much of it had been delivered over the last few months.

"It appears that way, yes," Messing said. Cue my relief. "There will be a series of tests over the next few days, weeks, and months to determine if his body is rejecting the transplant, or if he's now making new normal blood cells. I introduced Tyler to Jasper because they both have similar issues, and it would be nice for each of them to have a friend during their stay here. Things can get pretty lonely after a while. All I can say is that it's worth being optimistic about things, despite more time being needed to really know if our attempt has worked."

Julie squealed and hugged my arm. Somehow, I kept thinking that there'd be a 'but' somewhere in this conversation, and I was right.

"But I think it's important for you both to know, even though I think Jasper's speech will make a full recovery, there is a chance that he may be left with a few challenges. Aside from that, all we need is time to allow the transplant to take hold, for Jasper to regain his strength, and hopefully, in the end, a clean bill of health that'll clear him of his JMML."

CHAPTER 44

I walked out the hospital's doors with no time to spare. What should have been an hour or so visit ended up being closer to the three-hour mark. If I wanted to make it to the lawyer's office, I pretty much needed to hit every green light on the way there.

I put in a call with Jake from my hands-free system and floored the accelerator, peeling my car out of the hospital parking lot.

My day felt like it couldn't get any better. It seemed like Alissa and her selflessness might have been the ticket to ensure that my son would live a long and happy life. Okay, so I was getting ahead of things, but why not? My woman's optimism was contagious.

Jasper wasn't getting worse. If anything, he was looking better. My parents were moving on up in life, and I found myself elated that the things I had spent so many years pretending didn't matter were happening at a whirlwind pace. Dreams I had long ago stifled were becoming a reality. Yes, there was indeed a lot to celebrate.

Jake stood in the reception area of his law firm's suite waiting for me. We sat down in his office, and after catching up we got to the business at hand.

All that separated me from my current life and the one I had always dreamed of living were a few stacks of papers and an empty dotted line on all of them. Taking my pen, I smiled as I spent the next half hour fulfilling a personal dream that I knew Alissa would have no problems following at my side.

This is going to be great.

"So whatever happened to that woman?" Jake asked, as we headed out toward the parking garage. "Al-something?"

"Alissa. She moved to be closer."

"Really?" His skepticism was present. "Don't you think it's kind of fast?"

I shook my head. "We'd known each other for nearly a year before we met face-to-face," I said. "No, and before you ask, it wasn't a dating site."

"Hey, I'm not judging." Jake held his hands up in a peace-keeping gesture. "I heard about Jasper from your parents when they dropped in earlier. I'm sorry. Why didn't you say any-thing?"

"I would have. Things have been a little hectic," I said. "He's doing much better, and his doctor thinks it looks like he might just pull through, all thanks to Alissa."

Jake eyed me with careful scrutiny. "You've really got it bad when you think your girlfriend is responsible for curing everything. She might have cured you of a broken heart, but I doubt—"

"Jake, you're an idiot," I said, pausing by his car and play-fully punching his shoulder. "One day you'll find yourself at a woman's feet and when that day happens, I'll be there to point the finger, laugh, and say, 'I told you so.'"

"Yeah, right," Jake said. "So what did she do?"

I gave him the quick rundown on what had happened from the time we found out Jasper had JMML, and how grim things were, to how Alissa had donated her marrow.

"She did that?" Jake was wide-eyed.

"Without hesitation," I said. "I never thought I'd lose hope about anything, but she refused to let me go down that slope."

"Wow."

I nodded. "I love the woman, man." I slapped him on the back. "Speaking of which, I better get going if I want to make that reservation I made for us tonight."

"Give me a call and keep me posted on Jasper. We should get together some time soon," Jake said in a dejected tone. He seemed to be preoccupied with pondering everything I had divulged about my current relationship. "I'd like to meet this new woman."

I nodded. "Soon."

Jake was fantastic in and out of the courts, and he had the pocketbook to prove it. He might have been a genius with his investments, as well as all areas of personal consumption: cars, homes, and anything else material. But he was shit with women, unless it entailed getting them into bed.

Jake had found who he claimed to be his one and only woman back when we were in high school.

Danica Withers had been petite and quite withdrawn from our social scene, but he had always been smitten with our cute tutor-girl-slash-cheerleader friend. What broke him was what transpired after one of their many dates.

Divulging his true feelings for her led to her reciprocation, but within a day, the girl had disappeared. Nowhere to be found.

I had been the unfortunate one to tell him her parents had left and taken her with them. As to where she headed, who knew. All I had to give him was the message from a letter she had left in my parents' mailbox for me to deliver. A letter he still kept with him in his wallet, or so I had come to find out about a year ago when I had to settle his tab with his credit card since he was too drunk to do so himself.

From her disappearance onward, Jake and I had been busy with womanizing the rest of the school's cheerleaders and other notable interests. For me, the day came where I put a stop to it, or rather Julie had put a stop to it when I fell for her. For Jake, it hadn't been that easy. He had fallen in love first.

To be honest, I understand how he had felt. I had felt the same way when Julie had first left me, and for months afterward, until I had begun to chat it up with Alissa.

As an adult, Jake had drowned himself in booze and easy women. Women who were only after two things: his pleasuring and the money in his pocket, and he knew it. If he hadn't been a best friend of mine, I would have never paid attention to the look that crossed his face right as I turned to walk back to my car. He may have been acting macho, but the look of envy in his eyes at the mention of my relationship with Alissa told me he ached to have a family life. He just couldn't quite get himself to go get it.

Yet.

Fear is a powerful thing.

CHAPTER 45

I got home and ran up to the bedroom to get ready; taking notice that the packages I had left Alissa had been opened. She would look amazing in my gifts, I had no doubt.

I scrubbed down in the shower, jumped out, wiped at the fogged mirror with my hand and set to shaving my face with my towel wrapped around my waist, wondering where she'd gone off to.

I was slipping my arms through my dress shirt when I heard her. "Pax?"

"Upstairs."

I turned toward the closet and reached for a sport jacket, took a look at my selection of ties, and then shrugged that idea off since I wore one every day at the office.

I buttoned and tucked my shirt into my pants and as I was donning my jacket, I turned to a sight that stopped me dead in my tracks.

"So," she said, and twirled around to show off the new dress and shoes.

It was a simple royal blue halter dress, but it fit her like a glove; hugging her bust, waist, and hips in the right places until it flowed outward to her mid-thigh. Her legs looked endless in the black peekaboo-toed heels she paired with the outfit, and I loved the fact that she had left her hair down.

She walked up to me, and that's when I realized I still hadn't said a word. My lips pulled up into an admiring smile of approval for how great she looked.

"Well someone was quite busy today."

"You look beautiful." I pulled her in by her hands to kiss her cheek. "I'll take that as you missed me?"

She nodded. "Are you ready?"

"Yeah."

I watched as she turned and walked out of the bedroom with me following, hot on her heels. The accentuated sway of her hips and her sultry-like movements made me salivate.

Tease.

CHAPTER 46

We were seated in the back of the restaurant which, to her standards, was the best seat in the house. We were secluded with a wall covered by curtains on one side and a four-sided fireplace obstructing much of the view to the trickling in of the patrons on the other.

The waiter had delivered our dessert and Alissa turned her attention back to me. "So tell me." She leaned forward on her elbow as she drummed her fingers on the side of her cheek in suspicion. "Why do you look like the cat that ate the canary?"

I ached so much to tell her everything that had happened today, but it wasn't in my original plan. It was hard, but I found myself able to reel in a bit of self-control and opted to tell her about what I was willing to share. The rest could wait until the kinks were straightened and everything was perfect.

"Dr. Messing says Jasper's not getting worse and everything points to an optimistic turnout," I said. "My son has also made a new friend to room with during his stay."

She dropped her fork onto the plate we were sharing and wrapped her hands around my face and kissed me. "That's fantastic!" My heart fluttered at her reaction. "Have they said anything about his slurring?"

"Messing doesn't think it'll be permanent, but he confirmed that it was because of the clot," I said and cupped her cheek with one of my hands while hers had found their way down from my face to my chest. "But even if it is—"

"We can work on that," she finished for me and kissed me softly.

What started as a soft peck of elation escalated to a gentle make out session involving only our lips.

"I don't know if I should have bought you that dress." I exhaled a loud breath over her swollen lips. I turned and took a quick bite of the cake set before us. "All I can think about is what I got you to wear underneath it."

She blushed, but was quick to recover. She crossed her legs and tilted them so our knees touched. Alissa began rubbing my thigh as she watched me look down between her well-exposed leg and her soft moving hand.

She leaned toward my ear and the subtle scent of perfume and woman, the one that was uniquely hers, surrounded me. A seductive octave lower, she asked, "Do you think I'm sexy, Paxton?"

I gulped the remainder of my food down and found myself nodding, my mouth having run dry.

Alissa wasn't one to speak like that. She made her characters do that stuff in her novels. I was wondering if that side of her would ever come out in an unexpected setting, and I guess I got my answer.

"Do you crave me like I crave you?" I gave her another nod. "Here's what I crave, Paxton." She nipped my jaw and pulled away enough to look me in the eyes. "I want your lips all over me. I want to feel your hands caress my skin. I need your hard throbbing dick inside my wet pussy." She smirked when my fork fell out of my hand and I was forced to clamp my dropped jaw shut to swallow the sudden abundance of saliva that had materialized. "Paxton, I want you so deep inside of me that when we fall apart, we can see each other's soul. And when we're done, I want to do it again, and again, and—"

I cut her off. It was all just too much. Her words, the tone of her voice, the dress, not to mention the fact we hadn't been intimate like that in half a week, which was unusual for us since she'd moved in. Yes, we were normally like a couple of rabbits.

I grabbed the back of her neck with one hand and crushed my lips to hers. "Waiter!" I lifted my hand up and never once allowed my eyes to stray from hers.

"Yes, sir?" the waiter asked.

"We're ready to head home."

"Is there something wrong with the cake, sir?"

"No."

"Oh," the young man said, but didn't make a move to leave.

"Pack it up and we'll take it home with us." Alissa winked at me and the waiter scampered off to do her bidding. "I have a feeling we might be able to use a little sugar boost later."

"Damn, you're so sexy when you take charge like that." I kissed the side of her neck.

She graced me with a baritone laugh I had never heard from her before. It told me that I had no clue what she was capable of, and the more I thought about it, the more I wanted to see what she could do.

"I'm glad, because this is just the beginning." She pulled away, smiled, and then nodded her head to let me know the waiter had returned.

CHAPTER 47

Alissa turned it up a notch and it got quite hot on the drive home, despite cranking the A/C. If anything, it made it worse for me with her nipples sticking out through the thin material of her dress, making her look even more irresistible.

The devil woman had her hand under the skirt of her dress and was pleasuring herself while the other fondled her breasts. There was no way we were going to get home if I assisted her, and you better believe I was dying to.

As much as the thought of pulling over and taking her then and there appealed to me, I didn't want that. I knew she was putting on a show for me and as much as I wanted to take control, I knew what awaited us at home would be far better than if I took it from her on the spot. She deserved so much more after all that she'd done for my son and me.

"Oh, Paxton! I'm so wet for you right now." I groaned. "I can't wait for you to— Oh! Pax!"

"Baby." I gulped. "You're killing me here."

When I turned to her at the next set of lights, she was watching me. She smirked and took her glistening fingers and put them to her mouth to suck on one of them.

"God help me." Turning my gaze to the car's ceiling, I smashed my head against the headrest to my seat before looking at her again.

She brought her hand up to my mouth and I grabbed her wrist with one hand and held her gaze as I tantalized her two coated fingers with my teeth and tongue like a rabid dog.

Fuck she tasted fantastic!

"Just so you know, you'll have to hold off a bit longer once we get home." Her smile was wicked.

"Fuck me," I groaned.

"That's the plan."

A car behind us honked and I realized we were still stopped at the intersection. The light had gone from green to yellow and I chose to run the damn thing.

No more waiting.

The light shifted to red while we were in the middle of the intersection, leaving the car behind us stuck at the line, and its driver honking their frustration.

Alissa giggled while looking through the back window of the car.

One swift tire-squawking turn around the corner and we were home.

My woman was out of the vehicle before I could even shut my car door. "Sit on the couch and wait for me, I won't be long," she said, as she unlocked the door and hurried upstairs, leaving me to do as she'd requested.

"Baby," I said up to her from my perch on the couch, "you better make this quick or I'm going to find you and fuck you senseless, thanks to your shenanigans."

"I'm hoping you still will," she said her voice getting nearer, as I tilted my head back and breathed the ever-growing tension in my shaft and balls to a more bearable level with my eyes closed, "when you see this."

I lifted my head and opened my eyes.

There she stood, between my legs wearing nothing but her black heels, the lace bra and underwear I had bought her, and one of my dress shirts. The woman was sex on a stick, and I was hungrier now that she had served herself up on the night's menu.

I pulled her by the hips as she straddled my thighs, our eyes locking, time standing still.

"I don't know what's gotten into you tonight, but I do have to say that I like it very much." My hands grabbed her ass and squeezed. "I also have to add, I should go lingerie shopping for you more often if everything looks that good on you."

"You have great taste."

My hands moved up and under the shirt, feeling the heated skin along the length of her spine as she tilted her head back. I pulled my hands away, which brought her gaze forward. I reached to push the shirt she wore off of her shoulders.

"I think you're a little overdressed," she said, and her nimble fingers proceeded to unbutton my shirt.

I helped her get the garment off of me by leaning forward and she captured my lips in a searing kiss. I let her have full control, for the time being. She nibbled at my bottom lip, pulled away, and those bright eyes clouded with lust stared back at me.

"Pax," she said, and with that simple utterance of my name I knew she was relinquishing her control to me.

I pulled her face down to mine and kissed her hard, fisting a hand in her hair to gain better access to her neck. She released a sharp intake of breath as my teeth grazed the tendon there.

When I knew she would stay in position, I let go of her hair and let my hands roam as I rubbed a light, soothing pattern on her back. If she wanted my hands and lips all over her, then that's what she would get.

As I tasted, kissed, licked, and nipped the skin above her breasts, my hands unlatched her bra. I pulled it off of her, my fingertips skimming her bared skin in the process.

"You're beautiful." Her curl-tipped hair had fallen over her front to cover her breasts and with the flushed look on her face, the sparkle in her eyes, and the fact that she straddled my waist, she was like my very own version of Lady Godiva.

After a few self-indulgent kisses, her hands undid the buckle to my belt in a hurried fashion. Her lips had taken control and my body flushed with heat. I wanted her, true, but I needed her that much more.

When she pulled away, I saw the pain of her lust raging in balls of fire in her irises. She ached for me as much as I ached for her.

She pulled at the button to my pants and I stilled her hands. "Not here."

I grabbed onto her ass and she wrapped her legs around me as I rushed us up the stairs.

I threw her down on the bed while I hurried out of my trousers and crawled up to her sprawled form. She now sat with her back against the headboard, a seductive smile on those swollen lips of hers, donning nothing but the tiny bit of lace at her hips and her high-heels.

Allie squealed when I pulled at her ankles to bring her closer to where I was.

"You want my hands all over you, huh?" I asked in a husky tone, and she nodded her response.

I ran an open palm, starting at her knees, and up her legs to the inside of her thighs. Her hips arched up when my lips added to the mix by kissing her belly. I divested her of her lacy thong, letting my hands and lips do all the stimulating as I tortured her skin.

"And is this what you were looking for by wanting my lips on you?" I threw in a few licks to go with the continuation of my oral ministrations, climbing back up her body. She answered me with a whimper when I traced her navel with my tongue.

I hovered on my elbows, my face mere millimeters from hers as my fingers played with her hair. "How was that?"

"I think you forgot something," she said and smirked up at me.

Smartass.

"I did?" I said, aloof because I wanted to see more of her

taking charge, and she nodded in response. Our power exchange was intoxicating.

She didn't disappoint.

Sliding her hand between our bodies, she took hold of my cock and began pumping it with a firm grip. My take-charge attitude faded fast, and she knew it just by the confident gleam in her eyes.

"Oh," I said with my voice a quiver.

"I want you to take this dick of yours." She licked her lips. My eyes followed the movement. "I want you to slide it into my pussy. I want you to feel me surround you, clamp down on you, as you make me wetter with each long, full, stroke. I want you to bury yourself so deep inside me that we don't know where one of us ends and the other begins. I want you to—"

I slammed myself as far as I could go inside her. I was done listening to her loquacious torture.

"Oh, God!" She half-cried and half-moaned.

Our eyes fused together as she took me to the hilt, my balls slapping the crease of her ass with each penetration. With slow, but strong and controlled, thrusts, I pulled myself almost out and then plunged right back into her sopping heat.

Our mouths ate away at each other like men starved of water after spending a lengthy time in the desert. There wasn't enough of each other to quench our thirst. The flames were fanned and built to an unbearable inferno.

Her eyes rolled into the back of her head as her lids fluttered to a close.

"Open your eyes, baby," I said between panted breaths.

I rammed into her with so much fervor that each bottomed-out motion was accompanied by the sweet sound of her moans and my grunts.

It wasn't long before I managed to push us both over the edge of that cliff, into the pit of carnal rapture. I could have sworn I saw the sparks fly in her eyes as if it were my own rendition of the Fourth of July.

As we came down from our high, I rolled over and draped her over my body, allowing us to bask in the afterglow of our passion.

She started to get up and I pulled her back down. "Where do you think you're going?"

"Dessert," she said, and gave me a chaste kiss.

I released her from my arms and smacked her bare butt as she backed away, which made her turn to eye me over her shoulder.

I smirked. "Hurry back," I said, and watched those naked hips of hers sway out of the bedroom.

I don't know where her sudden confidence had come from, but I enjoyed this metamorphosis into a more vocal and confident version of Alissa. Her meek and demure side was a definite favorite of mine, especially when it was accompanied by her blushes, which she still graced me with at least once a day. But this self-assured side of hers was a plus. It was a side I hadn't witnessed with any of the women I'd been with.

Thinking back to the car ride and the fact that she had fingered herself right there in front of me, I felt myself rise with the need to have her again. Aside from the occasional porn flick, I didn't realize how much voyeurism would appeal to me. Then again, was there anything Alissa did that I didn't like? No, not really.

Lost in my reverie of the fresh memory, the scent of her arousal still surrounding me, remnants of our earlier copulation, I hadn't noticed her return.

"I sure hope you plan on helping me eat this, but judging by that tent you're pitching, I'd have to say that you're not hungry for sweets just yet." She leaned up against the doorway in her naked glory. She licked the bit of icing off of her finger before walking up to the bedside.

"Actually, you couldn't be more wrong." I took the plate

with the cake from her with one hand and pulled her down on top of me with the other.

We settled in bed with the TV on mute.

"I'm thinking about making it a rule where you're naked when we're both home." I kissed the crown of her head.

Her body shook with silent laughter while my fingertips tickled the skin of her bare back and she cuddled into me.

"Only if you're naked with me," she said, and dropped a kiss on my chest. "So, are you going to tell me what else you're hiding?"

"There's nothing to tell." I hoped I was more convincing than I sounded to myself.

She looked up at me and said, "Sure, and that's why you're not twitching like your itching to tell me what's going on."

"Sweetheart, it's for me to know and you to find out. I promise that you'll love it when the time comes."

CHAPTER 48

Two weeks had gone by and everything was going great. Jasper's health was getting better every day. Dr. Messing approximated that he'd be able to come home in the next couple of weeks if his neutrophil count kept going up and stayed high enough, as well as his engraftment, which was a fancy term I learned meant that his body was agreeing and accepting the transplant more and more.

At Julie's demand and with Messing's help, we found a specialist to work with Jasper on his slight speech impediment. It didn't matter that his issue might be temporary to my ex-wife. I believed it was safer to err on the side of caution, but I also didn't want Jasper to feel overwhelmed by this sudden extracurricular.

And that's exactly what had happened at the beginning.

Those initial visits had not been fun with the boy breaking down in frustration, which only aggravated his 'condition' as Julie referred to it. The minute my son got flustered, excited, or suffered a sudden surge of any emotion, his slur grew exponentially.

I resented Julie for a while. I wanted Jasper to have his normal life back as much as the next person, but, in my opinion, a four-year-old didn't need that kind of pressure that early in his life. Imagine my relief when about five sessions in, Jasper was making progress and was adapting well to the change in his routine. That did wonders to still my conscience on having gone along with Julie's idea.

Earlier in the week, Jasper should have started preschool. He was all too disappointed to learn he couldn't go, and more than upset he didn't get to make new friends. My son had voiced that all his classmates would have their friends by the time he got there, and there would be no one left to be his friend. Try and explain to a four-year-old that it was possible to have multiple friends and reassure him he wouldn't be cheated in his delay to experience schooling and friendship.

It was Saturday, and after two weeks of keeping things bottled up, it was time for me to come clean with Alissa.

My plan had been set in motion on the day I had signed those papers at Jake's office. My parents had time to set their affairs in order, which was why I delayed telling Allie in the first place. The fact we were busy with work and visiting Jasper whenever we weren't at our respective offices posed as another reason as to why I hadn't given her the news sooner. My final reason for holding off on telling her was the fact she was the queen of surprises, or so I'd come to find out since we'd become official. I felt like having some fun with the delivery of my news, and it was high time that I surprised her myself.

"What's going on in that head of yours?" she asked, as she snuck her arms around my torso and I handed her a thermos filled with coffee.

She got on the tips of her toes to kiss me.

"How much I'm going to miss having you around today," I said, as I walked her out to her car.

"I'm only working a few extra hours until dinnertime," she said. "You'll get a whole day alone with Jasper, one I think you both can use since I've been in the picture."

"You'll meet me over at the ranch when you're done?" I asked from the front step and she settled herself inside her car.

"I will," she said through her car window while backing

out of the drive. "Give Jasper a kiss from me and I'll see you by five, not a minute later."

It was nearing five now, and Mom was in the kitchen while Dad and I sat in the living room, our beers in hand and talking about our latest life changes.

My stomach did a flip when I heard the light knock on the front door, but the minute I opened it to let Alissa in, a sense of calm washed over me.

What would she think of what I'd done?

"You're early," I said looking at my watch and noticing it was ten to five.

"I couldn't stay away." She shrugged her shoulders.

"And you didn't call?" I asked and tried to get a read on her.

"It was your day with Jasper. How was your Man Day?" She smiled and her arms wrapped around my neck while looking up at me.

"Great." I kissed her smiling lips. "Better now that you're home."

"But we're not home."

"Home is wherever you're with me."

"Charmer." She patted me on the cheek before giving me a small peck on the mouth. "I can only imagine what you want when you start spouting that stuff."

Chuckling, I said, "And you eat it up every time."

"Right you are, handsome." She winked.

I took Alissa's hand and escorted her into the living room. She was looking around and I could tell that she was deep in thought. "Pax?"

"Hmm?"

"Are your folks moving?"

"Why yes we are," my mother said. Alissa turned with me to face the woman who had now joined us with a tray of drinks. "It's time to move on, sweetie." She smiled at Dad. "This house was built for a family, and I'm sure the new owners will love it as much as we have for all these years."

"I had no idea it was for sale." She squeezed my hand.

"If you ask me, we practically gave it away." My dad eyed me.

"We're not getting any younger and chose to live life a little more," Mom said, and grabbed my father's hand in hers as she sat on the arm of his chair. "When we heard about the new owners, we jumped on their offer."

"Lucky family," Alissa said.

"Yes, they are," Dad said. "That little boy will love it here as much as our sons did. I hope they have more kids. This place needs at least a couple more on top of the one they already have."

My mother giggled. I was beside myself with what Dad had just blurted out.

Alissa nodded. "A house like this does deserve a large family. I hope to have something like this some day."

"I'm glad to hear that," Dad said. "I guess wishes do come true."

Alissa looked between my parents, and then at me, and then did the same thing over again.

I couldn't hide the smirk from my face any longer. All the woman did was smirk back, but I saw the glimmer of confusion in her eyes, which transformed into a gleam of suspicion. The three of us were grinning like the Cheshire cat by then.

"What's going on?" she asked, but no one spoke up as we could tell she was reviewing the conversation in her mind. "Paxton?" Alissa turned to me.

The kid-like excitement that had been building all day got to be too much for me.

"Here." I handed her a velvet box.

"Paxton, one thing at a time please." She rolled her eyes.

"Now tell me what's going on and then I'll open it."

"The answer is in the box, sweetheart." I pushed her hand-covered box toward her body. "Open it."

She stared at the box and rubbed the velvet with her fingers. She looked up at me with suspicion.

"Open it already."

She did.

Her brows furrowed.

She picked up what was inside and held it out in front of her. "What's with the key? I already have one for the house."

No one answered.

The next minute seemed to go on for an eternity.

I watched as those wheels turned in that pretty little head of hers and then…

"Welcome home," I said when she looked up at me with a disbelieving grin on her face.

"You're serious?" she asked.

"As a heart attack." I laughed. "It's been ours for two weeks already. I wanted to tell you when the time was right."

"Why you—" She smacked me on the chest and then turned to look at my parents. "Please tell me this is a joke."

My parents both shook their heads, indicating the negative.

"I was dropping something off when Dad mentioned their plans for a change of scenery. I jumped at the chance when they offered the house. They signed the deed over to me on the same day I took you to dinner," I said.

"This is what you were up to?" I nodded.

She cupped her cheeks in her palms and shook her head. "What do I say to this?"

I grabbed her chin and brought her face so she looked straight at me. "How about 'when can we move in'?" I suggested, and offered her a sweet smile.

"You're simply too much. This is too much. When *do* we move in?" she asked with watery eyes.

I wiped the stray tear that began to trail down her cheek

with the pad of my thumb and grabbed her cheeks in my hands.

"Tonight seems as good a time as any," I said before kissing her. "I have another confession however."

"No more surprises please," she whispered the last with her forehead against mine. My parents laughed at her overdramatic request.

Oh, how I love this woman.

CHAPTER 49

The look on Alissa's face when I told her that we weren't going back to the townhouse to spend the night had been priceless. My confession had spurred some excitement on her part.

As soon as she had closed the front door on my parents, I turned Alissa around and pushed her up against it for a scorching kiss.

"What are you doing?" she asked, as I trailed my lips down the side of her neck.

I chuckled against the pulse-point next to her jugular. "I would have thought it obvious."

"I know what you're doing, handsome, but shouldn't we be trying to pack things up over at the other house?"

"Already taken care of," I mumbled against her neck.

"What?" She pushed against my chest.

"I hired movers. They should be here…oh…" I looked down at my watch, "in the next hour or so to drop our stuff and pick up the rest of Mom and Dad's, which leaves us with—"

She wrapped her hands around my face and pulled me down to her lips. "You're unbelievable," she said against my mouth, before closing the gap and pressing herself into me further.

"And you're perfect for me," I hummed against her neck when my fingers made contact with the hem of her dress. "Have I ever mentioned how much I love easy access?"

She grinned. I felt her warm and confident hand reaching

down, undoing the button and zipper to my jeans and setting me free. As I held the bottoms of her thighs, she guided me inside her slick heat and maintained the rhythm. With her wrapped around my body while I pinned her against the cool varnished wood that bore entrance to our new abode, I felt like I could do anything.

My face was buried in her neck as her hands clasped the back of my head, gripping my hair in a painful yet pleasurable manner.

I gave one last potent thrust that sent us both reeling to the pinnacle of all orgasms, which resulted in my knees giving out.

I followed the vertical alignment of the door down to the floor where she straddled me, as I sat on my knees leaning up against her.

The purring in her throat made me look up at her and our eyes connected. Insatiable hunger was still present in those orbs of hers. She squeezed herself around my fading manhood and bit down on her bottom lip. In all my times with a woman, I can say no one had ever been able to either keep me hard or get me back in the game that damn quick.

No one except for Alissa.

Round two had begun…

Before we knew it, we were on the floor, sitting beside each other with our backs against the front door, trying to gather our wits, not to mention our breath. Alissa's head leaned against my shoulder while mine rested on her hair.

The doorbell rang, making us jump. "Shit, the movers!" I said.

CHAPTER 50

I woke first to the sun peeking through the blinds in our room.

Disoriented, I stared at the lavender color on the walls and recalled where I was.

Home.

We've got to do something about these walls.

Waking up in my parents' old bedroom felt odd, but those thoughts faded as the wicked ambitions that engulfed my lower anatomy began to flutter through my mind when I felt Alissa's leg nudge mine.

She was sound asleep on her back.

I crawled under the covers like a man on a mission. If I had it my way, the entire house would be christened with our carnal delights before the end of the upcoming week.

After a quick trip to the hardware store, Alissa and I partook in getting Jasper's room all set up for his homecoming.

"Sweetheart, you know we don't have to get it all done today, right?" I said, as I watched her continue with the second coat of paint on the two remaining walls.

"I know, but I figured that we could surprise Jasper with his very own finished bedroom by the time he gets out of the hospital," she said atop her small three-step ladder. Her excitement was contagious.

"Allie, he's not coming home for another few weeks at the

very least. We have time." I shuffled sideways concentrating on the trim and keeping a straight line.

Who knew that Murphy's Law would dictate things the minute I decided to help my woman out with her project? Inevitably, that's what happens when two people work in a small room, with ladders, paint brushes, rollers, and cans.

Here I was making progress on the trim to the second coat of Jasper's bedroom walls when I tripped on the drop cloth, which caused me to nudge the bottom of the tiny stepladder that Alissa had been standing on. One minute she was struggling to keep her balance without touching the wet wall and the next, I had dropped my brush and paint bucket to try and catch her as she fell.

Her bucket flew up in the air, her brush remained in her hand and my mad dash to catch her sure as hell didn't work as planned. I landed on top of her as her bucket of paint landed and splattered everywhere beside us, transforming us into two rather curious looking masterpieces, instead of Jasper's walls.

"Are you okay?" I asked, and eased some of my weight off of a howling Alissa.

Her face was red with belly laughs. "Oh no, look at the floor!" she said between giggles.

"I don't give a shit about the floor, woman. Are you okay?"

"I'm fine," she said, and then chucked her paint brush at me as I got up off of her and kneeled between her legs.

"Hey!"

She gave me an innocent look. "What?"

"I'll show you."

All in all, what started out to be a day-long bedroom makeover, turned out to be just that with a side of two grown adults walking around looking like a juvenile's paint spatter project.

As Alissa was making us an early supper, I had made my way outside to fix that old rickety gate like I'd been meaning to before I opted to become Picasso. What should have been a quick fix turned out to be an hour and a half long endeavor, seeing as I hadn't anticipated the lack of supplies.

By the time the fence was as good as new, I came in to find the living room unpacked and transformed. In truth, there wasn't much to change in the room. Still, Alissa had managed to make my childhood home feel even more like our own while I was out.

The large stone fireplace mantle was filled with photo frames of Jasper and me, my parents, one of Julie, Todd and Jasper, and two I hadn't seen until now. An old photo of Theo and me, and the other of Alissa, Jasper, and me which had been taken over a bowl of pancake batter, a while back, with flour all over our faces. I smiled at the memory.

"What do you think?" she asked, as she entered with two plates and glasses on a tray and set them down on the large coffee table. "I figured I'd finish up with this room first since we'll be aching to sit down and relax tonight."

Grinning, I said, "I think we need a real photo of the three of us."

"I like that one," she said after her first bite of sandwich. "I hate posing. The candid and spontaneous shots are the best, but I'm all for the traditional shot as long as we keep this one."

I nodded. That shot showed so much of our personality and happiness in that moment. She'd even stacked books on the shelves. "All we're missing now is a fire in that hearth," I said.

"I'm definitely looking forward to those cooler nights."

CHAPTER 51

A month and a half passed in the blink of an eye, and Dr. Messing brought us all back for a progress report on Jasper's health.

To say that Julie, myself, and the rest of us adults were on edge was an understatement of epic proportions.

It had been a month since Jasper's release from the hospital.

Two months since my beautiful girlfriend might have altered the course of our lives forever, by taking a leap of faith, in an attempt to save my son's life.

"So," Dr. Messing said with all seriousness in his tone. Alissa and I reached out to each other and linked our hands, thankful that Jasper wasn't in the room with us and was outside with one of the nurses in the reception area. "I've run a full exam, the necessary blood work, and the scans," he said and fell silent.

I wanted to stand, reach across his desk, wrap my hands around his shoulders, and shake him like a rag doll. The suspense was killing me.

Come out and say it dammit.

The moment of truth was here.

Life or death?

The man seated across the desk from the four of us steepled his fingers over my son's file. His lips were in a thin line.

And then…

As if my heart wasn't already beating out of my chest, it kicked up to a stampeding rhythm.

This is it.

A smile.

An honest to God genuine smile spread across the man's face!

"Everything looks promising so far," Messing said. "Of course, I'd like to keep seeing Jasper and monitor his progress, but I see no reason why I should see him more than every couple of weeks. His numbers keep going up every day and his energy seems to be coming back slowly, but I see no need to keep him from school. I'd recommend starting him a day or two a week at first, so he doesn't exhaust himself, starting now. Come January, if nothing happens, and his numbers keep climbing, I may be able to give the little guy a clean bill of health."

"He's cured?" Julie asked.

"I wouldn't say that," Messing said. "He's on his way to remission, but it's pointing that way, yes."

I was elated. Relieved. Hell, I don't know what else I could tell you to pinpoint the exact emotions that reeled through me in that moment.

My body began to shake, releasing the pent-up stress, worry, and anxiety that had become a permanent fixture in my everyday life since Jasper's diagnosis.

Just when I would have thought my reaction to be one of jumping up for joy and taking this man into a bone-crushing hug, my body had fallen to complete mush.

The muscles in my legs were lost.

The cheering and excitement in the room was nothing but a pool of muffled sounds that came from a distance as the blood rushed through my ears.

And then I felt *her*.

Arms wrapped around me and kisses peppered my face.

I snapped out of my shock-induced stupor and found myself staring into Alissa's bright blue teary eyes.

I wrapped my arms around a kneeling Alissa and lifted her

so she sat on my lap. My first bone-crushing hug belonged to her.

"It was you. All you. You saved him," I said over her lips, my hands cupping either side of her face before kissing her hard.

"I'd like to think that I had something to do with it also," Dr. Messing said as he stood, his hand held out to me for a shake. I grasped it and pulled the guy in for a man hug.

"That you did, thank you," I said and smiled at him.

I let Alissa stand up where Julie pulled her into a hug.

We were escorted out of Dr. Messing's office with another set of directions on what we could now let Jasper do, and what he should hold out on for a little while longer. Suffice it to say he wasn't a complete bubble boy, but it wasn't too far from the truth. Regardless, my son was home and his health was improving every day.

The four of us stood in silence as we watched Jasper amuse himself with Tyler, his hospital buddy, when we exited Messing's office.

My son looked up and smiled at us.

I took a knee and he got up and took a giant leap into my arms.

"Did Dr. Messing tell you?" Jasper asked without a hint of a slur. He'd done so well with his speech therapy, I couldn't be more proud of him.

"He did, champ," I said before I kissed the top of his head a couple of times in quick succession. I ruffled his hair and released him so he could hug his mother and everyone else he pleased.

Alissa was the last one for his attentions, but she certainly wasn't the least. After a giant hug, he backed away, grabbed her face in his tiny hands and gave her a big juicy kiss on the lips. "Thank you for fixing me."

The look on her face was of absolute hilarity.

Her eyes were bulged, her face had blushed to a beautiful

surprised crimson, and her mouth opened much like that of a fish out of water.

Kissed speechless by a four-year-old.

My four-year-old.

"I think the girls are in trouble," she said, as she stood and I wrapped an arm around her waist laughing at what had taken place.

"I think you might be right on that one," I said, but I couldn't be brought to dreading the time he and I had to have discussions about women and his behavior with him. "It seems that I need to have a talk with him again about whose woman you are."

In a mood to celebrate, the five of us headed out for a family lunch.

I called my parents and told them the fantastic news while en route to Jasper's favorite restaurant: *McDonald's*. Relief was an understatement for them; Dad had to hang up because Mom had gone into relieved hysterics.

After our meal, I sat with Julie and Todd as we watched Alissa and Jasper in the playhouse. He had demanded she be the one to go in with him, and when one of the workers tried to prevent her from going up the tubes and down the slides, he kept the advantage.

"My sick is gone." He pointed to Alissa. "She fixed me and I'm not dying. She has to play!" The worker had no clue how to respond to the child's statement, and after some few seconds of Jasper standing with his chin held up high, his arms crossed over his chest, and a tiny foot tapping the padded floor, the teenager let them both have their way.

I was unsure about how he got the whole bit about dying, seeing as no one had told him, but I suspected my ever-so-observant four-year-old had picked up on the hushed exchanges and the grim aura that had surrounded us for the last little while, not to mention the way he felt through all of it. It saddened me that he had managed to pick up our negativity considering all we ever tried to do, when the outcome was unknown, was to stay happy, upbeat, and positive, not to mention, make every day a special day for him.

After lunch, Alissa needed to head into the office to tend to a few things for a corporate event she was overseeing in the following week. I took the opportunity to whisk Jasper away with me and have a few hours on the town with him while Julie and Todd headed home.

When all was done, I had everything I needed. Julie had agreed to Jasper staying around until after dinner, knowing that Alissa had promised to be back in time for us to eat together.

It was time for us two guys to head home and get to work.

"I'm really going to need your help on this one, little man," I said and looked back toward my son, who was still bouncing around in his booster seat.

"Allie will love it right, Daddy?"

God, I hope so.

I knew that everything would end up being fine. Perfect as a matter-of-fact. It always was.

So I chose to say, "You know it, champ."

CHAPTER 52

I was upstairs tending to some last minute details when I heard a car drive up the driveway.

It can't be her.

One look out the window proved that it was. A look at my watch also proved that she was over an hour earlier than what she had previously mentioned.

Without a backward glance, I ran downstairs and out the back door.

"Jasper, she's here," I said. "It's showtime!"

Alissa and Jasper rounded the side of the house, judging by the sound of their voices.

"You should see what Daddy got today," Jasper said.

"Where is he?"

"He's getting ready. He said he'll meet us at the pond."

"*Getting ready*? Getting ready for what?"

"You'll see," he said as they drew closer.

And then they came into my direct line of sight.

I had hid behind the other side of the house, my heart pounding out of excitement—out of nervousness—in the race of my life, or so it felt like it in that moment. I slowly followed them, keeping my distance so I wasn't made.

Jasper escorted her to the pond like I had instructed him to. They made idle chitchat about his afternoon with me, while sitting on the bench, and then Jasper sprung it on her.

"Allie?"

"Yes, handsome?" She swung his hand back and forth in hers.

"You remember what you said about wanting to be my mommy?"

I'd never seen a head snap so quick, it was almost comical.

She swallowed hard, shock all too evident at where the conversation had headed. "What of it?"

"Will you be my mommy?"

"But you have one already, sweetie."

"I know," Jasper said with such simplicity. "But Daddy asked me to ask you."

"To *ask* me *what*?" Her mouth slammed shut and she stopped dead in her tracks and looked down at Jasper, who was smiling up at her with that heart-stopping grin of his that could bring anyone to give him what he wanted. My heart melted at the sight. "You've always been mine, Jasper." She hugged him to her, kissing the top of his head before cuddling him into her side. "Tell you what, my answer is still the same. Yes, I would be happier than happy if I got to be your second mommy. Yes, I love you. And yes, if Daddy ever wants to get married, the answer I gave you the last time we talked in that hospital bed hasn't changed, and will always be yes."

After her heartfelt reassurance to Jasper, the two sat in silence for a moment before she added, "Jasper, you do know I love you and Daddy with all of my heart, right?" She cupped one of his cheeks with her hand.

"I know that," he said and pushed her back, grinning up at her.

"Now where's your father? You said he was here."

With a quick jump to give her a hug and a kiss to her cheek, he backed up and ran toward me as I approached. I had watched the conversation unfold only from about ten feet away.

Alissa turned to follow Jasper's movements and gasped as I took my last few steps up to her like a man on a mission.

Her eyes scanned me from top to bottom, her brows creasing as she was trying to dissect what the two of us were up to, but I knew damn well that she had caught on. If not in its entirety, then at least she had an inkling of what was about to happen.

Jasper pulled on the bottom of my shirt and held out his hand to me as I came to a stop a few feet away from her. I nodded to Jasper as I dropped it in his hands. He skipped the few steps over to Alissa.

"This is for you." He held out the box, bouncing on his haunches.

It was an identical-looking velvet box to the one I had opened only a month ago.

She looked up at me with skepticism. "This isn't another key, is it?"

I laughed. "No, but before you look inside, there are a few things I need to say first." I held out my hand for her to take.

I closed the gap between us until we stood toe to toe.

Jasper was still bouncing around. I knew that if I didn't do it soon, I would burst.

"Daddy wants to marry you! Daddy wants to marry you!" Jasper said, and my head snapped in his direction, but when I should have been ticked off about my ruined surprise, I couldn't help but laugh as I watched him dance around us in enthusiasm.

I turned my attention back to the person who meant the world to me, aside from my son. Her gaze was stuck to my face, as if trying to read me like I was one of her favorite books. "Is this true?" she asked about Jasper's outburst.

I took the box from her, looked down as I opened it, brought my gaze back to hers, and pulled her into me by wrapping my free arm around her waist. "He sure didn't lie. I've been thinking about it for a while now, and I don't know why I waited so damn long. Alissa Hidgins, I was first taken by you with your words in writing, and then your smile when we met in person. I—"

"Please say yes! Please say yes!" Jasper chanted and continued to dance around, which made Allie look down at my son and giggle while I watched her face this time around.

"Son, this is twice I try to talk and you've managed to ruin my attempts," I said and turned my words to Alissa. "I'm sorry, it should have been better. It should have been perfect. I sh—"

Alissa kissed me, halting all of my words. She pulled away, but I could still feel her breath on my lips.

She mouthed that ever so life-altering three-letter word on my lips before pressing her lips back to mine while she wrapped her arms around my neck.

"Really?" I asked and grinned as I pulled away and pressed our foreheads together. She nodded with that radiant smile of hers. "Oh, thank God!"

She laughed then smacked me. "As if you'd think I'd say no."

I kissed her again before I let her go and backed away. "Let me at least do this right, since Mister Ants-in-My-Pants over there is a little overexcited today."

And I assumed the position.

On bended knee, I took the ring out of its box and held it up to her between my thumb and index finger.

"I love you, Alissa Hidgins," I said. "Please tell me again and that you'll be my wife?"

"You bet I will," she said, and threw her giggling self down at me with a little too much force, which caused us to topple over into the long grass. "I love you so much, Paxton Lowell."

"I never doubted that for a single second." I slid the ring on her left hand ring finger and kissed the top of it as we laid there gazing at each other. "I love you too."

"Alissa sandwich!" Jasper said with much enthusiasm.

My son's pile-driving antics caused us to laugh and Alissa to slide off of me so Jasper ended up wedged between the both of us.

We spent the next few minutes tickling Jasper into a fit of

giggles that had grown contagious all around. I had been the first to get up and assist my beautiful new fiancée to her feet, who in turn assisted my son. I scooped him up from where he stood, wrapped my free arm around Alissa, and walked back toward the house with her cuddled into my side.

It may not have been the perfect proposal to any onlooker, but in retrospect, it had been perfect for us.

CHAPTER 53

Later that evening, I had gone to fetch us a drink while I left Alissa on the back patio swing by herself.

Upon my return, something made me pause and observe her.

She was calm, peaceful, but most of all, I saw the happiness radiate off of her as she tilted her face up to soak up the sun's setting rays with her eyes shut.

One step and the creaking of the board below my feet ruined the magnificent image before me, but it had been replaced by an even better one; the one of her with a smile I now knew she bestowed upon me alone.

Jasper was gone.

The dishes were done.

It was she and I and the calm of the countryside.

As I watched the rays shimmer across the surface of the pond, I smiled at the memory of a day a few months before.

Leaning against my shoulder, Alissa looked up and eyed me. "What's that smirk about?"

"I was just thinking about the time by the pond," I said and watched as her blush manifested itself.

I ran the back of my hand over her cheek.

"Damn, that look never gets old."

She laughed. "I'm glad, because I don't think it'll be going away any time soon. It hasn't yet."

I grabbed a fistful of her hair and pulled her head toward mine, capturing her lips with my own as she melted into me.

She pulled away giggling and then shot up to her feet. My

brow arched and with one glimpse into her eyes, I knew the seductress was back.

She backed away with a smirk on her face and pushed her shorts down her legs and kicked them to the side.

"What are you doing?" I asked.

"I would say it's pretty evident, my dear husband-to-be," she said with a husky laugh. I was stunned at her statement. "Race you."

She took off running. Her laughter filling the air as she pulled her shirt over her head and threw it to the side.

I shook my head at her retreating form.

Would I ever figure that woman out?

Probably not.

Did I want to?

What would be the fun in that? I have to admit, I sure love chasing after the discovery of what made Alissa tick. I doubt that a lifetime with her would ever allow me to know every answer, but I was damn well going to try to do just that.

My feet set themselves on a path up to where she had headed. I hadn't run after her, but I can guarantee you that I did walk at more than a leisurely pace.

"I'm highly disappointed in you," she said and crossed her arms over her chest. "I guess there's no more fun left in you now that you're about to be a hitched man."

I shed my T-shirt and dropped my shorts along with my underwear and smirked at her while she ogled my naked body.

"I'll show you no more fun." I rushed her as she stood on the edge of the dock.

I grabbed her by the waist, making her squeal, and twirled us around until balance left us altogether and we tumbled into the water. We surfaced laughing like kids, my arms still around her as her heated skin created a contrast between us and the coolness of the water.

"I guess I was wrong," she said and pecked me on the nose.

"You're damn right, you were."

My smile turned into a smirk as my hands snaked up and

popped the clasp to her bra. I kissed her shoulder as I slid the garment off of her and chucked it onto the dock.

I grinned and said, "Your bottoms, my beautiful soon-to-be wife."

She laughed. "You'll have to work for those," she said and stayed right where she was.

EPILOGUE

As the candles surrounding us in the bedroom burned low, Alissa lay in my arms, cuddled and sated, as was I. It was in this moment that my curiosity from earlier in the day had inched itself to the forefront of my mind.

"I never got to ask you what brought you home early," I said and kissed the top of her head. I felt the slight tension in her body, and it dissipated just as quickly as it had appeared. It made me crook my head in question as I looked down at her. "Is everything okay?"

She lifted her head and looked at me. The sight of her bottom lip held hostage in her teeth had me groaning, which caused a soft chuckle from her.

"Everything is perfect."

I wasn't convinced. "Then why do I get the feeling you're hiding something from me?"

She smiled shyly and her blush suffused her face. "Maybe because I am?"

Well, that wasn't the tone or the answer I was expecting, but instead of bracing myself for something negative, the shy smile she offered with her answer brought forth an excited, almost impatient urgency for me to hear her answer.

"Well?" I asked, and pulled her so she lay over me, and then tilted her chin so her eyes stayed glued to mine.

"*Well*?" she mimicked.

"Come out with it, woman, before I fuck it out of you," I laughed.

My free hand ran down the middle of her back until I

reached that bottom of hers and palmed a cheek tightly.

"You might want to do that when I'm done talking, or leave me altogether." She pulled her chin out of my hand and kissed the middle of my chest before laying her head on it.

"Now why would I leave you? You and Jasper are the best damn things that have ever happened to me," I said and cradled her head, running my fingers through her silken hair. "I wouldn't have asked you to marry me otherwise."

"That's good to know, because..." she began, and then lifted her head to look up at me again. "I think I might be pregnant."

My heart beat at a staccato pace.

Did she say what I think she just said?

"You're what?" I asked a little above a mute whisper.

"I might be pregnant," she groaned and hid her face in my chest, my hand once again cradling her head in its spot as I stared at the ceiling in shock.

We stayed there, silence overcoming both of us for a few minutes, and the oddest reaction took hold of me.

I started to laugh a full-out belly laugh.

She lifted her head and her eyes narrowed on me with a fuming gaze. This would be the second time she had gotten pissed off at me since we've been together, and even though I had never wanted her feeling that way, I couldn't ignore the passion that surged through those eyes of hers, despite her blatant irritation.

I rolled her onto her back and began kissing her. The image of her growing round with my child, *our* child, stirred something within me.

"Oh, sweetheart," I said between kisses. "If you're not pregnant, I plan on getting you there very soon after we say 'I do.'"

"Now wait a damn minute, don't I get a say?"

I lifted my head to watch her face and realized she was feigning insult.

I descended my kisses to her stomach and rubbed the area where our baby would be growing with my hand. She giggled.

"Have you taken a test?" I asked and cuddled my head to her stomach, my fingertips running a pattern up and down her side.

Nodding, she confirmed, "Two."

"And?" I looked up.

"Both were positive. I have an appointment to confirm with an OB next Tuesday."

"Can I come?"

She cupped my cheek and smiled as I looked up from her belly in hope. "I wouldn't have it any other way."

I turned my face and kissed the inside of her palm.

"Damn, woman, you make me so happy," I said, kissing my way back up her body. "And you're right."

"About what?" she asked.

"I do want to fuck you." My hand cupped her core and I slid a finger into her, causing her to arch into my hand and moan. "That's right, love," my voice rumbled as I watched the emotions flutter across her face. "Let me hear you."

THE END

ABOUT THE AUTHOR

Born and raised in small town Northern Ontario, Canada, Carey Decevito has had a penchant for reading and writing for as long as she can remember.

A writer of erotic romance, paranormal romance, romantic suspense, and member of the Ottawa Romance Writers, this lover of food will throw in a bit of heat, a dash of sass, a pinch of comedy and a dollop of real-life experience in order to provide her readers with a story that will mess with their emotions from start to finish.

Family and friends are her lifeblood but Carey also enjoys conquering the outdoors, sports, traveling and playing tourist in Canada's National Capital region. When life gets crazy, she seeks respite through her writing and submersing herself in the latest addition to her library. If all else fails, she knows there's never a dull moment with her two daughters, her goofy husband and their cat and dog who she swears are out to get her.

Once Written, Twice Shy is the first book in *The Broken Men Chronicles* series.

FIND CAREY ONLINE

WWW.CAREYDECEVITO.COM

night break

nightshade

1

CAREY DECEVITO

PROLOGUE

DALTON

One Year Ago…

If I had to deliver that fucker's obituary, this is how it would read:

Rick Donnelly—Wannabe war hero, traitor, terrorist. May he burn in hell.

In truth, he was the scum who managed to kidnap my friend Theo Lowell's nephew, Jasper, then made off with the man's woman, all for the sake of petty revenge and furthering his stance in organized crime.

Now, he was nothing but a piece of shit, sprawled forward, split in half, and wedged between Warehouse Ten and the front end of Theo's brother's pickup truck.

Dead.

Collapsing to my back, Theo held onto his woman, Morgan, at my side. Allowing a long, drawn-out breath to escape, it helped ease the tension in my body as I dealt with the pain in my hand and leg. The damn bastard might be dead, but he did some damage before Morgan drove a truck straight through him. My shooting hand now had a hole through it, and since I was reaching for the gun in my ankle holster at the time, the fucking bullet managed to hit my bad knee.

It's over. Thank God for crazy-assed women, great friends…and random strangers.

Jasper was safe.

Morgan was safe.

And Theo could settle into the life he thought he'd all but lost only hours before.

Sounding on the verge of tears, he uttered, "Huss?"

With our adrenaline dropping from the night's festivities, I couldn't blame his emotional state. The same gamut of emotions was reeling through me too, and I hadn't had to track down two loved ones, nor had I had the displeasure of being held hostage, having to free myself, then do the same for the woman I loved. All this with some unknown cyber vigilante, who'd popped out of nowhere, to help him out. One we'd been forced to have blind faith in.

I'm your girl, Mr. T.

Yeah, Hussy was our girl tonight. Definitely.

"Yeah?" she said through that voice distorter of hers.

"Thank you." Theo's voice lodged in his throat, leaving the man incapable to add to his words.

It took a few seconds to get a response, but when it came, albeit in that robotically masculine voice again, it was just as overwrought with the same jumble of emotion that Theo and I seemed to be experiencing. "You're welcome, Mr. T," she whispered.

Hussy's earlier concerned outburst to my being shot jumped to the forefront of my mind. This spurred me into action. I didn't know why I felt compelled to reassure her, but I found myself unable to stop myself from doing it. Hussy wasn't one of my team at Nightshade Security, yet tonight, she had come through for all of us. Despite never having met, a bond had been forged between the team, Hussy, and myself. Plus, I've always been one to listen to my gut, and it's proven me right every time, so it was why I said what I did next.

"Huss?" I managed.

Her distorted voice caught. "Yeah?"

"I'll be fine." I swallowed the ball of emotion that had made my voice come out sounding like gravel. "But I'm going to need your name, honey."

What I got next was an unaltered, breathless sounding, "Kip," that made my lungs seize, my body tighten, and a part of my anatomy take notice in a very visceral way.

I had no idea who this woman was. She'd only spoken a single word—the nickname she'd given me based on my last name—Kippers. But that's all I needed. I can't explain the electrical charge that rolled through me, or the sense that something greater was at play. I simply needed more of that voice. I needed more of *her*. "I want to know—"

I heard a subtle thump on the other end of the line, followed by a long sigh.

I never thought that a sigh could hold so much untold emotion, but hers did.

Exhaustion.

Wistfulness.

Hesitation.

Defeat.

Fear.

"Don't," she whispered, and I could have sworn I'd heard her add a "please" to that. "Let's just leave it at this." I didn't want to. A gnawing feeling in my gut told me that I needed her still; that I wanted her. "I only did what needed to be done. It's what I do."

Something told me that pushing her right then would be ineffective, so I gave in, much to my displeasure. But I did it in a way that left the proverbial door open and the ball in her court. "Okay, Huss. If you ever need anything—"

I could tell that she was contemplating my words. "I won't." The tone of finality in those words had disappointment weighing me down until she continued, "Tell you what, I'll be in touch if something ever comes up."

Disappointment fled and hope took its place. This was as good as I was going to get. "Okay."

Silence dominated the next ten seconds before Hussy broke it. "I'm going to sign off now."

"Huss?" I was desperate and I didn't care. I wanted to reach through the communication device shoved in my ear canal and yank her to where I lay, so I could see the face that belonged to the voice. I wanted to figure out why she was how she was, what made her tick, what set her off. Hell, I'd have been happy to wait out the medics and the slew of first responders with her voice in my ear, telling me everything was going to be okay, just like Theo was doing with Morgan.

But before I could do or say anything, the line went dead, all coms were down, and sirens could be heard in the distance.

I could feel Theo's gaze aimed at the side of my face. He probably wanted to know what the fuck was going on with me.

Ignoring the man, I thumped my head onto the dock in sheer frustration, and closed my eyes. "Bye, Huss," I whispered.

CHAPTER 1

D E V O L I N

Present Day...

Come on. Come on. Come on!

"Come. *On!*" I bounced in place as I watched the progress bar run its course, and then punched the air in victory once it hit one-hundred-percent. "Gotcha!"

Disconnecting the thumb drive from my laptop, and slamming the top down on it, I scooted out of bed and proceeded to stuff the lot into my satchel.

There was no other option than to go straight to *him*.

This was life or death, and everything hinged on what I did next. I'd long since made a promise to myself that I'd never risk making contact with the team I'd bonded with after one night of mayhem. But promise or not, this information I'd just dug up wasn't something I could relay to him over the phone.

It needed to be seen.

Analyzed.

Discussed.

That meant that I needed to see Dalton Kippers. In the flesh. Talk to him. Show him what I'd found, what he was in for.

Then, I needed to get far away from him, and move on already, because this crazy obsession I had developed over the man was getting out of hand. My best friend, Skylar, had told me as much on multiple occasions. And when Skylar deemed it fit to force her wisdom upon me, I needed to listen. It's been nearly a year since I helped Dalton and his team rescue Jasper Lowell and Morgan Smyth for Christ's sake!

On a snort, I shrugged off where my thoughts were heading and closed my bag.

"What are you doing?"

The breath in my lungs seized. "Sky!" Hand clutched at my chest, I turned to face the woman, waiting for my erratic heartbeat to calm. "You scared the living shit out of me."

Skylar leaned against the doorjamb, dressed in wrinkled hot pink scrubs from a hard day's work, smirking. "Well, at least we know one of us is capable of getting that ticker of yours up above a slow trot now, don't we?" She breezed into the room, nodded toward my satchel, a glimmer of curiosity entering her gaze. "What's going on?"

I bit my bottom lip, knowing the guilt showed on my face for what I was about to ask of my dearest friend. Then I blurted, "Sky, I need your help."

"Do I need to worry that the cops will be coming in here to cart your ass off to jail?" she asked.

"I need to get out of here for a few hours."

"Dev, you know I can't—"

"It's life or death, Sky."

Skylar's eyes widened. "Dev, what in the hell have you gotten yourself into?"

I headed toward the cabinet, that passed itself off as a closet, and grabbed the pair of jeans and t-shirt I'd been wearing when I had been admitted. My irritation at the lack of immediate support showed with each jerky movement I made. "Can you or can't you help me out?" I turned to look at her from over my shoulder.

Skylar crossed her arms over her chest, taking a seat in the chair closest to my hospital bed. "You look flushed. How're you feeling, and tell me the truth."

Oh no, not that no-nonsense tone of hers. If I told my

friend, who incidentally was a nurse, that I was feeling 'off' for lack of a better description, there'd be no way Skylar would let me walk out of there, say nothing of her covering for my absence with Doris, the nurse that was currently on duty. Damn woman was so old, she should have retired a decade ago, but seemed to find it amusing to torture her patients. That's why Skylar and I had dubbed her Nurse Battle-Axe. Because of this, and the fact that I did need to get out of there, I went with, "I'm fine," and hoped that my bad acting, let alone lying skills wouldn't give me away.

Unfortunately, the lack of conviction my words held, and the pause I had to take to brace myself against the wall to wait out the wave of dizziness that hit me, didn't help my cause.

"Uh-huh…"

"I'm not kidding, Sky. I need to do this." I whipped my pajama top off and flung it at the bed, slipping my shirt on. "This case…it's *big*."

"Dev—"

"No!" I persisted, yanking down my pajama bottoms, then headed to the bed for needed support. Leaning on it, I slid my legs into my jeans, wiggling them up over my ample hips. "*He*'s in danger, Sky."

Her eyes rounded as realization hit her. "He, as in *he*?" I nodded. "I thought we'd discussed this, Dev." She sighed.

"No, *you* discussed it. I merely listened. You told me to move on and I will. Just…" My frustration came out in a huff. "I have to see this through. It's my fault he took this case in the first place, so by default, it's my responsibility to make sure he knows what he's heading into. The people he'll be dealing with…" Another sigh accompanied my shake of the head. "They're not good, Sky."

"Okay." Skylar paused mid-thought. "Say I let you leave. How the hell am I supposed to keep Doris out of here?"

"She knows you come in here after your shifts. She never bothers to check in on me when you're here, you know that."

"So you want me to…?" She let her words hang so I could fill the gap.

"I know it's not right for me to ask this of you, but can you stay here, as in this room, until I get back?" Biting my lip in that nervous tick of mine, I continued, "And I'll need your keycard."

"Devolin!" she scolded.

Both of us looked toward the room's door and listened for a short moment to see if Skylar's outburst had generated some attention.

"I'll take the back way out and come in the same way. The emergency stairwell is just outside that door."

"I can get fired for that," she whisper-yelled, shooting the door another glance. Still, the woman pulled her access pass and handed it over.

I snapped it up from her hand then shrugged. "Just say you lost it if anyone asks."

"Yeah, yeah. You're lucky I love you, woman," she grumbled.

Knowing I had her where I wanted her, I grinned. "So you'll help me out?"

On a curt nod, Skylar got to her feet. "Yeah." Her eyes did a full head to toe appraisal before she shared my smile. "But we need to do something about your hair and makeup first."

I blew out a relieved sigh, hoping my eyes conveyed my appreciation. I really would have left against hospital advice—sure, I'd return after my duty was done—because a life, if not lives, hung in the balance and it was all my fault.

Sneaking out of my room, and down the stairwell, proved to be easy enough. Nurse Battle-Axe was out on the floor and away from the nurses' station. Heading down two floors, I exited the stairs, and made my way toward the bank of elevators that would take me the rest of the way down to the main lobby. When I got there, I jumped in the first cab that I spotted, rattling off my home address.

Upon my arrival, adrenaline running at an all-time high, I

hurried to my vehicle. Finding it parked in its usual spot of my mother's garage, I noticed the bay next to it was empty and thanked the powers up above that I wouldn't have to deal with dear old Mom right away.

Hitting the fob, I opened the door, dropped my bag on the passenger seat, then settled into the driver's side.

"Hello, baby," I cooed to my newest acquisition, the leather upholstered finish and new car smell that had yet to fade, even after nearly a year of ownership.

Hitting the button that would open my bay's door from the controller on my visor, I put the key in the ignition and turned it. Sending my destination from my phone to the car's GPS, I took a few short seconds to enjoy the purr of the Charger's engine. Then I shifted my ride into reverse.

Nightshade Security Investigations—Dalton's company— was closed, so I made my way to the former corporal's home to find that it too lacked the one man I was trying to locate. I did take the time to admire the two rockers on his front wrap-around porch and the American flag hanging in a place of pride on one of the support pillars framing the steps.

I hope I'm not too late.

I wasn't sure what I'd do if Dalton had already skipped town. Just as quickly as that thought popped into my head, another followed it.

Theo would know where he is.

Reprogramming my GPS for Theo and Morgan's place, I reared out of the drive and floored the gas pedal. Fifteen minutes later, my lead foot caused me to nearly miss the entry to the driveway, as I reached my third, and hopefully, final destination.

It wasn't until my finger released the doorbell that I realized how truly horrible I was feeling. To make matters worse, my nerves had also kicked in, and I had a fleeting thought that perhaps I should have given myself a quick cursory glance in the mirror before exiting the car. There were no do-overs on first meetings, after all, and I was about to meet more than just Theo and possibly Morgan today, seeing as it looked to be that they had a visitor, judging by the third vehicle parked at the front of the house.

As luck would have it, someone was home.

I would have cried out my relief at the sight of the pregnant woman before me, but a whispered, "Morgan," was the only thing I could muster as soon as the door opened.

The woman's eyebrows furrowed in apparent confusion. "Do I know you?"

I shook my head, indicating the negative, because that's all I could do. I was too busy fighting the sudden bout of nausea and dizzying heat. Next thing I knew, my vision tilted, then dimmed, and my knees gave out.

At the feel of a cool damp rag sponged against the hollow of my throat, over my forehead, my cheeks, and then back again, some of my faculties returned. The sensation was like heaven on my overheated skin. I sighed at the same time a, "Mr. T," escaped me.

"W-what, did she say?" I recognized Dalton's voice immediately. Unable to get my eyes to cooperate and open, I heard a thump come from right beside me, accompanied by the heat of another body warming the side of my torso.

"Danger…Kip," I mumbled, and then everything started to fade again.

Before I was able to embrace the darkness that swooped in, I felt the palm of Dalton's callused hand gently cup my cheek as he whispered, "Huss?"

CHAPTER 2

DALTON

With a lot of convincing to get the medics to allow me to be there, here I was, sitting in the back of an ambulance with who I suspected was Hussy, the cyber ghost I'd set Brycen to tracking in his spare time over the last year.

Her name: Devolin Payton Taylor. At least that's what the ID in her bag said when I managed to sneak a look at it after the paramedics had located it. I wouldn't be surprised if she'd faked her own identity, seeing as she seemed hell-bent on remaining anonymous.

Leaning forward onto my knees, I peered at the woman splayed out onto the gurney before me. Out cold.

Morgan had told me that Hussy looked panicked when she first opened the door to the woman. Then she'd collapsed and Theo had called 911. Morgan rushed to get me a cold cloth, and I'd been left with an unconscious woman. Her head rested in my lap, as I tried to decipher what her few short words meant, and why she'd chosen now to show herself.

Devolin whimpered in her sleep, causing me to reach out and grab the hand closest to me. Her very tiny, dainty, exceptionally soft hand.

My eyes trailed up from her digits, her arm, her shoulder, the delicate neck that held a thrumming but steady pulse, to her face. Her license said she had green eyes, but I wondered if they'd shimmer like emeralds, taper closer to the hazel side of things, or would be bright like aquamarines. Beyond that, her lips were full, dark pink, almost rosy, reminding me of bubble gum. A fleeting curiosity of if she'd taste as such washed over me, but I shrugged it off. It was her hair that had me begging to set it free and run my fingers through it. It was a deep auburn, with streaks of darker reddish hues mixed in. Her skin was pale, but I knew, with the small line of freckles over the bridge of her cute nose, that her complexion wasn't that much darker when she wasn't ill, as she seemed to be now.

What the fuck is the matter with you? Scolding myself internally for waxing poetic about an unconscious woman, one I'd had a past with, yet had never met before. I bowed my head, trying to devise a plan of action, now that I had bullied my way into being by her side.

DEVOLIN

I woke up in what looked like the back of an ambulance, my hand clutched in a firm and warm grasp.

Allowing my head to drop sideways, I found myself looking at Dalton, who sat beside me. His head was bent forward. He was leaning onto his knees, one of them bouncing out of what I surmised was anxiety. I can only imagine what went through his, Theo's, and Morgan's heads when here I had shown up out of nowhere, and then before I could explain anything, I pulled a Sleeping Beauty maneuver on their asses. That thought had me rolling my eyes, cringing internally.

Dalton had yet to notice that I'd woken up, so I took the opportunity for a more thorough perusal of the unguarded man before me while I had it.

His dark brown, almost black hair was due for a cut, slightly falling over his eyes. I wondered how it would feel between my fingers if I were to brush it away. Dalton had a chiseled jaw with a slight square shape, full lips, strong and masculine features that guaranteed him to look mean one minute, yet soft when the time called. His nose had a slight bend to it, most likely from combat, as with the small scar on the side of his right cheek, by his hairline. I could only assume since I'd been unable to access most but not all of his service records. He looked infinitely better in person than in any of the photos I'd dug up. Trust me, I'd searched those babies out, if only to indulge in my insane obsession over a man I've never met, but had spoken with once.

Damn!

Dalton must have sensed that I was conscious for his head shot up and his steel grey eyes connected with mine. "You're awake." The silk of his voice ran over me, goosebumps exploding on my skin, making me withdraw my hand from his so I wouldn't give myself, or my reaction to him, away.

Double damn! Wait; was that my voice? Embarrassment filled me as a grin broke over his face, solidifying the fact that I had spoken aloud. But that look though… Had I felt anywhere close to one-hundred-percent, that look on his face would have melted my panties. I'm sure of it.

As it was, my mouth had gone dry, my tongue feeling as if it had tripled in size. "Uh."

"If you're going to look, I'd rather you be doing it while I can watch." His grin transformed into a smile.

My mouth opened for a rebuttal to his bold statement, then closed because words evaded me.

Light danced in the man's eyes. "The jig is up, Huss." His words were filled with pride. "Or should I say Devolin Payton Taylor?"

"How'd?" He patted my hand then twined his fingers through mine, setting off another set of goosebumps, but I knew how he found out. "You went through my stuff."

He followed his curt nod with, "How are you feeling?"

I tried to pry my hand from his like before, but he didn't

give this time. "Where's my bag? I—I need to show you something."

"I asked you a question, Devolin."

I pulled at my hand again. Stuck. "Just let me—"

Instead of the gentle tone he'd led with, this time, his words brokered no argument. All alpha-like. "Don't. Brush. Me. Off, Devolin."

"But—" My words ceased halfway out of my mouth as his lips formed a thin line in warning, his hand squeezing mine as an added measure.

I tried to lift my head, but collapsed back onto the stretcher's pillow as the nausea and dizziness, that had been absent since my waking, set in again. For the first time today, I started to really worry. This was all too reminiscent. Closing my eyes, I begged. *Please don't let it be back. I can't deal with this right now.*

"What is it?"

My eyes snapped open. The paramedics had to have given me drugs or something. It could be the only reason why I couldn't keep my thoughts to myself.

Dalton leaned closer, the squeeze on my hand a gentle one. "What's back? What's the matter? Come on, Dev, talk to me."

He couldn't know. I didn't want him to know. I was there simply because I felt responsible in warning him, to keep him and his team at NSI safe. I should have known that exploring my connection with Dalton couldn't lead to… And what was it that I wanted it to lead to? A happily ever after? I snorted at the thought then averted his questing gaze by turning my head to look up at the ambulance's ceiling. No, there would be none of that romance book nonsense for me. If I was having a relapse of some kind, this solidified why I had to push him away. I was best off making sure he had what he needed for that case of his; then disappearing from his life like I'd done the first go around.

Impatience clearly showing, Dalton groaned, "Devolin."

I closed my eyes, soaking in the warmth growing inside

me, all due to the sound of his voice. Trying to breathe away my nausea, I silently prayed he'd say my name again. "You smell good. Like soap, mint, and man," I whispered.

"Devolin." He sounded humored.

I chose to ignore him, until I felt his other hand cupping my cheek. Then I couldn't.

Before I could react, deflect, possibly shove my foot in my mouth further, "Sir, we're at the hospital," came from one of the medics at the front of the vehicle. "We need you to clear out." The back door to the ambulance opened with the other attendant standing there.

"Wait!" I cried out as Dalton began to back out of the rig. "My bag!"

"What is it with you and that bag?" the man grumbled, and then lifted the messenger satchel to show me that it had been with us all along.

"Take it. There are things on the thumb drives that you need to see." The medics proceeded to unload my stretcher from the rig as Dalton stood at my side. "It's about the Wentworth case."

His body stiffened, eyes narrowing on me. "How do you know about that?" he clipped.

I wasn't about to apologize for doing what was right, even if he made me feel like a scolded child just then.

Showing my stubbornness, I jutted my chin up and said, "It doesn't matter. You need to do it right away." I'd be damned if something happened to him, or a member of his team, when I'd been the one to put them in this mess, all thanks to a personal connection.

"Fine. I'll get Brycen to meet me here, then you can show us what you've got when the doctor gives you the all clear."

"No!" Being around him was the last thing I needed. Hell, if working together on that one mission had caused me to lose my head about him, I feared what working with him and his team in person would do. "Just take it. Take the laptops and the thumb drives, too. There's more stuff on those. Brycen will know what to do with it. You won't need me. Just leave me my wallet. It's all I need that's in there."

The man got right in my face, anger, or was it exasperation, emanating from him. It caused me to jerk back into the stretcher's cushions. "You're not getting away from me this time, Devolin," he snapped, his nostrils flaring.

"That's not—"

"You two can do this later," the driver stated. "Miss Taylor, we need to get you back to your room and checked out."

"What?"

Ignoring Dalton's outburst, the medics wheeled me toward the hospital entrance.

CHAPTER 3

DALTON

I was fucking obsessed.

Years ago, I swore I'd never get like this over a woman again and now look at me. Taking that same old stroll down that same old road. Yet, despite how it turned out for me the first time around, here I was, spending the last year using my own company's resources to track down someone who would be deemed, by anyone with a functioning brain, a ghost.

From the moment the mission to rescue Theo's nephew and Morgan ended, White Hat Hussy had disappeared from the deep web, never to be seen or heard from again. Well…sort of.

It was bad enough that her voice has haunted me since *that* night.

The silky, smooth, low and sultry cadence, with a subtle Northern lilt, was never far from my mind. I heard it while out on missions. It was there again when I fell asleep.

Truth be told, I had no idea why, or how for that matter, this woman had infiltrated my thoughts. But random things reminded me of her. I found myself imagining what she looked like. I wondered how old she was, or if she thought of me as often as I did her.

It had been months since I'd seen sign of life from her. A

year since I'd last heard her voice. The guys at Nightshade Securities still gave me hell when I inquired if they'd turned anything up. They thought I'd fallen off my rocker. Maybe I had.

Then again, Devolin made it impossible to forget her.

When my ass landed in the hospital, after being shot, she sent me flowers. I'm not talking about one of those *get-well* bouquets, either. Hell, she'd gone overboard, embarrassing me in front of the others. Even Morgan, a florist for Christ's sake, asked me if I intended on becoming a rival of hers, what with every surface available—and some of the floor—being covered in vase after vase.

But Devolin, our little cyber angel, had gone the extra mile. I hadn't been the only one to suffer her wacky sense of humor, or been blessed with her generosity.

With Shane, she'd help close a bunch of cases that had either gone cold or lacked information to proceed with their current lead. For Morgan and Theo, she'd sent the man a *Mr. T* doll, and a few other more meaningful gifts in celebration of their nuptials. Hell, Brycen might not have thought of it as funny at the time, but the rest of the guys from that night, myself included, thought it was hilarious how she'd infiltrated the computer wiz's system, repeatedly, only to leave dancing babies for him to find. Shit, even Theo's nephew hadn't been left untouched. Jasper had a custom blanket delivered to him, with each one of us guys' names on it. The note it came with, typed up mind you, commended him on his bravery. She also told him that if things ever got scary again, all he had to do was hide under the blanket and that he'd be safe.

Each gift or act had thought put into it. Maybe that's why I was hung up on her, I don't know. Which is why, with every delivery, I pushed the guys to track her down.

But each box or envelope lacked the return address they needed. And forget fingerprints. Each service utilized had no way of providing the billing information, or any information for that matter, because she'd gotten into their systems to erase the data. Items were paid for in cash. The surveillance systems were of no help either. The damn woman had thought of everything to make sure she stayed incognito.

Yet, now I'd found her.

Technically, she found you, dumbass.

And by the looks of things, she wasn't doing very well. So naturally, when a nurse approached me, volunteering to show me to the waiting room, I followed her.

It wasn't until my ass landed in a seat of the Chronic Care Ward, that worry hit me. About the same time it did, so did my stubbornness.

If Devolin thought she could get rid of me, she was mistaken. I'd sit there and wait for as long as it took until I could get to her. I didn't want answers on the Wentworth case from what Brycen could find on her devices. I wanted answers straight from the source. Devolin.

CHAPTER 4

DALTON

About two-point-five seconds after the nurse left me in the waiting room, I pulled out my phone and dialed up Brycen. I might have wanted Devolin to give me the information, but depending on the severity of her illness, it might not be soon enough, and time was of the essence with this particular new case.

Within half an hour, the man was sitting next to me, pounding away at Devolin's hardware. Shortly thereafter, another nurse—one named Doris, according to her nametag, who looked like a witch with an axe to grind—came by to convey a verbal message that Devolin was fine and she wanted me out of there.

Nope. It wasn't going to happen. I told the old battle-axe as much too, and sent her on her way with a handwritten note to boot.

With Brycen playing around on Devolin's computers, we weren't going to be moving anytime soon.

Turning to my computer specialist, I asked, "What can you tell me?"

The man looked up, his eyes wide with a look of wonderment. "Is this chick for real?" The confusion on my face must have shown, because he didn't hesitate to elaborate with a shitload of enthusiasm, so much so, his hands became part of the conversation. "I wish I could borrow her brain for a day. She's a fucking genius, D!" For him to say that about someone he'd loathed for the better part of a year was something else. "This tracking software she's created puts mine to shame." He shuffled closer, tilting one of the laptops so that I could check things out. "This, is what I've been missing. This is what we need for NSI, D. You should see the codes she's written. Fucking hell! If you won't offer her a job, I will."

The problem was that I had planned to do that a year ago. Before I could, Devolin shut me down, citing that parting ways after Morgan's rescue was best for everyone. As I've mentioned before, I hadn't stopped at that, but she was like smoke. There one second, gone the next. Invisible. Today had been the biggest break I'd gotten where she was concerned.

Before I could share this with Brycen, I spotted my half-sister heading my way. "Sky?" Getting to my feet, I took a few steps toward her, then waited.

Skylar greeted me with a hug. "What are you doing here?"

I squeezed her back, answering, "Waiting on someone."

She pulled back from me, her eyes filled with worry. "Is it one of the guys?" Then she peered over my shoulder, eyes going wide, reflecting recognition. Her face filled with shock. "That's Devolin's bag!" Clearly agitated, her arm shot out and her finger pointed in Brycen's direction. "Those are her computers! What's he doing with her computers, D?"

What in the ever fucking fuck? Skylar knows Devolin?

My stance widened, my arms crossed over my chest, and my eyes studied the woman in front of me. Skylar bit her lip nervously, her eyes darting between me and my partner, who was diligently tapping away on one laptop, then switching to the other, muttering nonsensical things to himself, all the while oblivious to this latest development.

"How do you know her?"

"She told me she was fine," Skylar explained, and tried to move past me to get to Brycen, but I shot out an arm to stop her. She sighed and looked up into my eyes. "Dalton…is she in trouble?"

Despite her evident concern, I didn't answer. Instead, I repeated my earlier question. "No bullshit, Sky. How do you know her?"

Fire flashed through her eyes as my sister's trademark stubbornness kicked in.

Getting onto the tips of her toes, her index poked me in the chest. "She's a friend." Another poke. "A good friend. The best I've had in the last two years as a matter of fact." She kept punctuating each point with that finger of hers. "Tell me what's going on. Whatever you think she's done—"

"Sky—"

"No! Listen to me, D." She wasn't backing down. Like a dog with a bone that one. "She wouldn't do—"

I was officially past the point of exasperation. "Would you shut the fuck up and listen to what I need to say?"

"You can't take this away from her, D," she whispered. "It's all she's got. She's been sick for—"

"Sick?"

"Yeah, sick, and not the cold or flu kind, D. You do realize you're in the Chronic Care Ward, right?" She paused, shaking her head before letting it drop to her chest. "I just…" A sigh. "I just thought that this last time would be it," she whispered, but I heard her loud and clear. "She doesn't deserve this to be happening to her. She doesn't need more shit in her life." Her eyes flew up to mine and I was faced with a protective Skylar. "You need to leave her alone. Whatever it is that you caught her doing, she's doing it for good, you get me? Leave. Her. Be. Dalton." She finished this with her chest rising and falling rapidly, eyes shining with unshed tears.

Grabbing onto her shoulders, I pulled her into me, hugging her, offering her comfort. "Had you given me a word in edgewise," I said softly into her hair, "I'd have told you that Brycen, the guys, and I have been looking for Devolin for quite some time now." Skylar's body went solid as a rock.

Nodding against her head, I continued, "She helped me out a while back." I chuckled. "She's given us quite the runaround, too." Pulling away, I set her back, a subtle smile on my face. "Aside from the fact that I wanted to track her down to thank her for getting involved, I—"

Skylar's eyes widened. "This is about Theo and Morgan, isn't it?"

What the fuck?

"I heard her that night, D." Her voice shook. "I was working the nightshift, and planned to stop by on my break like usual, but I heard her. The panic in her voice. The resolve in it…her defeat. I had no idea what she was doing, but I knew it had something to do with her computers."

"Skylar?" She turned to face the same nurse who'd given me Devolin's message earlier. "Your girl's looking for you."

Skylar nodded to the woman, "Thanks, Doris," then turned to me once more. "I…"

"Go," I told her. "Make sure she's alright. We can talk about this later."

She nodded. "Can I ask you something?"

Smirking, I nodded. "Doesn't mean I'll answer."

"D…" She rolled her eyes.

"Fine."

"She's the one with the flowers and gifts, isn't she?" Her lips quirked up at my slight nod in response. "I'm going to tell you this, but I swear, I'll hunt you down in your sleep and kill you if you tell her this came from me…"

That's when I knew I had an ally in Skylar.